Toadhouse Trilogy

The Toadhouse Trilogy

Book One

Jess Lourey

The Toadhouse Trilogy: Book One
ISBN-13: 978-0615644578
ISBN-10: 0615644570

This is a work of fiction. Names, characters, places, and incidents either are the product of the author's imagination or are used fictitiously, and any resemblance to actual persons, living or dead, business establishments, events, or locales is entirely coincidental.

Cover design by Leonardo Pérez, 2012.

Visit the website: www.jesslourey.com/toadhouse/ttt.html

Dedications

For Zoë, Amanda, Esmae, and Xander, with much love.
You teach me grace, joy, and patience, and remind me of magic.
Also, in loving memory of Grandma Didier.

Prologue

The sky is the color of blueberries and cream. The sea below is a soothing, bottomless pool of aquamarine with a surface broken only by silverfish in a darting game of catch-me. A single island rides this sea, a roughly circular thrust of land with trees stippling its rocky edges. The island's hardwood perimeter gives way to the easy rolling of grassy hills, which crest at the base of a single mighty tree at its center. The tree is colossal, impossible to ignore, a wise ruler holding court. Here the air smells like freshly-bloomed lilacs, and underneath that is the tangy scent of the ocean.

From a distance, the great tree most resembles a gigantic weeping willow, its arms protective and vast, but up close, the way the wood shimmers and speaks gives it away. The girl presses her ear to the rough brown bark and hears the murmur of a million languages. Words flow out lovely like leaves, gathering, growing, becoming lacy fronds the color of honey and emeralds that weigh down the branches and rustle like pages in the breeze. It is the Ogham, and this is its home.

The girl's baby brother sits a few feet away from her, sheltered from the sun, fat and happy, letting the soft grass tickle his fingers. He wears a serene smile, and when a bright purple ant with orange legs skitters across his hand, he laughs from his belly. Nearby, a herd of gentle gwartheg y ulyn munches on grass, mooing contentedly. The girl glances over at the glorious white beasts and a sly smile lights up her features.

"A full clan of gwartheg without their herdmistress?" she says in a deep, mocking voice. "But the Daoine Sidhe must never leave their posts!" She plants her hands on her hips and marches around the tree in an exaggerated high step. "I am the king, and I demand that everyone adhere to their assigned roles. The herdmistress must at all time stay with the foolish gwartheg to keep them from overeating."

The baby crinkles his eyes. He begins sucking on a corner of his hand. The girl halts with her chin tucked into her chest. She lays one arm across the base of her spine and gestures with the other as if speaking to an army.

"Not only the fairies must stay at their posts, you understand. Where would we be if the wooly bears stopped predicting the weather and the praying mantises no longer led lost children home? Come, now, everyone knows that the cwn annwn must howl at the moon! This is how it has always been, and so it must always be." Suddenly bored with the game, she skips in a pattern known only to her. Never does she venture beyond the tree's sheltering arms. She twirls her party dress and enjoys the feel of the cool white cotton against her calves.

The breeze picks up, sighing through the leaves of the Ogham, and she realizes that she can make out entire sentences without having her ear pressed to the bark. She laughs with the joy of her discovery. Her laughter triggers the baby, who giggles from the belly again. She skips over to him and puts her hands on his soft plump cheeks.

"You think everything is funny, little brother." She returns the daisy chain she made to his head. "You don't know that you're the funniest of them all."

He grasps for the flower ring and brings it to his eager mouth. She places a gentle hand over it. "Nope, not for eating."

She balances the crown back on his head, sensing it before she hears it—the voice of their mother. Lilting and musical, the sound rings distantly through the shimmering curtain separating the Ogham's home from hers in Tir Na Nog. Playtime is over. She sighs and scoops up her brother, setting him on her hip. The daisy chain falls to the ground. Expertly balancing the boy despite her small size, she reaches for the crown.

She's reluctant to leave the protective arms of the tree. She wasn't supposed to sneak away from the celebration and she definitely wasn't supposed to come here. Only those of pure royal blood are allowed under the branches of the Ogham. She can't see the harm, though. She wanted to find out if her brother could hear the words, too. That's all.

"Think they've saved us some treacle cake?" she asks him.

"I doubt it."

She whips around as a ragged cloud shambles over the sun, cooling the air. Her stomach drops. Fear Darrig stands at the edge of the Ogham's shelter, his rat face almost entirely cloaked by his crimson hat. He was supposed to be attending the celebration but has followed them instead.

"Na dean maggadh fum," she murmurs. It's a terrible thing to say, a protection against monsters, and she's immediately ashamed.

She's heard it explained time and again that his appearance is not his fault and that as an elder, he deserves respect.

Fear Darrig smiles as if he's just remembered something. "You're not supposed to be here."

He minces a few steps closer, glancing everywhere but into her eyes. Her baby brother whimpers and squirms in her arms. She feels a surge of heat in her chest, and quiets it.

"We were just leaving," she says.

"I could..." he stops a few feet away. An oily look smears his eyes, but still he holds his gaze at something just beyond her shoulder. "I could tell you a secret before you go. Please. I get so lonely. Just set your brother over there, on the other side of the tree, so he can't..." He pauses, and a giggle escapes his mouth. Across the field, the gwartheg shift restlessly. "...so he can't hear the secret I want to tell you."

Her face burns. She is certain, instantly and with peculiar shame, that she never should have come here, never should have brought her brother. The realization feels like drowning. She slowly steps backward. She would give her favorite amber bracelet, the one her father crafted, to return to the party and be with adults she trusts. She turns so that her body shields her brother.

"I don't want to hear a secret," she whispers.

"Pretty girl, the prettiest girl in all of Tir Na Nog, is it because I'm so ugly?"

She gasps. Can he read her mind?

In that moment, he eats up the distance between them. The breeze turns into a gusting wind and the words of the Ogham speed into a dizzying cadence. Warbled warnings caress her skin. She feels as though she will faint but she can't, not while holding her brother.

Suddenly Fear Darrig clamps one hand around her wrist. His mouth draws near her ear. She smells the forbidden food and the sourness of old eggs. Her faintness grows.

"There is one uglier than me, fair child, uglier than a hundred of me. And he's coming for you." His hot breath stirs her hair. "But that's not the secret I want to tell you. I want to tell you the prophecy, the one everyone has kept from you and your simple brother. You see, the reign of King Finvarra will come to a very bad end. It's been foretold that the marked child will be his demise. The marked child! What do you say to that, pretty little girl?"

She ducks her hands beneath her brother's flowing white shirt. The back of each is etched with a perfect pink defect in the shape of a tiny curl of ivy. She'd been born with the identical risen flesh on each hand, or so she was told.

Fear Darrig releases her and throws back his head. His quivering giggle grows into a cackle so loud and black that it unsettles the adar llwch gwin nesting in the far trees. They take to the sky with trebling shrieks, and their great golden wings momentarily blot out the sun.

Something tiny severs inside of her and the world begins to spin. The Ogham is yelling now but she can no longer make sense of the words. Her brother is crying, his head tucked into her neck, his fat arms tugging at her. She wants to flee, but her blood has been replaced with hot clay, and a hopeless paralysis binds her as surely as chains.

Then she hears it again, over all other noises—her mother's voice, closer, just on the other side of the ethereal curtain. The call is impatient, safe, elemental. The girl struggles up through her torpor. She tries to yell but no sound comes out. In a last desperate effort, she grasps her brother tightly and falls backward, her blood thumping, one silent word on her lips. The two of them slip between the sun and the shade.

The last thing she sees before returning to Tir Na Nog is not the Ogham but Fear Darrig's leer. His eyes are pinned to hers and a smile dances like an insect across his face.

Beware the marked child, he mouths, over and again.

Chapter 1

Aine dives into the hollow of the tree, scraping her elbow on the rough bark. She bites back a curse. Her heart is thudding. She curls herself small, like a chipmunk. The den reeks of mushrooms and a basement she can't remember visiting. Through force of will, she steadies her breathing. That, or her smell, will surely give her away. She cradles moss over her raw elbow to mask the iron odor of the fresh wound. In this hunt, out of sight does not equal out of mind.

Footsteps sound almost immediately, surprisingly quiet. *Swish, swish.* The grass is parted. Two quick sniffs seek her scent. She swallows her breath and melts into the cave of the tree, becoming bark and branch.

It works. He steps past the gnarly sycamore with its girl heart.

She waits a handful of beats before poking her head out. No sign of him. Just dense hardwoods forming a canopy so thick only ferns and horsebalm sprout beneath them, and an occasional patch of grass where persistent sunbeams have fought through. The dappled light gives the forest an underwater quality, making it both vibrant and hazy. The ground is peppered with fallen branches, each one a potential thundercrack if stepped on.

She breathes deeply, quietly. The hot Alabama air fills her lungs like water. Hopping out of the wooden cave, she grabs a pinecone from the forest floor and tosses it in the direction he disappeared. She clings close to the protection of her tree, waiting, listening. No response. He is either out of earshot or standing still as a rock, waiting for her to expose herself. It can't be helped. She can't hide forever.

She shivers with the risk of it and darts toward the relative safety of the river, dancing between twigs as silently as a deer. Her body ripples in and out of shadow and light. Dust motes float lazily through the sun rays piercing the forest, undisturbed by her passage.

As she flies, Aine catches a flash of movement close to the earth and fifteen feet to her left. She drops to a crouch, expelling her breath in measured puffs. She scans the area. Her heartbeat picks up. Has she misjudged his location? Is he actually shadowing her, smug, like a cat with his mouse?

The slight movement snags her eye again, this time accompanied by a tiny crunch and the color brown. She relaxes. This creature is much too near the ground to be her pursuer. Probably a rabbit. She pushes herself up, brushes the damp forest from her palms, and dashes toward the river.

But the flash returns—the flicker of movement, still to her left, following her.

It's no rabbit. That means two hunters are on her trail. She glances around, ears tuned to the smallest sound, harmonized to the sighing breeze through the sweetgum leaves, honed on a crow's squawk. The air is its own living force, torpid and sweet like syrup.

But she senses only animal and nature, no human sight or sound.

The identical scars on the back of her hands itch. The marks are dime-sized lines with two diagonal lines intersecting each. The defects resemble poorly-done stitching more than anything. That's in fact what Grandma Glori had told her they were, leftovers from a childhood accident. Aine'd gotten into the habit of hiding them at school, and now, she ignores the itching. Tiptoeing to her left, she crouches and waits for more movement. Nothing. But she doesn't mind being still. It provides its own safety.

Scritch scritch.

The crunching has returned. Whatever tiny thing is following her moves steadily, like a fox, scurrying only when it nears an open spot. It could give away her position if she doesn't scare it off. She turns the cards and tracks it rather than letting it track her.

Step.

Crouching step.

Step again.

The forest is quiet. The oppressive heat licks at her neck and flattens her hair into strings, but she's patient. And she's rewarded.

The creature breaks free of a cluster of tree-shaded ferns and scampers behind the safety of a rock pile before moving into the deep forest ink. Aine snares only a glimpse of it, an impression really. Still, what she sees shocks her. She rubs the back of her hand across her forehead. The thing she is stalking is not a four-footed creature. It walks on two legs. In fact, it looks exactly like a three-inch human doll come to life.

"Gotcha!"

She twirls. "Spenser! What're you doing?"

"Jeez, you don't need to get all wet. That's how the game's played, remember? You hide, I find." He smiles broadly, his eyes focused a little to her left, and slides his hand down his white cane. He requires the tool to navigate the woods only when he is moving fast and worried about clapping a tree. Otherwise, he knows the forest well enough by sound, texture underfoot, smells, and memory.

Aine curls her forefinger into her thumb and flicks him on the side of the head, her tone loving even if the words are not. "Now whatever I saw is gone. Thanks a lot."

He rubs his head, his expression apologetic. "What'd it look like?"

Aine glances around, but the woods are still. Her sweet little brother has scared away even the worms. No way will she tell him she thinks she saw a tiny man wearing a loose white shirt and brown britches. The speckled afternoon sun must have teased her eyes. It was ridiculous for a sixteen-year-old to be playing hide-and-seek anyhow. She'd never live it down if her friends saw her. If she had friends.

"It wasn't anything," she said. "You coming?"

"Nah. I'm going to the river. I wanna dip my feet in. It's hotter'n a witch's oven out here." He cocks his ear toward the distant shush of water.

For the first time in her life, Aine feels anxious about the woods. "Grandma'll want us back soon."

It's a lie. Their grandma is always happy to toss them out of her weathered farmhouse. She says it's because kids need exercise, and adults weren't put here to entertain them. *That's what big sisters are for. I babysat my brother when I was your age. I almost raised him myself, in fact. You'll be fine, and stronger for the experience.*

Aine thinks there's more to it than that. She notices her grandma never smiles when she and Spenser are around. Yet, Aine has on occasion heard laughter filtering from the house when she and her brother were exiled to the woods, Grandma Glori's chuckles mixed with those of Mondegreen, her ever-present male companion. The retreating laughter makes Spenser smile. It makes Aine resentful.

She first met her grandma when she was eleven. The pixie-faced woman's silver hair is the only sign of her age. Cropped short, it curls around her ears and frames her small, keen face. Other than the gray, Grandma Glori appears ageless and carries herself as stiffly as a soldier. It isn't that she is unkind. She doesn't hug or touch the children if she can help it, that's true, but she loves Aine and Spenser in her own ten-foot-pole way. That's what she tells them, anyhow. She also has the life she'd lived before they'd come to stay with her, which Aine infers consisted of never leaving her property, fierce gardening, and afternoons of playing card and dice games with trusty Mondegreen.

Spenser shakes his head. "You know she'll be mad if we return early. Just a quick dip? I'm melting like butter."

Aine is in no hurry to return to Glori's constant annoyance with her—*you didn't clean fast enough, your brother needs someone to play with, the potatoes are too salty, you only earned a "B" on this paper, you can do better, you can do better, you can do better.* The thought makes her shudder. She also doesn't want to feel scared in her own forest. She decides the tiny clothed creature she'd thought she'd spotted earlier was nothing more than a chipmunk and a trick of the light.

"Fine," she says. "Race you!"

Spenser can navigate the woods surprisingly fast, blind or not, but Aine is the wind. The sycamores and blackjack oak blur as she passes, her light footsteps barely scaring up the smell of rotting leaves and damp. She's at the edge of the river, her breath even, when he catches up to her. Sweat dampens her clothes, but the water flowing down from the Appalachians promises icy relief.

Spenser rests his cane on the rock where they always leave their shoes. The huge gray boulder is an unusual sight in this part of the river. Here, the water is wide, deep, and calm, the banks sandy and knotted with reeds. Up a half a mile and around a tree-spotted bend, the river turns dangerous, a churning white foam that eats massive rocks like this one and spits them out as river stones.

Grandma Glori has warned them against that part of the river, and particularly the whirlpool that swirls like a tornado, always, beneath the point where the rocks became a cliff and the forest stretches up and into a mountain. Spenser calls it the Cthulu pool after a story in *Weird Tales*. He is taken with the image of an under-water dragon with the arms of an octopus, waiting to pull the unsuspecting into its clutches, and regularly begs Aine to walk with him to the banks of the whirlpool. When she does, she has to yell to be heard over the rapids.

She also has to keep an extra eye on Spenser. He is drawn to the water's edge like a sailor to a siren. He has always loved water. A bath-tub will do in a pinch but if he gets near water deep enough to duck his head in, Aine has a hard time pulling him out. He twirls like a seal, jumps and spins, twining his fingers through water plants and massaging his feet along the rocks and sand. He has floated so still in this river, completely underwater except for his nose and eyes, that fish give him little pecking kisses. At least that's what he told Aine in one of the sweet speeches he frequently offers to fill the empty air.

Aine doesn't mind the river. She'd just rather be lost in a book if she had to choose: on an adventure, solving a mystery, following bloodthirsty Captain Flint across the raging seas or sharing secrets with the March sisters, ultimately escaping this boring life of play-ing children's games with her brother, no matter how tender he is.

The day she leaves home forever, she'll bring him with, of course. She has had that planned almost from the moment they'd been dropped at Glori's. As soon as she graduates and is able to support Spenser, the two of them will hit the road to look for their mother. Maybe she could land a job as a teacher or a librarian. She'd never much taken to people but her love of books would surely open some doors. Wouldn't it?

"Last one in is a rotten egg," Spenser calls, stripping off his outer clothes and diving in.

Aine sighs and retrieves his shirt and shorts. After folding them and stacking them on the boulder with his suspenders, she sets his shoes beside the pile. She does the same with her book bag and shoes before stripping down to her pale pink camisole and knickers. The birds are unusually quiet, which she chalks up to the terrible heat. She dips her toe into the water. The iciness is delicious. She's a good swimmer, not nearly as strong as Spenser, happier on land.

Her brother appears on the surface and spouts a plume of water like a nymph. "You coming?"

"Workin' on it," she says.

He laughs at nothing in particular and disappears underneath the glassy surface. A twig floats over the ripples he's created.

Aine wades in up to her calves. The coolness climbs through her blood, and the sluggish breeze that licks at her neck no longer feels like a threat. Smooth river rocks massage her feet. She scoops a handful of water and bathes her scraped elbow. She is studying her reflection in the water, long hair coming loose from its braid and serious eyes, when she hears it.

The crunching again. Behind her.

She twirls and scours the reeds for any sign of the squirrel wearing clothes. Only a gentle breeze bends the grass. She sneaks back toward the bank and crawls up low and quiet. If she can just get one good look at this creature, she won't have to be so nervous anymore.

She is stalking the sound when the scream pierces the air.

Chapter 2

Spenser leaps out of the water and stares upstream. "What was that?"

"The Cthulu pool! Stay here." Aine grabs a fallen branch, as thick as her arm and longer than she is tall. She rushes up the river and toward the bend. The branch slows her down, but she still makes amazing time. A flash of color in the water moves toward the angry mouth of the river. Someone is being sucked toward the whirlpool. She leaps over thistles and around slippery moss. The glimpse of color appears again, accompanied by another scream, this one weaker but laced with pure terror. It's a boy, and he's drowning.

The closer to the churning rapids she gets, the louder the crashing of water becomes until it is an industrial roar. She has to trust that her brother isn't following her, is safe back in their swimming hole.

Only when she rounds the bend does she realize her terrible mistake. She can't reach the whirlpool from here, not even with the branch. It's twenty feet from the bank. The churning rapids gnash their teeth and froth from the rock-battered water splatters her face. The sound of hungry water is terrifying. There's no safe way to cross the river.

Her eyes scour the whirlpool, her throat tight. No boy. Then she spots him. He's clinging to a glistening rock near the rim of the violent swirl. The water sucks greedily at him as his fingers slip. His small arm muscles pop from the effort.

"Don't let go!" she yells. "I'm coming!"

She'll have to run back toward the swimming hole and cross where it's safe. Will there be enough time? She's dashing back, exhausted from running with the heavy branch, when she spots an otter flash in the water. She isn't going to stop, but then she catches a glimpse of pink. It's not a river otter. It's her brother, slipping toward the sucking whirlpool, his tender little body disappearing between rocks and under froth. Aine's stomach clutches.

"Spenser!"

He doesn't hear. The rapids have swallowed him whole, rushing him toward the whirlpool's ravenous maw. Aine doesn't hesitate. She plunges into the water, tucking the branch under both arms. Her foot is sliced by a sharp rock and her balance is sucked away. She drops under the water. The branch batters her but keeps her from being pulled too deep. She kicks at the ground and finds it surprisingly close, but the current won't let her to stand. Angry, she kicks again. She's going to save her brother!

Rocks assault her and clutch at her clothes, but she powers forward, winning against the water. Her ears and nose are stuffed with raging, suffocating liquid. Suddenly, she's thrown up and out. She slurps greedily at the air, disoriented by the clamor of the rapids. She's been sucked into a secondary pool, a weak reflection of Cthulu, where the water spins ineffectually around a cache of sticks and leaves.

"Spenser!" she shrieks.

The river bottom is slippery, but she can stand. She releases the branch and scours the seething rapids for any sign of her brother. She sees only roiling water capped with white, gigantic rocks jutting up like prehistoric teeth and the swirling, hypnotizing, racing Cthulu pool. She has to plunge back in. She's going to put her hands on him and pull him out. She's not going to let anything in this world hurt Spenser, even if it means swimming to the center of the earth.

Just as she dives, she hears him. "Aine! Here!"

The voice is thin over the thunder of the rapids. She catches herself mid-dive and shoots up her head. She spots Spenser, across the river and down. He is standing shakily on the far bank, a bloody boy in ripped short pants lying still at his feet. She pulls herself out of the pool and runs faster than she thought possible, ignoring the pain in her foot and the blood trail she leaves. Rounding the bend, she dives in even though the water is rough. She crosses, dashes up the bank, and reaches her brother's side.

"What do you think you were doing?" Her voice is a mix of anger and relief. That's when she notices that Spenser is on the verge of crying. Out of the water, the danger past, the reality of what just happened settling in, he looks scared. She hugs him tight.

He is shaking in her arms, his words muffled. "It's a good thing he didn't get sucked all the way into the Cthulu pool, Aine. It doesn't have a bottom. It goes on, deep and forever. I don't think I could have swam out if I'd gotten any closer."

Aine wants to yell at him some more and make him promise never to put himself in danger again. Instead, she gives him a hard squeeze then leans over the boy on the ground. She knows him from the edges of school, a friend of a classmate who appears outside the playground every spring and disappears every fall. She remembers his name, an unusual one at that: Tru. He is about Spenser's age, maybe a year older, and small like her brother. His hair is sandy brown now that it's wet, so light it's almost clear when it's dry, and the ordeal has left him mottled with bruises. Aine rolls him onto his stomach, slapping his back once, then twice.

Tru begins coughing.

"Are you okay?" Spenser asks.

He coughs some more and throws up a slithering silver pile of water. He flips over onto his back and runs a shaking hand over his body as if to check that everything's still intact. "I don't reckon that was the swimming hole?" he asks. His thick Southern twang is a marked contrast to Aine and Spenser's accent-free speech.

Spenser shakes his head. "No. Sorry."

"It's our river," Aine says, suspicious of this trespasser now that he is safe. Nobody is allowed on Grandma Glori's extensive property, no one but her, Spenser, and Mondegreen. "You shouldn't be here."

Tru tries to stand but his legs quiver too much. He holds out his hand instead. "Name is Tru, ma'am."

"Aine." She takes his hand. "This is my brother Spenser. Did you break any bones?"

Tru makes a show of stretching out his legs, examining his elbows, and twisting to see his back. The activity seems to restore him, and he slowly stands, using Spenser for support. "I think I'm fine."

"Then you should go."

"Aine!" Spenser's color is coming back. "He almost drowned."

Aine plants her hands on her hips. Grandma Glori will be furious if she finds out a stranger was on her property. Yet, Spenser is right. She can't send Tru off until she's certain he's okay. "All right. He can come to our rock and get warmed up."

18

Jess Lourey

The walk back takes several minutes. All three of them seem new to their legs. Now that the danger is past, Aine feels the pain of the river rock cutting her foot. She makes a point of stepping naturally so that Spenser doesn't hear her limp and worry. The sun shines brightly on the river's edge so their clothes dry quickly. No one speaks for a time. When they round the bend, and the roar of the rapids diminishes, Tru ventures a comment.

"It was hot enough to cook an egg on my head. I didn't think I'd hurt anyone by practicing my swimming. Just learned how to yesterday. Didn't know this was private property. Didn't even intend to go down this far. I started in the river at the edge of town, just floating. Guess I lost track of time and then the current got me."

"It's a strong river," Spenser agrees.

"Thank you," Tru says. "I'm mighty sorry if I upset your sister." He's thoughtful for a moment. "Hey, you two know what a knock knock joke is?"

Aine purses her lips. If she could see herself, she would be surprised how much she resembles Grandma Glori just then. "We haven't got time. We're going to let Tru collect himself and then send him on his way."

"Please," Spenser says.

Tru forges ahead. He focuses his attention on Spenser. "I say 'knock knock,' and then you say 'who's there.' I tell you a little about who's at the door, and you ask who that is. Like this: knock knock."

Spenser is already grinning ear to ear. "Who's there?"

"Amos."

"Amos who?"

"A mosquito just bit me!"

Both boys dissolve into giggles. Aine rolls her eyes and moves to

19

the boulder so Tru can't see her smile. On the way, she realizes that she is wearing her underclothes in front of a strange boy. He's a wet little tail-wagger, but still. She's become too wild over the summer. She steps behind the rock and quickly slips on her blouse and skirt.

It takes exactly that long for Spenser and Tru to become best friends. They're at the edge of the swimming pool and piling words on top of each other like dominoes when she emerges. Spenser is talking about his rock collection, and Tru is describing his, and they're reaching for smooth river stones and passing back and forth the ones they think are special.

Aine climbs on top of the boulder and watches. She is astonished her brother has no scratches or bruises. He must be an even stronger swimmer than she thought, and for that, she's grateful. On the whole, Spenser approaches life the same way he approaches Pixy Stix: eagerly, without thought, forgetting every time that if he takes it whole, he'll gum up the works and not get anything. He is a puppy of a boy, blind since birth. He is also kind almost all of the time, friends with everyone at school, and every adult's favorite. Aine would be jealous if she wasn't so proud of him. She flips open her book bag and yanks out *Dracula*.

"Aine," Spenser begs from the riverbank. "Can we swim a little bit?"

Aine's scars itch for the second time that day. She scratches absently at them, and a flash of brown snags her eye. She looks past Spenser's shoulder at the edge of the forest. She stops scratching and puts down the book. The brown is the same shade as the tiny creature she'd spotted following her earlier, but it seems much larger now. She remembers the crunching sound she was stalking before Tru screamed for help. She is suddenly uneasy again. "Tru, I'm afraid you need to go home. So do we. Now."

She's watching the brown and spots a snatch of white with it, just a glimpse between the sweetgum branches. Whatever was following them has now become as tall as a grown man. An unfamiliar coldness settles into her chest.

"All right," Tru says, stepping out of the water reluctantly. "Maybe some other time."

Aine jumps down and watches the boy walk toward town with slumped shoulders. She keeps glancing at the forest. Whatever is in the woods hasn't moved. She steps to the water's edge and helps Spenser with his shoes, never pulling her attention from the brush.

"I'll make you a glass of lemonade when we get back," she says.

Spenser considers the offer. "Extra sugar?"

"Yeah. Just come on. Let's hurry." She pulls him away from the riverbank and leads him over a log carpeted with moss. As they head toward the farmhouse, Aine glances back to sweep the forest one last time. She sees nothing but trees and ferns and horsebalm.

Chapter 3

"What are you two doing here?"

Grandma Glori had been pacing the hard wood of the kitchen floor when they'd returned, her pleated, sage-green dress billowing behind her. She'd moved so quickly that the tiny, delicate gold cylinders hanging from her earlobes whistled as she passed.

Mondegreen, her ever-present companion, is leaning against the oak cabinet, his face tense. He is a bear of a man who always wears his newsy cap on backward and slips sweets to Aine and Spenser when Glori's back is turned. His is a comforting, even-keeled presence, and there is no better judge of Glori's moods. His visible distress combined with Glori's agitation makes the back of Aine's neck tingle.

Spenser begins to explain. "Aine—"

She gently squeezes his arm to quiet him. He's going to tell Glori that she saw something strange in the forest, and about Tru's near-drowning. Aine senses that this isn't the time.

Grandma Glori stops her pacing, her eagle focus spearing them.

Worried creases bracket her mouth and eyes. Something bad has happened. Aine steps in front of her brother. He is usually Glori's favorite, if such a thing can be judged, but protecting him has become a habit.

"Yes?" Grandma Glori arches an eyebrow. "Aine *what?*"

"Sorry, Grandma Glori," Aine says. "Spenser was just going to say that we're near the end of *Babbitt,* and he wanted to come back early so I could finish reading it to him."

She surreptitiously squeezes Spenser's arm again so he won't call out her fib. Every day she reads to him from books Glori chooses but they are barely halfway through *Babbitt.* They only read it at night when Glori can check up on them, and both of them are enjoying the story about as much as creamed peas.

It's not unusual for Spenser to dislike a story that doesn't feature swords or monsters. He's a boy. Plus, it's difficult to fully enter a story that someone else reads aloud, and they can only afford a handful of books in Braille. Aine, though, has hardly met a book she didn't love. She gets teased mercilessly at school for always having her head in a novel, or two, as well as for the scars on her hands. She tells herself it doesn't matter, none of those kids matter, but sometimes she envies Spenser for the friends he's gathered in place of books.

She can't change who she is, though. She's always been transported by stories. They remind her of her mom. Aine had been eleven, two years older than Spenser's current age, when a social worker had dumped the two of them on her grandma's slanted porch. Their mom had run off with a stranger and wouldn't be back, Grandma Glori had said with pursed lips and flashing green eyes, and nobody could locate their father. The words hadn't fit in Aine's head. Moms didn't just leave. Especially *her* mom.

Lavender. That's what Helen had smelled like. When Aine had hugged her, she was wrapped in the scent of a warm summer evening. She remembers that. She also remembers Helen reading to her and Spenser every night. She's almost sure of it.

Spenser claims not to remember anything about Helen, even when Aine coaxes him with details about the beautiful blue shade of her eyes and the soft golden hair cascading down her back. Not even when she hums *Aspri Mera Key Ya Mas* and rubs his head like their mother used to. He just twists his mouth in that way he has and plays with his rock collection or his hermit crabs.

It makes Aine sad that he doesn't even try, but the truth is that she remembers very little about their mother, and she wonders if she's embellished her scanty memories. Something like a fog comes over her when she thinks of Helen, or her own life before Grandma Glori. She'll glimpse a bit of an image or a single memory but it'll slip away like a breeze before she can get a good look at it. What few recollections she does have she fought for until she shook and sweat trembled on her forehead. She guards those memories dearly and replays them every day so they don't swim off like the rest.

One thing she will always be certain of, though. Their mother hadn't run off. She loved Aine and Spenser too much for that. But Glori refuses to reveal any more about Helen on the rare occasions she entertains their company, and so Aine always has a pain just behind her eyes, a heaviness that she carries like a bag of rocks even when she smiles. She's confident that the pain will disappear when she is old enough to leave with Spenser and find Helen. She can't wait for that day.

"*Babbitt?*" Grandma Glori resumes pacing, but more gently, and her eyes blur for a moment. Outside cicadas sing and the oppressive heat cooks the mimosa trees until they release their bright, honeyed scent. "That is a glorious book."

Aine releases the breath she hadn't known she was holding. Glori suddenly seems herself, collected and in control. Mondegreen's shoulders soften as well, and the room relaxes. Maybe the two of them had been fighting. It would be a first but not impossible. Aine is leading her brother away when Glori's face tenses again.

"But you can't read it now," she says. "I need you to go to town."

Spenser can't suppress his gasp. Aine barely swallows hers. They have a routine on Grandma Glori's farm. They attend classes during the school year. In the afternoons and during the summer, they play in the woods and by the river and read books and stay out of Glori's way. Like Glori, they do not leave the property, sending Mondegreen to complete any necessary shopping. Upon first arriving at the farmhouse, Aine had found it strange that they were allowed to go to school but nowhere else, and she had questioned Glori about it.

"I'm too old to teach you to read, and I don't care what anyone else says about that," Glori had replied. "Other than school, there's no need for you to expose yourself."

Glori'd been baking an apple pie at the time, and Aine remembered the smell of cinnamon and allspice descending like a delicious fog, melting her resolve, her need for answers. Since then, whenever she thinks of Glori's routine and how small their world is, she smells the apple pie spices and decides that everything is just fine until she turns old enough to support Spenser.

"We get to go to town?" Spenser asks, pulling Aine back into the moment. He sounds excited, thrilled by the possibility.

Aine is surprised he hasn't picked up on the tension in Glori's voice, but it's not completely unlike him. He is so often searching for the good that he overlooks the bad. "Why do you want us to go to town?" she asks warily.

Glori trades a glance with Mondegreen. Their mouths are tight. "For salt," Glori finally says. "A 5-pound bag. Enough to make a circle around the house."

Aine stares. "Why do you need a circle of salt around the house?"

Glori doesn't answer. She strides to the kitchen table and yanks three quarters out of her coin purse. They're shiny and impossibly important. The Great Depression has hit Monroe County harder than most. Three quarters to rub together is a luxury. Glori hands the coins to Aine, who drops them into the pocket of her skirt quickly and carefully, as if they'll dissolve into dust if handled too much. This is all strange and fast and wrong.

"Do you want us to go now?" Aine asks. She's uncertain how to go about leaving the house to go shopping.

"Yes."

Suddenly she's swept into Glori's arms. Her grandmother smells comforting up close, like lilies and paper. Aine is shocked by the embrace but it's over before she can react. Spenser is caught in a similar hug but is too quick for Grandma Glori. He squeezes back and holds her. For a moment, she lets him. Then she pulls away and returns to Mondegreen's side, her voice husky.

"Hurry back," she says. "Don't talk to strangers. Take care of each other, no matter what."

Aine is unaware that her hand is hovering over the pocket containing the money. A trickle of sweat runs down her back, and the air in the kitchen feels impossibly close. "Grandma Glori, what's happening?"

"Nothing," Glori says, meeting her gaze. Her eyes are steely. "If

Mondegreen and I aren't here when you return, know that we'll come back soon."

"But where would you go?" Spenser has finally sensed the anxiety. Glori and Mondegreen, their guardians and the closest thing to family they have, are scared.

Mondegreen smiles reassuringly, but it cracks a little around the edges. "Just for a walk. It's such a beautiful day. No need to worry."

Aine knows it's exactly time to worry when an adult tells you not to. She also is certain Grandma Glori isn't going to reveal anything more. "Come on, Spense."

He takes her hand. After she bandages the wounds on her foot and elbow, they step outside and follow the dirt road to town.

Chapter 4

The walk to town is steamy. The whirring bugs stick close to
Aine's skin and make her feel crawly. Keeping the insects from
landing on Spenser is a full-time job. She avoids discussing their
mission by entertaining him with a story about two fish who realize
they can fly. She soon has him giggling, but her tension at Glori's
strange behavior lingers, giving way to apprehension the closer to
town they get. They've walked the dusty trail many times, but only
to go to school.

The coldness has returned to Aine's chest despite the tropical heat.
She keeps glancing behind her at the safety of the retreating woods.
They leave the road for a shortcut across a cotton field. The harvesting
has just begun, so they hold their arms up to avoid snagging their
clothes on the burst cotton bolls. The field smells dusty and brown.

On the other side, they step onto a dirt road which takes them
past a row of neat shacks, and then travels alongside the junkyard,
and then runs in front of the loneliest house in the county. It's barely
more than a lean-to, and gaping holes covered with oilcloth serve as

windows. A large family lives there but Aine has never seen a one of them in school. Their front yard looks like an offshoot of the junkyard, all done up with rusting metal and garbage. A corroded engine sits on a rotting trailer, an icebox with its door hanging open spills nesting material onto the ground, and a collection of steering wheels line the walkway with their pointed ends tilted upward like medieval ramparts. Red flowers used to grow in jars perched on the sagging wooden fence, a startling contrast to the decay, but they're gone now.

Just looking at the house makes Aine feel empty, and she tugs at Spenser's hand to hurry him along. Finally they reach town, and there is no more pretending. Aine feels out of place, underdressed, ugly. She hesitates with Spenser on the edge of town until a group of Negro women pass, their dresses starched and bright. They are laughing but grow quiet when they draw near Aine and Spenser, careful to avoid eye contact. They are almost past when the closest woman, her face nearly hidden by a gigantic straw hat decorated with a green velvet ribbon, sneaks Aine and Spenser a mischievous grin and a tip of her hat.

"Hello, Miss," she says.

Aine smiles back in surprise. The kindness gives her enough courage to walk across the town square. The single general store, the Jitney Jungle, stands like an obelisk in their path, its jaunty red and white sign daring them to cross the threshold. Aine squeezes Spenser's hand and walks up the front steps, past the lazy, staring white men spitting their tobacco onto the porch floor, and into the enormous store. Spenser huddles close to her.

She and Spenser stand apart. Despite Spenser's friendliness, they always have. The time they spend reading, the way Aine always makes sure they appear clean and proper despite their games in the woods, the scars on her hands, the way they speak—none of that matters at Grandma Glori's, but here, it marks them as different. Outsiders. Aine wants to melt, but instead she walks forward, head held high.

Despite her discomfort and fear, a slow smile creeps across Aine's face. The inside of the Jitney Jungle is a wonderland—immaculate tins of sardines, beautifully-packaged cuts of beef, bright, violet rectangles of Choward's Scented Gum. Everything is neat and orderly, bright and clean. It smells smoky and sweet and exotic. A twirling Emerson Electric pedestal fan brings blessed relief. Her smile widens to a grin. She feels like she's stepped into a magical land so different from the dusty school or the isolated farmhouse. Who knew this marvel was so close?

"Well if it ain't I-knee and Spenser, out of the witch's cauldron."

Aine pivots on her heel, the grin dropping from her face. Wilbur Peppertree has appeared from behind a display of toilet tissue and Octagon soap. He's a grade ahead of her and three years older, built like an ice truck and not much smarter. She avoids him like she avoids most people, but she still knows a little about him. His dad is a dirt farmer, probably also a bootlegger, and Wilbur has no more right to be in this store than they do.

He also knows full well how to say her name correctly, though she's used to it being mispronounced, either unintentionally or as a taunt. Right after her name is butchered, classmates usually begin to tease her about her hands with their ugly scars, or her eyes that they say are too green, or her legs that are too long for her body and make her look like a river bird. Wherever else it goes, the teasing always ends with a handful of her classmates reminding her that she doesn't have any friends.

When she was younger she'd wished she did. She'd try to explain that her grandma wouldn't let anyone come over. Eventually she found it easier just to be quiet and absorb the taunts. She'd get out of this town soon enough—just one more year of school—and until then, she had her books. She tugs Spenser's sleeve and begins walking toward the grocer's counter, careful to hide her hands in the folds of her skirt. Spenser, however, digs in his heels.

"My sister's name isn't I-knee. It's pronounced 'Ah-nee.' Rhymes with 'Bonnie,'" he adds helpfully in Wilbur's direction, a puzzled smile on his face. "It's a family nickname."

Wilbur Peppertree grins, displaying yellowed teeth. "It's a family nickname," he mocks, doing a poor imitation of Spenser's drawl-free way of speaking. The words sound as if they're exiting through his nose. "Well I reckon it is. That don't make it any better. It's still the stupidest name I ever heard. Probably that's the sort of stupid name you get when you don't have a mama or a daddy who even loved you enough to stick around, just a witchy old grandma."

Aine doesn't like the way he looks at her, the way all older boys and most men look at her, as if they can see right through her dress. She resists the urge to cross her arms over her chest and tamps down the little fire starting inside of her, something she's had to practice many times.

"We're here for salt," she says clearly, her hands curling into fists.

"Looks like you'all made a trip for biscuits then, I-knee," Wilbur says, drawing out the mispronunciation. "This store don't sell no salt."

Spenser turns to his sister, alarmed. "Aine, what are we going to do? Grandma Glori told us not to come back without it."

Wilbur laughs wickedly. "Can't get no salt for your witchy grandma, eh? Are you going to cry, blind baby?" He pokes Spenser with a meaty finger.

Aine shoves between them with her chin jutting at Wilbur. She speaks in measured tones. "You know that's a lie. They sell salt. And you can either leave us alone so we can buy it, or come fall, you can watch me tell everyone in school that you're a bedwetter."

Wilbur blanches and glances nervously around. "You better watch your back, Aine, you horrible little witch baby with those ugly scarred hands."

He backs out of the store, his face a muddy mixture of shame and anger.

Aine notes with satisfaction that he has finally pronounced her name correctly.

Spenser's hand slips into hers as the store bell jangles, marking Wilbur's departure. "Is he really a bedwetter?" he whispers.

"I have no idea," Aine says honestly. "I know he's a bully, though, and bullies usually have secrets. That's the way it is in books, anyhow. Come on, let's get the salt and hurry home."

Wilbur has stolen the brightness from the store, so they make their purchase and leave. The return walk lacks the anticipation of the hike to town. They hug the treeline, and more than once Aine needs to steer Spenser from traipsing straight into the forest. They feel safe there, unlike on this hard-baked country road where their backs are exposed. A great crested flycatcher trills at them from the heights of a sycamore tree, its song a repeated *weep weep, weep weep*. The perfume of the August flowers is nearly suffocating, and the bag of salt flung over Aine's shoulder has begun to wear a groove.

"What do you think was wrong with Grandma Glori?" Spenser finally asks. "She was acting so strange."

"Nothing. She has a right to an off-day, doesn't she?" She cuts her eyes to her brother, hoping he won't ask any more questions that she can't answer.

"You think that's all there is to it?" His voice is hopeful.

Aine grunts. She has seen Grandma Glori really upset once before. Twice, actually. The first time was four years ago, when Glori spotted an ash tree taking root on the edge of the woods. She'd made the children dig it up, and then anything that resembled it, and burn the whole pile. The second time was when Spenser brought home a pocketful of iron jacks with a rubber ball. Glori screamed at those jacks like they were made of poison and forced Spenser and Aine to walk them to the edge of her property, then another ten feet for good measure, and scatter them like dandelion seeds.

Other than those two times, Glori has been as steady as a train. Until today. Something is going on, something to do with the itchy feeling Aine got in the woods and then by the river, somehow connected to the white and brown shadow following her that was first small and then large. There's no point in worrying Spenser about it, though.

They finally reach the clearing surrounding Grandma Glori's house. The huge grassy field is as large as the town square with the two-story farmhouse planted in the middle like a lonely tree at the end of a dirt road. The house is plain but sturdy, constructed of unpainted wood and asphalt shingles with a porch running the length of it. Grandma Glori and Mondegreen frequently take to the porch on humid summer nights. They sweep the area with their eyes and drink iced tea from sweating glasses, commenting on how nice it is to be able to see what's coming from every direction.

The cleared area also means the house can be spotted from a distance, which Aine presently finds reassuring. She is drenched in sweat. The dark hairs that have wriggled free of her braid are plastered to her face. Spenser doesn't appear much better. He stops abruptly. His cotton shirt is almost transparent with moisture.

"Do you hear that?" he asks.

Aine is too exhausted to stop and listen. "No. What?"

"It's quiet. There's no one in the house."

Aine feels a cold oil slide down her back despite the baking heat. Spenser doesn't always pick up on conversational subtleties, but he's got ears like a bat for everything else. If he says the house is empty, it's empty.

"Grandma Glori said they might not be here. She said not to worry." Aine speaks the words firmly, but they strike a terror in her. She and Spenser have never been alone in the house, other than when Glori was outside working, always within earshot. Aine remembers a time when she wasn't afraid, when her mom filled her with confidence and laughter, but that thought slips back into the darkest part of her brain and disappears and she's left wondering only what to do with the bag of salt.

"I'm sure you're right," Spenser says, patting her arm. "Everything will be fine. Should we pour the salt around the house, like Grandma Glori asked?"

He tugs his penknife out of his shorts and hands it to Aine. She cuts off a corner of the bag, making a large enough hole to pour a controlled stream, and walks around the house. The crystals smell pungent and send sharp, coppery puffs into her nostrils as they fall. There's just enough for one complete circle, the line thin but unbroken. The salt distributed, they have no choice but to walk up the front steps and into the kitchen. The front door is unlocked, but then, when hasn't it been? Glori's not once left the property since Aine and Spenser came to live with her.

"Hello?"

Aine's voice echoes back. The world suddenly seems impossibly huge. If Glori is gone, they have no one. Aine locks the door that's never been locked, pulls the curtains tight over the windows, then distracts herself by bustling over to the cupboards.

"Cheese dreams okay for lunch?"

It's Spenser's favorite meal. He agrees happily, slipping off to gather his hermit crabs, Pinch and Shelly. He carries their terrarium into the kitchen. They scratch at the sides of their cage and crawl over each other to get at Spenser while Aine cooks. She cuts four slabs of homemade bread and next unwraps the papered white cheese that Mondegreen buys in town. She cuts two slices and arranges them on the bread before slapping a generous pat of butter into the cast iron pan and holding a lit match over the gas burner.

Spenser is humming a soft song, and something about it reminds Aine of their mother. She grabs at the memory, fighting for it. Helen, walking with Aine, her arm around her young daughter. They're somewhere lush, green, but it's not Alabama. Lots of people are around, beautiful, tall people in flowing clothes, people who smile and laugh. They're all friends. Helen leans over to whisper something into Aine's ear, something sweet, maybe important. Aine strains to hear it, and then it's gone. All of it.

The cheese dreams are black and smoking, their acrid scent fouling the kitchen. Aine worries it will stink up the whole bottom floor, what little there is of it, and she'll have to hang all the bedding and clothes on the line until they smell fresh again.

Spenser fans his nose against the smell and then stops politely. "It's okay, Nini. I can scrape the burnt off."

Aine feels a surge of annoyance. She hates his baby nickname for her, hates that they're trapped in this place, hates that she doesn't know where Glori is or when she'll be back. If their mom was here, she wouldn't have to do this all alone. She slides the blistered sandwich out of the pan and pushes it toward Spenser but is attacked by conscience at the last moment and yanks it back just as he reaches for it. She's suddenly very ashamed. The tension of this strange day is getting to her.

She is scraping the worst of the burnt off when a loud creak on the front porch announces a visitor. The person takes two careful steps, then is still.

Both she and Spenser freeze.

The silence is deafening.

The knock, when it comes, echoes like a guillotine.

In the five years since they'd come to live in Grandma Glori's house on the edge of the woods, only two people besides Mondegreen have ever visited. One was the mail carrier and last winter, a lost traveler came knocking. Both times, before answering the door, Glori had warned them. *Hear that sound? You don't ever answer it. For anyone.* The world is full of bad people, she'd told them repeatedly, terrible people who will take children away forever to a dark, screaming place where no one will ever love them and the whispering monsters will feed off their tears. *The bad just needs a chance, so don't ever open the door.*

No one has knocked other than those two times. Until now.

"Shush," Aine whispers, unnecessarily.

She is grateful that she locked the door and hadn't yet opened the window to let the burnt smell out. The heavy green curtains save them from being spotted by the intruder. Her thankfulness lasts only a moment. Why couldn't they have been in their rooms upstairs, safer? The old farmhouse's steps creak like a rusty saw, so there's no point in hiding up there now. There's no other way out of the farmhouse, either, other than the windows.

Spenser is as white as bone. He's gripping the edge of the table. In a burst of insight, Aine realizes he has their mom's long, elegant fingers, the beautiful hands of a piano player. She hurries over and hugs him, her heart pumping in her ears.

"Whoever it is will leave soon," she says quietly into his ear. "Probably just the mailman with a package, like that last time. He'll leave it out there. Let's go into the living room, away from the windows."

Spenser nods gratefully even though they both know it isn't the mailman. Grandma Glori made clear the one time he stopped that he was never again to deliver mail here, to her house at the end of a windy dirt road no one can find unless they know where to look. She insists on a post office box in town, and that's where all her packages and letters are delivered. Mondegreen picks them up and brings them to her.

Still, it feels safer to move away from the door. Spenser grabs the rock-filled cage containing his hermit crabs and allows Aine to lead him to the living room. The knocking sounds fainter once they are crouched against the far wall pressed up against the chifferobe, but it doesn't stop. *Rap rap rap. Rap rap rap.* Aine feels a matched knocking, only louder, through her ribcage. Spenser doesn't let go of her hand.

"Should we hide in the root cellar?" he asks. His chin quivers despite his best efforts.

There's no way to reach the root cellar without going outside. He's so scared he's not thinking straight. "We need to be really quiet, Spense." She squeezes his hand. "If we sit here and don't make a noise, the person will go away."

Like a magic spell, the knocking stops the moment the words leave her lips. The silence feels louder than the rapping had been. Spenser smiles tentatively, his cherry lips a cupid's bow of hopefulness. "You're right, Aine. It stopped. I knew we'd be safe here. No one can die in a living room. Whoever it was has—"

An unfamiliar face appears in the window over their heads.

Chapter 5

Aine screams, a short, involuntary sound, before she grabs hold of herself. She shoves Spenser out of view and stands between him and the window. "Stay still," she says, low and careful. "There's someone at the window." Her lips barely move. She doesn't want the intruder to see her talking to anyone. He might have only spotted Aine.

Spenser is too scared to reply.

The face disappears. It had been a man with matted blonde hair and wild eyes.

"Quick, back here," Aine commands, pushing Spenser to a more protected spot behind the woodstove. He doesn't know the size of the space he is being shoved into, so she has to tuck his arms and legs in for him. His knee scrapes along a sharp corner, drawing blood.

"Will he be able to see me?" Spenser's voice is small and painfully frightened, the paper-thin sound of new ice cracking.

"Not if you're quiet. Trust me."

"Hide with me, Aine. Please." He reaches out, his hands desperate. Plump tears slide down his cheeks.

"There's no room. I'll be back for you. Don't make a sound."

She peels off his hands and darts forward to hunker in the doorway between the living room and the kitchen. The living room had been an excellent choice for moving away from the front door but is a terrible place to hide, all open spaces and light. A glance assures her that Spenser is still invisible, but not to anyone who is looking hard. If the man forces the front door or breaks a window, he'll be on top of Aine in a few long strides and there will be no one to save her brother from a lifetime of pain and fear and unspeakable horrors. She feels faint, like she will throw up if she moves too quickly.

Moments later, the knocking at the front door resumes. "I know you're in there," the man says, his voice raised. "I saw you."

Something about the way he talks is unsettling. Aine realizes he lacks the Alabama accent she is so used to hearing. He instead speaks with the clear rhythm used by her family. This doubles her fear, making it thick, but Aine walks through it to distance herself from her brother. She is almost certain Spenser hasn't been spotted. If the man thinks she's the only one inside, he won't hurt her brother. That thought keeps her moving forward.

"Who are you?" she calls from the other side of the kitchen door in a steady voice that belies her anxiety.

"I need to see Gloriana. Is she here? It's urgent."

"She's not home." *You should go away. Please go away.*

The man curses. "Mondegreen?"

"Not here." *There is someone else on this earth knows my grandmother and Mondegreen!*

A thump against the door makes Aine jump. He has slammed his fist against the wood. "Tell her I stopped by, then," he says darkly.

"I don't know who you are."

"That's about right then." Sarcasm or frustration shades his words. "Tell her Tone has come by with a message: Biblos has arrived."

The final three words crackle and hang in the air.

The porch creaks heavily, followed by receding footsteps. Aine counts to twenty, then springs through the cloud of anxiety and darts to the kitchen window before fear and doubt suffocate her. She peeks around the hand-sewn curtain. The man is storming down the driveway.

Because the house sits in the center of a three-acre clearing, she is able to watch him for some time before he steps off the road and melts into the woods. Her chest does not loosen at all. She moves farther to the right so she can see the front stoop. She is startled to see Tru sitting on it, his chin in his hands. She lets the curtain drop and takes three deep breaths before opening the door a crack.

Tru stands and brushes the back of his dusty shorts. "What was that guy doing at your house?"

Aine beckons him forward. When he's within reach, she yanks him inside and locks the door behind him. "What are *you* doing in my house?"

Tru smiles a crooked grin. "You let me in."

"That's not what I mean. I told you today when you were by the river with Spenser…Spenser!" She races into the living room and finds her brother still behind the stove, rocking gently, tufts of ripped-out hair twined between his fingers.

"Come here. It's okay. The stranger left." After some coaxing and with the help of Tru, she coaxes her brother into the bathroom. She cleans the wound on his elbow and tries to wash the fright off his face. "It's going to be all right, Spenser, I swear. He left. He just had a message for Grandma Glori is all."

Spenser doesn't appear to hear. He is whispering so quietly, repeating the same words, that Aine has to lean in to make sense of them. "What's that? I can't hear you."

"Alone, alone, we're all alone," Spenser sings tunelessly, quietly. Her brave brother who saved Tru from the Cthulu pool has been replaced by a small, scared, nine-year-old boy.

Aine bundles him into her arms. "We are not either alone. We just have to find Grandma Glori. Tru, tell us why you're here and what you saw outside."

He shrugs. "Just that man. I was watching from the woods when he came up, fixin' to stop by myself. I spied him knocking, then he disappeared behind the house before comin' back front. When nobody answered, he took off down the road. I figured you weren't home, so I set on your porch to wait until you got back. I have one of Spenser's rocks. It got mixed up with mine by the river."

He holds out a smooth brown stone. It looks to Aine like every other river rock, but Spenser's face relaxes when Tru slips it into his palm. "Thank you," he says.

"It's nothing. Hey, what's with the salt around your house? My aunt did that once. Keeps slugs out of the root cellar, she said. You got slugs?"

"Sure," Aine says. She's already tuned out Tru to formulate a plan. They can't stay in the house and risk being cornered again. They must go out into the forest and find Glori. Aine grabs her book bag from the hook behind the door. She leaves the book, pencil, and paper inside and adds bread and cheese along with a slab of ham wrapped in butcher paper. She rifles around three kitchen drawers before discovering a pocketknife to cut the meat.

She slings the bag over her shoulder, and then notices the mess from the burnt cheese dreams. She cleans it up quickly, issuing instructions to the boys. "Okay you two, we're going for a walk in the woods. Maybe even back to the river. It's late, but it's still hot out. You two ready?"

They nod, both of them solemn-faced. Aine is grateful they aren't asking questions. She steels herself before unlocking the door. She curls her hand around the warm doorknob and slowly pulls it open.

An unexpected shape stands in the doorway.

Aine jumps back before she realizes it's Glori. The woman is stooped as if in pain, and her eyes are deep and ashen.

"Grandma Glori!" Spenser must have caught her scent because he runs forward. He grabs her in a vise lock. "We came back and you weren't here! Someone came to the door. He knew you. He knocked, but we didn't let him in. You told us not to—"

"Stop." Glori's voice is imperious but tired. She allows Spenser to hold her, directing her attention to Aine. "A man came. You saw him?"

Aine nods. "He was younger than Mondegreen, older than me. He said his name was Tone and to tell you that Biblos has arrived."

Her words punch Glori. The woman falls into the sash of the door, releasing Spenser. The boy steps back awkwardly. "So I'm right," she mutters.

Mondegreen appears behind her, concern etching his mouth. He reaches for Glori. "What is it?"

Glori pushes him away. "Biblos is here. Tone delivered the message. Tell me you found Gilgamesh!" It's a command, not a question.

Mondegreen removes his hat and runs his hands through his hair. "I did. I found him in the forest. I tuned up the toadhouse and told him to wait for us. If Biblos is here, it's time to go. Now."

Aine steps closer to Spenser. She drops her arm around him and feels his trembling. None of this makes sense. The sun is shining, the air smells of mimosa, and her world is being turned upside down. "Grandma Glori, what's happening?"

Glori doesn't appear to hear. "Gilgamesh *has* come through," she says under her breath, relief coloring her voice. "I knew it." She snaps to attention and notices Tru. "Who is this?"

"Tru, ma'am." He offers his hand but Glori does not respond. He curls under her gaze until his hand drops to his side. "I'm a friend of Spenser and Aine's."

"What are you doing here?"

"Just visiting, ma'am."

"You shouldn't be here," she says, but she's clearly already dismissed him. "Mondegreen, I can't go with. I have to fight Biblos, slow him down. Take them to Gilgamesh. Flee this story."

A cry escapes Spenser. "We can't leave you!"

A young stranger steps onto the porch. "It's time to go," he says.

His voice is low and commanding despite his age, the urgency in it unmistakable. His shoulder-length dark hair is pulled back into a ponytail. His striking features are accented by a thin, beet-colored scar that curves from his left temple down to his chin like the letter "c." He appears only a year or two older than Aine, except for his eyes. They are dark and rimmed with strain.

His white shirt is loose and the collar hangs open, hemmed and embroidered at the edges. A silver necklace is visible under the cloth. He is wearing old-fashioned brown britches. As Aine takes in his appearance, she gasps. He is the creature who followed them in the woods. He was first small and now is regular-sized, not as big as Mondegreen but well-muscled, lean and lithe like a cat. Although his impatience is written across his taut flesh, he holds himself with confidence. Aine can't stop staring.

"Gilgamesh." Glori smiles, and it transforms her. Her cheeks regain some color, and her voice is again strong. "You've found us. You know what to do?"

Gilgamesh nods, studying Aine and Spenser curiously. "Up close, I see they've grown to look more like their father than their mother. The boy especially."

"Don't get sentimental on me," Glori says. "I summoned the four shadows and sent the message to Finvarra. He knows what I only guessed before Tone confirmed it: Biblos has found us. And here I was, after all these years, thinking we'd be safe."

Glori turns to Aine and Spenser. He is clutching her, his expression confused and scared. Tru has melted into the space behind the cabinet. "Listen to me," she says. "Our time is now measured in minutes. I wish it hadn't come to this. I had hoped to keep you safe and hidden forever, but I couldn't. Biblos is here, and he is coming for you both. Go with Gilgamesh and find the keys. They will bring you to your mother."

Aine's eyes blaze, and she finds her voice. "You know where our mother is?"

"Peace, child. It isn't as you think."

The thick green leaves outside rustle in an ominous murmur. A crash sounds in the forest, far off, but not too far. Gilgamesh shifts his weight and reaches for a weapon that is not there. Mondegreen steps off the porch to study the woods.

"Can't you just tell us where she is?" Spenser begs.

A roar sounds in the distance like a gigantic engine that's just been fired. It rumbles toward them. The sound is unrelenting, destructive, and moves inexorably closer. The ground trembles.

"He's closer than I thought. We must leave now." Gilgamesh steps around Glori but seems uncertain how to force Aine and Spenser to move.

"Where to?" Aine cries. Spenser is pressed against her.

Glori squeezes Aine's shoulder with great strength, and puts her face in close, speaking quickly. "Gilgamesh will take you to your mother, but it won't be easy. This was the plan of last resort. You were supposed to be hidden here, safe in this story until Biblos was captured and you could return to your true home. It hasn't happened that way, and there's no crying over what you can't change. You must find three objects. Each one is a key to the next. They will take you to Tir Na Nog. I can only reveal the clue to the first one, because that's all I've been told. It was too dangerous to leave any keys out for Biblos to capture."

The booming sounds come closer. The treetops shake and the smell of sulfur fills the air. Glori does not flinch. "You're listening?" she asks.

Aine nods. She is so frightened that she has to remind herself to blink.

When next Glori speaks, her voice fills every bit of space inside Aine's head. "The adventure of a lifetime is tied to a powerful rod. Reach wisely for the precious one, and remember that man is not god."

Aine reels back. "What does that mean?" she asks desperately. "A rod? From where? How will we know if it's the right one? How will it bring us to our mom?"

Glori continues in a majestic, disembodied voice. "When what you find is true, the next object will be revealed to you. There are three, and they will bring you to your true family." Her mouth sets in a firm line and her voice returns to normal. "That's it. That's all the information I was given. Remember to always take care of your brother, and keep in mind that what we seek is usually right under our noses. Now, go!"

"Not without Pinch and Shelly." Spenser has hidden behind Aine, clinging to her, but his voice is resolute. An ashen gray has settled under his eyes.

"Spenser!" Aine knows his stubborn streak. It rarely appears, but when it does, it's there to stay. "Are you sure? We'll have to carry it everywhere."

His lip quivers. "I can't let anything happen to them, Aine. I have to bring them."

"Where are they?" Gilgamesh demands, his voice like gravel. The cacophony in the forest has become as loud as the rapids at Cthulu's pool.

Aine points toward the living room. Gilgamesh disappears and returns with the terrarium.

"Now," he says, with finality.

Aine turns to the woman she's called Grandma for five years. She needs an explanation, hope, a reason. Glori has never been affectionate but she provided for them and loved them in her own way. She is the only family that they've known since arriving at the farmhouse.

Rather than consoling Aine, Grandma Glori steps to the porch, turning her back in her granddaughter. She faces the terrifying noise in the forest, lifts her hands, and begins murmuring. A murder of crows appears from behind the house. Shrieking, it flies like an arrow toward the tree-thundering.

Gilgamesh urges Aine and Spenser ahead and down the porch

steps. Tru follows closely. "Run. Our transportation is in the deep of the forest, to the west, near the sycamore tree you hid in earlier. If we don't get away from here, all is lost."

"Defend them with your life, Gilgamesh!" Glori commands. She still has one hand in the air. The other is holding a clear glass marble as large as a grapefruit. Aine has never laid eyes on the object before.

Gilgamesh doesn't pause. He keeps a tight grip on Aine and Spenser, pushing them forward, away from the house, ignoring Tru at his heels. Mondegreen runs north, toward the frightening thundering in the woods, his hands in the air. Aine glances over her shoulder and sees white symbols appear above his head. Flashes of color, so blue they're almost purple, fly toward Mondegreen from the deepest part of the forest, and smoke floats toward the sky. Whatever is chewing up the woods will be in the clearing in seconds, and Mondegreen is charging to meet it.

Aine stops near the forest edge, just for a moment, a warning on her lips. In that second a knife of blue cleaves the air and pierces Mondegreen's stomach, 200 yards away. He cries out and doubles over. Another flash of blue, this one an electric rope, wraps around his neck. His eyes bulge and a trickle of blood leaks from his mouth. He falls face-first.

The blue weapons crawl off of him like worms and fly toward Glori. She drops the marble and curves her right hand into a claw. She clutches at her chest as if removing her heart and flings her hand at the woods. A roar of pain flies back.

"You can't help her," Gilgamesh says, surprisingly close. "I will carry you if you don't move. Do not let her sacrifice be for nothing."

But Aine cannot look away.

The blue maggots squirm toward the house and her grandma.

Then a strange thing happens. The salt ring stops them. They puff and squeal when they get near it. Glori ignores them and sketches shapes in the air. The forms resemble Mondegreen's, intersecting lines and twisting ivy, except hers are a rainbow of colors and twice as large.

The breeze begins to hum. Glori keeps her eyes pinned on the forest, beyond Mondegreen's still form, attention absolutely focused. The trees begin to part. The roar in the woods has become primal and huge. The air around Glori is so thick with the shadows of shapes that it pulses.

Whatever has killed Mondegreen is about to emerge into the clearing.

Aine's legs move instinctively and she jogs toward her grandma. She can't leave Glori to fight that horrible, unseen creature by herself.

A bellow of pure hate echoes out of the woods.

Glori's eyes widen and the blood seeps from her face. She is staring straight north, into the woods. Aine knows her grandmother has just laid eyes on the monster. She tries to see the creature herself but she is too far away, the angle all wrong. She spots only the blue glow of a flash before a strike, growing, stretching, stinking. The sky darkens and the air sizzles. The monster is gathering a killing force.

Glori turns to Aine, and Aine sees it clearly on her grandmother's face: surprise mixed with resignation. But no fear. Later, she will remember being surprised there was no fear.

"I'm coming!" Aine yells.

A proud smile flashes across Glori's face for an instant before it is replaced with a look of supreme concentration.

But time has run out.

The blue force in the forest has arched and focused until with a crack, it's shaped itself into an arrow that sears toward Glori. The air crackles and reeks of fresh lightning. The acid blue bolt screams directly toward her grandmother. Glori has time to snatch only one shape out of the air, only one final chance to save her own life.

"Scaoiligí!" She hurls the word at Spenser and Aine.

Aine feels it hit her. She drops to her knees. The sensation is good, powerful, itchy. She smells a blast of cinnamon and allspice then breathes in air purely for the first time she can remember. The vibrancy of freshness and green overpowers her senses. She raises her eyes to Grandma Glori and they lock stares. Aine is aware of a deep connection that lasts only for only a moment. It feels like love.

It is in that instant that her grandmother is sliced in two by the scissoring blue blades, her hand a claw reaching into the air. The giant marble is rained with blood.

Time stands still for a moment that lasts forever. Then the two halves of Glori's body drop to the porch with a terrible thud. The air is saturated with the metallic odor of new death. Aine's eyes cloud and she is unable to breathe. The suddenness, the permanence. She is stunned beyond reaction.

Grandma Glori has been murdered.

Chapter 6

True to his word, Gilgamesh tosses Aine over his shoulder like a sack of grain. He grabs Spenser's hand and pulls him into the forest's encompassing protection. Tru follows, but not closely enough. He pumps his legs, but the blue energy hurtles like a bullet toward his head. He trips over a root, and his clumsiness saves him. A midnight-blue light shrieks past his head, leaving a smoking lock of his hair on the ground.

A ravenous chuckle rattles the sky. A lonely, rotten-sweet smell, like overripe fruit and hot tar, reaches them. It's followed by a strange, scratched, taunting voice that sounds as if it's everywhere even though the monster must have just reached the clearing.

"Where are you, little sweeties?" it calls. "Mondegreen and Gloriana died too quickly. Don't make me pursue you, too. Hunting works up an appetite, and you don't want to make Uncle Biblos hungry for those boys' delicious ankles."

Fingers of terror slide down Aine's neck. "I can run by myself!" She pushes herself off of Gilgamesh's shoulder. She grabs the terrarium from her brother so he can jog more quickly.

"Move or die!" Gilgamesh shouts back to Tru.

The boy charges to his feet and makes up for lost time. They race over branches and ferns, Aine convinced the cloying smell of dirty rotting fruit is pawing at her hair. She pushes harder, following Gilgamesh through cuts and tunnels that she thought were known only to her and Spenser. She hears an echo in every step they take, certain the monster is upon them, feeling the hot breath of the creature who just murdered her grandmother and Mondegreen.

They near the sycamore tree she'd hidden in that morning back when the world was normal. The mottled bark winks at her, promising...what? She sees no transportation, no automobile or flying machine. She pivots to tell the boys they should hide in the tree's secret heart so she can draw the monster away when Spenser falls in an unceremonious heap a little ways behind her, helplessly tangled in a grasping root.

"Get up!" Aine says.

"I can't." His breath comes in labored gasps. "I need to rest."

"I'm bushed, too," Tru says, dropping next to Spenser. "I think I'll just take a quick nap."

"Are you insane?" Aine yells. She can't believe her ears. "We have a murderer breathing down our necks. If I have to drag you both away by your hair, I—"

"Don't take another step," Gilgamesh snarls, holding her back. "It's not their fault. I set a fairy ring for Biblos, to protect the toadhouse." He points to the cluster of mushrooms circling her now-sleeping brother and Tru.

She is suspicious of Gilgamesh, of all the upheaval, of people who do little more than leave when you need them most, of this sudden talk of her mother and keys and secret lands. Yet the terrible sound of splintering trees is coming closer, and the too-sweet sulfur smell has been replaced by smoke. She speaks, holding the phrase away from her body. "What do we do?"

With a wave of Gilgamesh's arm, the mushrooms disappear into the ground with a liquid pop. Gilgamesh throws Spenser over his shoulder and grabs the terrarium with his other hand before stalking toward the copse of pines.

"Leave my brother alone!"

Gilgamesh doesn't pause. "Biblos will do far worse things to him than I could ever dream of," he yells over his shoulder. "Help me and save yourself."

Aine wants to weigh her choices but realizes she doesn't have any. She slides her hands under Tru's armpits. The shriek of a tree shattering pierces the forest. The monster is hunting them, burning the woods in his wake. He will be upon them in minutes.

It takes the last of her remaining strength, but Aine manages to stumble behind Gilgamesh, dragging Tru under the shoulders, into the shelter of the pines. She lays him next to Spenser, her breath coming in deep, ragged gasps. The boys seem defenseless here too, resting on a pine-scented bed of longleaf needles. By the sound of it, the monster is within a few hundred feet and she wonders at her foolishness in following this stranger, no matter what her grandmother said. She and Spenser could have hidden from God himself in the forest. "You said you had transportation here?"

"Yes. The toadhouse. Get in." Gilgamesh jabs his finger at a clay sculpture tucked into the base of a pine tree. It's as big as a breadbox and shaped like a tight, upside-down bowl. It's green-gray with a tiny elfin curl on the top and a delicate paned window next to an open doorway. Opposite the window rests a golden square the size and shape of a box of matches.

Aine snorts. Her disbelief is too vast for words.

A thunderous roar followed by the cracking of trees jerks her thoughts back into focus. Biblos is approaching the other side of the pine copse. His voice breaks through the destruction with a roar.

"I know you are close, my sweet prey! I can smell you. When the parents don't play, their children must pay." His faint accent is like a narrow Mediterranean current flowing through his taunts, but his voice is metallic, thunderous, spiked with hunger. Sparks of color flash through the trees but the monster is not yet visible.

Gilgamesh's muscles flex all along his shoulders and arms like an animal holding back an attack. He speaks in a furious whisper, enunciating each word. "Get in the toadhouse. There's nothing left for you here!"

Her brain can't make sense of the situation. Gilgamesh growls in frustration, scoops Spenser into his arms, and leans through the five-inch tall gray-green clay door as if it is nothing. Aine sees a normal-sized Gilgamesh from behind and, through the window, a tiny Gilgamesh arm laying a teeny Spenser on a cot. It's like watching a man bend through a carnival mirror. He swivels to Aine. "Get in."

A shattering explosion rings out as a nearby tree blasts apart in a fountain of knife-sharp slivers. Biblos isn't certain where they are, but he's near. It's only a matter of seconds until he discovers their hiding spot.

"Not without Tru," she says, shocked.

Gilgamesh shakes his head angrily. "You can't take him with us. If you do, you'll kill the story and leave the boy homeless."

"What?"

"If you change the outcome of the story, it's lost. Once the book ends, everyone in it will disappear forever." He points toward the sky. "Like that smoke."

Biblos' voice reaches the pine copse, alarmingly close. "Eeny meeny, miny moe, gonna catch you by the toe. Are you behind this rock?"

Forty feet away, a boulder flies through the air and slams into the sycamore tree Aine had hidden in earlier today, destroying it. She is so scared she can't swallow, trapped between the monster in the clearing and a world she hadn't known existed. She wishes powerfully, hopelessly, for her grandmother to be by her side.

"I don't know what you're talking about," she says, "but I'm not leaving Tru here to die."

Gilgamesh looks to the trees for quick counsel before swiveling toward the toadhouse. His movements are terse and angry. "Fine. I can set his archetyper. If we return him to this book before his words run out, we might still save this story and him. But I swear, you don't know what you do, woman. Drag him in while I get the toadhouse running or we're all dead."

Gilgamesh dashes into the tiny structure and disappears from Aine's line of sight. She buries her confusion at why he called her a woman—Glori and Mondegreen had always treated her like a child—and grabs Tru's arms. Out of the corner of her eye, she sees a tiny Spenser rousing inside the toadhouse. He sits up and reaches around frantically. His voice, squeaky and terrified, escapes the small structure. "Aine?"

"Out here," she says. "You're safe, Spense, in a house. Don't step outside of it no matter what. I'm going to hand Tru to you, and you pull him in."

Aine smells the smoke. She catches an unnatural flash of silver and blue at the edge of the copse. She hears the triumphant roar of the monster.

Biblos has sniffed out their hidey spot.

Fear makes her stomach jelly, but it also makes her strong. She releases Tru's arms and instead sweeps him up, even though he is three quarters her size. She throws him at the toadhouse door. Her aim is true, and he flies through, shrinking, shoving her brother to the floor. Aine falls on all fours from the effort. If she can crawl forward a few feet, she will be on the threshold of the toadhouse. Gilgamesh is yelling at her to hurry, sweet black Annis, just hurry.

And then, the forest goes dead quiet.

The hair on the back of Aine's neck spikes.

She feels the hot breath.

She doesn't want to turn, would give everything she owns not to face what's behind her. Inside the toadhouse, Tru shrieks, a tiny tortured rabbit cry of pure fear, and Aine knows he is looking through the doorway at the monster directly behind her. She knows that she has no chance. She knows that she can't escape.

And so she turns.

Chapter 7

She understands what drove the blood from Glori's face when she first laid eyes on the monster.

Biblos is enormous, shaped like a man but nearly fifteen feet tall. He looms over Aine, who is still on all fours. His eyes are alight, crazy glowing blue embers burning below a jarring head of thick black hair. His features are handsome, sickeningly so for all his deformities. His skin is nearly covered by a long-sleeved, strangely outdated shirt and trousers, but where it is visible, odd letters freckle his burnt and scarred body and face. He has one normal hand. Where the other should be is instead a mutated tube of flesh that squirms and shifts like a melting worm. Thousands of blue-charged insects and slugs crawl over his feet in busy, writhing patterns.

A tiny voice calls Aine from inside the toadhouse. She is paralyzed. Her eyes are hot with tears. Biblos' lettered, fingered hand reaches for her, slowly, intimately.

"Biblos is not out of the game yet, eh pretty one? We will be spending much time together, you and I. I won't hurt you, I promise you that. I only want to take a little trip, just the two of us." His meaty hand slides around her leg, gently but with immense strength, pulling her close to him and farther from the toadhouse. He breaks into a grin at the contact, and she sees his perfect white teeth, his canines sharpened to points.

She nearly throws up. She forces down the bile, horrified that he will touch her with his worm hand. He leans in closer. His gigantic head moves toward her, his wet lips close, his hot breath reeking of composting food. When his face is only inches away, she witnesses his most horrifying feature of all: words crawling like dirty ants across the white meat of his eyes.

The sight unfreezes her.

She kicks with her free leg, striking his nose. He bellows. She twists her other foot in his concrete grip. Because he is soaked with sweat, she is able to free herself after paying a tithe of flesh. She turns, stumbles toward the tiny toadhouse, falls, and stands up again. How can she possibly reach it in time? Biblos lunges and catches a twist of her hair. It yanks free with a ripping sound. She cries out.

Aine launches herself toward the toadhouse, becomes airborne, feet and then inches from the doorway. She has no time for doubt. As she passes through the doorway, she feels a delicious shiver, something secret, something strong, something painfully sweet, and she realizes her upper body is shrinking. The miniaturization moves to her waist then below, and the sensation is all-consuming, squeezing and caressing every cell in her body. Safe, she is almost safe. And then the sinewy, slimy worm hand slides around her ankle, as tight and strong as a noose, and yanks her back into the hot forest and the red jaws of burning death.

An indigo flash reeking of sulfur and lightning hurtles over her shoulder and explodes inside the toadhouse.

She screams.

Chapter 8

Tru and Spenser have grabbed her wrists. Biblos' horribly strong slug hand remains curled around her left leg. Between them, the prize in this treacherous tug of war, Aine is only aware of the singular ecstasy of every inch of her flesh being shrunk and resized.

On the other side of the toadhouse, Gilgamesh is cursing and sweating over a glowing disk balanced on a tripod. Blue flames shoot unnaturally from it. The whole toadhouse spins like a leaf in a whirlpool. The world outside flashes and sparks, and the muscled grip on Aine's ankle loosens.

"Hold tight!" Gilgamesh warns without turning from his task. "If you lose her out there, we'll never get her back."

Abruptly, Biblos is no longer clutching her leg. In fact, there is suddenly *nothing* outside the toadhouse. The blackness is so thick and free of odor that it's an absence rather than a place. Tru and Spenser yank her in the rest of the way. She slumps against the wall and comes back to the horror of the situation. She directs the boys to sit on the cot across the room. The delight of shrinking was momentary and has left her bewildered, aching from the loss of her grand-mother, head throbbing where her hair has been ripped out, empty.

Gilgamesh continues his frenzied effort and speaks without turn-ing. "You almost killed us all." He forms a claw with the first three fingers of his left hand and, using the exact motion Glori had made shortly before she was cut in two, tosses Biblos' sizzling blue ball out the window. The disk he is toiling over no longer glows, but it is smoking.

"Because of you, Biblos had time to cast one of his blue spells, and it went straight to the plotter." His voice is a growl. "His curse has seriously damaged it, maybe irreparably. If you had left when I asked, he never would have had the time to invoke it."

Aine finds she can't gulp enough air, no matter how hard she breathes. Tears rush down her cheeks like rain. She can't help it. Her grandmother, her home. Gone. A monster after her and Spenser. The tears leave streaks of clear pink skin on her ash-coated cheeks. She wants to fly across the floor and smash Gilgamesh's face into what-ever that machine is but she's afraid to leave her safe spot against the wall.

He turns as if he's read her mind. He eyes her warily without leaving his post. Something shifts in his glance. "I wasn't entirely right earlier. You look quite a bit like your mother. You have her chin. And her eyes. I imagine her temper, too."

Aine finds her fingers going to the chin that she always consid-ered pointy. She flushes and drops her hand. After studying her a moment longer, Gilgamesh returns his attention to the machine.

"Where are we?'" Tru asks.

His skin is as colorless as his hair, and his eyes are saucers cra-dling fear. Spenser sits next to him on the bed and rocks as his mouth moves silently. Aine forces her brain to slow its racing and her lungs to accept rather than fight for air. The exercise works but her hands begin to shake, mildly and then uncontrollably. She stuffs them behind her back.

"I'm here, Spenser," she says. "We're going to be okay." The tremble in her voice gives away the lie, but she has to say something to reassure him until she can trust her legs to carry her across the small room.

She focuses on her surroundings, anything to distract. The interior of the toadhouse is simple. It's the size of a hunting cabin and as round as a plate. In the center is a rough-hewn table with two matching chairs that appear carved from whole timber. The cot where Spenser and Tru currently sit like seasick stowaways hugs the wall opposite Aine. Spenser clutches his terrarium. A bookshelf supporting a single tome is moored over their heads.

Next to the bookshelf perches a cupboard with its door swinging open. Inside are a mismatched plate, bowl, cup, and cutlery set and what appears to be a loaf of parchment-wrapped bread. Nearer the front door rests a ceramic chamber pot and a coat rack, the latter decorated with several thin-looking shirts. To her left rests the burbling, whizzing, previously smoking circular object propped on a three-legged stand that has captivated Gilgamesh. It reminds Aine of a mandala that she'd seen a picture of in a book, only as big around as her arms if she made a circle with them. Well, at least as big around as her arms at their present size.

She angles her neck slightly so she can see through the doorless doorway. Just gazing at the heavy nothing tightens her chest. The world outside is so black it appears blue at the edges, and there's something vacantly absorbent about it. It makes no noise, no whisper of wind or rustle of movement. Her panic begins to build again, threatening to suffocate her. Without realizing it, her fingers have dug into the rough clay floor with such force that her nubbed fingernails have bent backward. Again she calms herself through force of will, concentrating on breathing slowly and on the realities of the room.

"It goes without saying that we don't step out of the toadhouse when it's in motion." Gilgamesh leaves his duties at the mandala and glares at the gloom beyond the window. He appears larger here, with all of them shrunk and the walls providing perspective. His seriousness is unmistakable. "You step out, and we never see you again."

Aine doesn't acknowledge his observation. "What is that?" She tips her head toward the machine because she still doesn't trust her hands.

Gilgamesh glances at it, confused, as if she'd asked him what his arm was. "The plotter. It guides the toadhouse. Like a map and a steering wheel together, I suppose. It's powered by that gold box outside the door."

"What did Biblos do to it?"

"That blue ball was a word curse he'd summoned. The plotter runs on words, and he scrambled it somehow. It might be temporary, or maybe we can never land again." He scowls at her, as if he blames her entirely.

"That reminds me." He leaves his post in one terse movement and grabs a cereal box-sized mechanism from a shelf. It is laced with gold wires and bisected down the middle. One half contains something that resembles an hourglass fitted with tiny tubes and cups. The other half holds a minute metal book. Gilgamesh rearranges several of the wires, and the machine makes a clicking sound. "This is now Tru's archetyper. You see these letters?"

He points at the hourglass. It is full of what look like grains of sand to Aine, but she nods.

"They track the progress of his story. When enough letters make a word, the word falls down the tube and drops into this crucible. When there are enough words for a sentence, they enter this one. And when there are enough sentences for a page, they filter into the other side of the archetyper, and a page in the book turns. This one has 67 turns before Tru needs to be back in his story. If we don't return him before his letters run out, the book is dead."

"Aine," Spenser says. His eyes shine brightly, so brightly that she is certain he is in deep shock. "When you were bringing Tru in, Gilgamesh told me that we can go into real stories, that books are just places to visit like the Jitney Jungle or school. He says we're gonna go into three different stories to find those objects Grandma Glori told us about, and that'll bring us to mom. You'd like that, wouldn't you?"

The painfully strained, almost clownish smile on his face hurts to look at. She forces herself to crawl across the room because her legs still feel like rubber. Pulling herself onto the cot, she squeezes him hard. He melts into her arms, shaking so violently that she is afraid he will fall apart. "Shh, Spenser. We'll figure this out. I'm never going to let anything bad happen to you. I promise."

She rocks him and smoothes his hair with her hand. She directs her voice at Gilgamesh. Her tone is firm. "I don't want to hear about magic keys or books that we can enter like a house. Tell me something that makes sense. Like who is Biblos and why did he kill my grandma and Mondegreen?"

Spenser stiffens, but when he speaks, it's not a question. "Grandma Glori is dead. I thought so. I felt her go. What was the word she said at the end? Squealaghee?"

Gilgamesh wipes his hands on his pants and mounts the arche-typer on a nail-driven brass chain over the doorway that seems designed just for that purpose. When he turns, his face is grim. "Scaoiligí. It means to unbind. She set you two free rather than save her own life."

"Free from what?" Aine asks. "And who is Biblos?"

"I'll keep it simple, which is all I'm allowed. Gloriana—Grandma Glori to you—told you of three keys that you must acquire to open the doorway to Tir Na Nog, your real home. These keys are objects hidden in plain sight in the most famous works of literature. Glori-ana gave you the first clue to the first key. This toadhouse will carry us to the story where it's hidden. When we retrieve each one, we'll be rewarded with the clue to the next. After we retrieve the third, we can enter Tir Na Nog. The problem is that the Bookworm, as he calls himself, wants all of the objects as badly as we do, likely more. Plus he wants you and your brother. That's all I am permit-ted to tell you."

Gilgamesh abruptly retreats to once again fiddle with the plotter. "My job is to transport you to those objects and bring you to your real home. With a bit of luck, we'll have all three keys within the day, and your mother can tell you the rest herself."

"The Bookworm?" Tru asks. His voice stumbles a little, but he coughs and continues. "That's what you call that big gorilla who chased us into here? He looked like he was growing right in front of my eyes when he grabbed Aine with that awful hand of his." He shudders, but covers it up with another cough.

"Biblos Skulas is the name he's given himself. We call him the Bookworm. He can shrink and grow at will. He destroys stories, and he wants those three objects."

"Why?" Spenser asks, pulling away from Aine.

Gilgamesh slams his hand on the plotter. "Do the three of you always talk so much? I told you, with any luck, you can ask her yourself at the end of the day."

Aine considers letting him cool off but the questions are too urgent. "*What* is he?" There is no question who she is talking about.

Gilgamesh tightens his jaw. "He's just a man like me. He found a way to gather power from his victims and to harness his rage to work magic, but he's still just a man."

"Is there anything he's afraid of?"

Gilgamesh's words escape through clenched teeth. "Afraid? I don't know. Rocks appear to confuse him, and they make it difficult for him to track you. That's why most children instinctively collect rocks, though they outgrow that inclination too soon."

"He likes ankles, too." Spenser's voice is small but Aine is grateful to note that the empty puppet smile has fled.

Gilgamesh hitches his breath and his frustration seems to melt away, replaced by sympathy. "I'm afraid that's true. Biblos has developed a taste for the ankles and feet of sleeping children, along with other despicable distractions. But not to fear. There are agents like Mondegreen and Tone in every story, waiting to booktrap him. It's just bad fortune that he happened upon the story where you two were hidden."

"That's where I'm afraid you keep losing me, sir." Tru glances from Aine to Spenser and then flexes his hands as if to check whether they're real. "You keep saying we were in a story, and that I have to get back to it before that archetyper thing runs out, but that doesn't make any sense."

A flicker of melancholy crosses Gilgamesh's face, but he dismisses the question with a wave of his hand. "That's more than enough questions for a lifetime. We're nearing our destination. Secure yourselves. I'm not certain I've fixed the machine. No telling what sort of landing we're in for, if we can land at all. You don't want to crack your head open."

Aine takes the terrarium from Spenser's clutching hands and places it on the floor between her feet. "Secure yourself, he said." She removes her book bag and rubs her shoulder where it has abraded the skin, then wraps her arm back around him.

The smile he gives her is beatific. He leans into her shoulder, still trembling, but less violently. "Thank you for letting me bring Pinch and Shelly."

Aine examines him. His face is still peaked, and his deep, dark eyes ringed by eyelashes so thick they stir the wind when he blinks are crusted with dried tears. "Clean your face," she says mildly. For all she knows, they are on their way to a slave camp where ankle-eating is merely a warm-up, but her brother can't know she's terrified of this new reality, where monsters kill grandparents and readers enter stories.

An odd memory stirs her: Grandma Glori, three weeks ago to the day, reading to them. She'd never done such a thing before. She'd chosen Shakespeare, of all writers, and *A Midsummer Night's Dream*, a play Aine had never read. Glori didn't allow much time for comedies, but even though her reading was wooden, she couldn't ruin the fun of Nick Bottom's lines. Aine had found herself smiling, against all instincts.

Spenser fell asleep halfway through. Aine tried to hide that fact by leaning in front of him. She'd not wanted the moment to end, but Glori soon noticed she'd lost half her audience. She slammed the book shut and declared that was enough foolishness before stomping off to bed. Still, before she'd left, she had kissed both of them on their foreheads, another first.

Aine touches her face where she had felt her grandmother's lips, warm and dry and somehow magnetic. She wonders how old Glori really had been. Sixty? Seventy? She was as spry as anyone, always hurrying and never going anywhere, her close-cropped grey and white hair contrasting beautifully with her green eyes. Aine feels tears pushing up, and she scolds herself. *One story and a good night kiss don't make her a substitute for a mother.* This is what she has to tell herself, she decides, so she doesn't fall apart.

The black outside the toadhouse eases, allowing in light and color, and then a delicious rush of smells: air, coffee, paper, ink. With a thump that jars their teeth, they land. Tru is the first outside. Aine dons her book bag and holds Spenser back. She peeks out the door into a space that is most certainly not the woods of Alabama.

Chapter 9

"You've made it! And these are the two we've heard so much about."
Aine and Spenser arch their necks from inside the toadhouse.
The man speaking is a giant with deep wrinkles, trailing white hair,
and a long, grey-streaked beard cinched with a purple band. His
robe is the same color as his hair. When he smiles, the beard moves.
Surrounding him is an impossibly huge room lined with books
from floor to ceiling. The smallest tome is twice the size of the
toadhouse travelers.

The man reaches forward as if to pull out and embrace the miniature travelers and then stops, clasping his hands benignly. The
movement of his robes is powerful enough to lift Aine's hair. "I shall
wait until you resize, of course."

Aine steps out tentatively, keeping Spenser behind her. She stares
at her hands and feet, horrified. She is outside the toadhouse but
still miniature, the world impossibly large, the man in front of her
looming like a kindly titan. "We're still tiny! What's wrong?"

Gilgamesh steps past her. "It takes nine minutes and eleven

seconds to resize after leaving the toadhouse. Every time. It's a kink the engineers haven't worked out yet."

The old man nods in agreement, and Aine finds the gesture oddly soothing even though it stirs up tornadoes of dust at their feet. Behind him are more books than she knew existed, stacks and piles and trains of books teetering at impossible angles, stuffed into shelves, weighing down tables, filling every crack. An arc of novels traces the curved doorway at the front of the room, the tomes perfectly balanced into an upside down "U." The bindings are red, brown, white, blue, leather, paper, cardboard, cracked, shining. The room feels hopeful and cozy despite its vast size, drenched in the smell and potential of books, a faint and clean odor, like lemon soap.

Soft violin music plays in the background, and glass globes floating like bubbles give off both light and heat. They remind Aine of the large marble Glori had been holding before she died. She cranes her neck and sees that the roof of the huge, book-filled room is a dome. Beyond that is a sky the deepest indigo blue she's ever seen, so pure and complete that it pulls at her.

"What's up there, beyond the ceiling?" she asks, keeping Spenser close.

"Nothing and forever," the old man answers, dropping to a knee. His beard grazes the ground. "My name is Kenning. You're Aine, of course. I'm honored to meet you." He bows, a ridiculous gesture given that he is a grown man and she a three-inch version of herself. Tru giggles.

"That must be Spenser behind you. Welcome." He bows again. "Gilgamesh, I wish the circumstances were better but it's always a pleasure. And who is your stowaway?"

Tru offers his tiny hand. Kenning touches it with a gentle finger. "My name is Tru, sir."

"Welcome to Ellipses, Tru."

"What is this place?"

Kenning glances around. "Ellipses? It's a sort of library, I suppose, and a bit of a refugee camp. Most importantly, it's a safe haven. Gilgamesh, that toadhouse didn't sound good when you landed. Is that why you're here?"

Gilgamesh nods grimly. "It's begun. Biblos has located them, forcing Gloriana to release the first clue. Then he struck her down."

Kenning grows pale. "And Mondegreen?"

"Dead."

Kenning bows his head. When he raises it again, his eyes are resolute. "We knew this day would come. I'm afraid Mondegreen was your best chance at repairing the king's toadhouse, but I'll do what I can."

A rust-colored hairless cat appears at Kenning's feet. Its forehead is a maze of wrinkles, and its angled eyes studying the newcomers with curiosity and more than a little aggression. Its naked tail twitches.

"Sir!" Tru exclaims, jumping back. "You've got a rat runnin' free in your home!"

Kenning chuckles and rubs his hand along the animal's back. He stretches appreciatively but never stops scowling. "This is Archibald. He and I are the only permanent residents of Ellipses. Not to worry. He's used to seeing little ones. He won't harm you."

Aine feels her ears pop followed by a tingle and instinctively steps to one side. The wash of sharp pleasure that follows, as if every cell is being sliced and then sewn, is so powerful that she gasps. In the blink of an eye she has returned to her normal proportions, leaving only a slight buzzing sensation on her flesh. Her companions have also resized. It wasn't a gradual process, where she could watch actual limbs lengthening. On one side of an instant they were small, and on the other, they were normal size.

Unfortunately, they are now standing awkwardly on the table where the toadhouse landed. Gilgamesh steps down, then helps the others. He reaches for Aine first, but she is too mesmerized. From this perspective, the sheer number of books seems even more awesome than when she was tiny. She couldn't count them all in a year, let alone read them. Gilgamesh clears his throat, and she realizes he's waiting for her.

"Sorry." She takes his hands, surprised by the rough strength of them. Their eyes connect but only for a moment before he drops his gaze. She hops to the ground and reaches for a book to cover her sudden discomfort. She runs her hand over it, a thick volume whose title is written in a language she can't read.

Kenning gasps. He is staring at her hands. "So it's true. She bears the enigmata."

Aine ducks her hands behind her back out of habit. Kenning shakes his head gently, beckoning for her to show him the scars. "Please accept my apologies. I've only read about them."

She reluctantly holds out her arms. "Glori told me they were from a botched stitching."

"That is as good a story as any to protect you." Kenning leans in closely to study them. "A perfect Gort on each. Amazing. She is marked, just as the prophesy says. Has Biblos seen them?"

Gilgamesh shakes his head. "I'm not sure."

"You must keep both their hands covered in the hopes that he hasn't, at least until they return to Tir Na Nog," Kenning says. "In fact, you might as well cover the hands of all three to confuse their pursuer. I've got spare bindings in the room off of the kitchen."

Spenser steps forward, speaking tentatively. "What prophesy?"

"There's no time," Gilgamesh says, shooting Kenning a warning glance. "We need to mend the toadhouse well enough to ferry us to the necessary books. You can help with the repairs?"

"I'm no engineer, but I can try." Kenning gives Aine, Spenser, and Tru directions to the kitchen and instructions to take as much food as they can carry along with several rolls of bandages.

Gilgamesh stops them before they leave the library. Reaching into the toadhouse, he pulls three of the thin-looking shirts off the coat rack. "Take these. Some of the halls here are drafty."

Aine accepts the tiny shirt doubtfully. "This wouldn't fit on the cat."

Tru's eyes widen, and he stares at Archibald. "Cat?" he whispers.

Gilgamesh hands the remaining shirts to Spenser and Tru. "They change size to fit their wearer."

Aine doubtfully tugs the shirt over her arm. To her amazement, it stretches and becomes a grey sleeve that completely covers her arm. She yanks it behind her back and over her other arm, and it continues to grow until it is a perfectly tailored gray jacket. She helps Spenser into his, delighted to discover that his coat is navy blue. Tru's is brown. They leave the men and the cavernous book room behind, following a narrow hallway lined with bookshelves. A single globe follows them, offering a feeble light that casts their shadows in front of them.

Spenser slips his hand into Aine's. "I smell dust and books. Tru, what'd that cat look like?"

"Naked as a boiled chicken," Tru says with wonder still in his voice.

Aine takes the first right, as they'd been told. This hallway appears exactly like the last—never-ending, dark, and lined with books. As she walks, she realizes how little she knows about Tru. She's put him at ten years old, though he's the same size as Spenser. Because he doesn't go to her school, she doesn't know where he lives during the year.

"Tru, where're you from?" she asks.

"Mississippi, mostly. I stay in Alabama with my aunt in the summers."

Spenser reaches toward him. "Don't your parents miss you?"

He traces his hands along the spines of the books they pass, and feathers of dust fly down. "Naw."

"I bet that's not true."

Tru nods with resolve. "It is. They're nice enough folks and treat me okay, but they like each other a lot more than they like me." He shrugs and speaks matter-of-factly. "No one ever misses me. Hey, I'm real sorry about your grandma and her fella."

Aine cuts her eyes at Spenser. The tears are instant, but he doesn't make a sound. When he speaks, his voice is steady. "What'd he look like? Biblos, that is."

The name chills Aine, and the bile rises again in her throat. The worms, the deformities, the shock of black hair. She considers Spenser's question. "Like the ugly part of a man, if you pulled it out and gave it a body of its own."

"And huge. Don't forget that. He's a giant," Tru says. "It looks like he exploded and was sewn back together again. And that worm hand." He shudders.

Spenser stops abruptly. Aine tugs at him. "Come on, Spenser. We have to hurry."

His head is down, his voice a whisper. "You're not going to leave me, are you Aine? First mom and now Grandma Glori. Promise me you won't go next."

She holds him. His hair smells like fresh air and boy. Around them, the books go on forever. "Never," she says fiercely.

He nods, and they continue to walk. Aine ventures a question she'd been afraid to say out loud until now. "Do you two believe that we can travel into stories like Gilgamesh says?"

Spenser wiggles his shoulders sadly. "We sure did go somewhere far away, and real quick. Why couldn't it be a story?"

"Because that's impossible?" Aine asks.

Tru glances at her, his expression innocent. "Then where are we?"

"I don't know," she says. "But if we believe Gilgamesh, Grandma Glori gave us a clue to the first key: 'The adventure of a lifetime is tied to a powerful rod.' If we can figure out what she meant, and we'll have that first object."

"I think the rod is Sinbad's golden staff from *The Seven Voyages of Sinbad the Sailor*," Spenser offers.

The idea is so quick to come that Aine is sure he's been thinking a lot about it. She doesn't want to hurt his feelings, but she knows that he's guessing Sinbad because it was the last complete book she read to him, and he had loved it. She speaks gently. "I dunno, Spense. If everything we learned today is true, then we can't fool around, especially with that plotter thing not working properly. We need to travel directly to the correct story, and I don't think it's Sinbad."

"Then what is it?" Tru asks.

Somehow, Archibald has found them in the dark of the books, and he's sticking close to Tru, making him visibly uneasy. They continue to walk down the extensive hallway as they talk.

"Part of the rhyme was, 'Remember that man is not god,'" Aine says, thinking out loud. "That's sounds a lot like The Time Machine, a book by H.G. Wells. The Time Traveler in the book believes he is above humanity, travelling back and forth in time, and it turns out to be a terrible mistake."

"Does that story contain a rod?" Tru asks. He hurries to the opposite side of the hallway, and Archibald follows, tangling himself in the boy's feet.

"The lever he uses to control the machine!" Aine realizes, feeling triumphant. She hears Spenser's stomach growl fiercely, and it's answered by Tru's. She realizes that she and Spenser haven't eaten since breakfast. She digs the meat and cheese out of her book bag, unwraps them, and offers one hunk to Tru and the other to Spenser. "Plus, in The Time Machine, there will be riches of food everywhere if we can't find enough here, and the Eloi won't stop us!"

"Eloi?" Tru asks, biting into a corner of the cheddar.

"A gentle people who populate the future the Time Traveler enters. They'll feed us, we'll grab the metal rod off the time machine, the next clue will be revealed, and we'll be on our way! What do you boys think?" Despite herself, she feels a trickle of excitement, a tiny counterweight to the vast pain and confusion marking the day. The Time Machine is one of her favorite stories. She's read it three different times. What if they could really visit it? It wouldn't be the strangest thing that had happened that day, not by a long shot.

"If you think so," Spenser says. He tears off a piece of ham and trades with Tru, then wipes his hands on his short trousers. "And Aine?" He seems embarrassed but pushes on. "Did you hear Gilgamesh say we look like our father? Our father! I've never even thought about him. Who do you suppose he is?"

Aine flushes, remembering something else: the heat she felt at the base of her stomach when Gilgamesh told her she resembled her mother. Her mother had been beautiful. She is about to respond when she hears from up ahead the moans of someone in great pain.

Chapter 10

Aine runs ahead, hearing more moans and the chatter of many conversations as she nears. The sounds come from a room off of the hallway, a space half the size of the library but still gigantic. This room is also lined with books, but it's the people in the center who capture her attention. Over twenty men and women suffer various forms of distress. Some appear lost, while others are crying, several are lying on beds with their heads or bodies wrapped in bandages. Three men in robes move from patient to patient distributing water and checking on wounds. The smells of antiseptic and illness are strong. *The refugee camp Kenning talked about*, Aine thinks, *but refugees from what?*

The wounded people are all ages and races, wearing varieties of clothing she has never imagined outside of a book. Across the room, an Asian woman in a flowered silk kimono leans forward in a chair, her arm in a sling, conversing passionately with a woman in a powdered wig who is dressed in a glorious ball gown. The thickly brocaded dress is ripped and bloody down the front, and the woman wears an eye patch. Next to them, his eyes closed, lays a man who appears to wear nothing but his knickers without shame, though they're not like any underclothes Aine has seen before. They reach nearly to his knees and the fabric is shiny. His shoes are also peculiar, like to loafers but reaching over the ankle, with a star inside a circle printed on the outside of each.

"What's your need?" The voice coming from the hallway startles Aine. The speaker is also wearing a white robe, but is a woman. She pushes past them into the room with a stack of blankets in her arms.

"Uh, we, um, Kenning sent us. For bandages and food."

The woman doesn't seem surprised. "The kitchen is the next room down, and you can find the bandages in the storage room directly off of it. What story are you from?"

The question is a passing one, a nod to politeness, asked much the way people asked after her roots back in Alabama. The casualness of it throws Aine off. She isn't sure how to answer. "*Babbitt*," she blurts, thinking of Glori's love for the book.

"Ah, that's a splendid one." The woman's face drops. "Biblos has gotten to it as well, then? I suppose the only good news is that we'll soon have a copy of it in the library. All the destroyed books come here, if Kenning gets to them in time. Can I ask—were there any survivors besides you three?"

"I'm…I'm sorry." Aine feels terrible for her lie, not just because of the sadness it's brought to the woman's face. "We're not from *Babbitt*. I don't know what book we were in. Gilgamesh brought us here."

The woman sucks in her breath sharply and her eyes immediately drop to Aine's hands. They widen. "Leave, now, before you're seen." She moves forward to usher them out, but it's too late. They have caught the attention of two men resting on cots nearby.

"Did I hear Gilgamesh's name?" The man closest to the wall sits up. Gauze covers his head and his right eye. He is missing one of his legs from the knee down, and the bandage covering it is steeped in red. Still, his voice is light. "What's that young lad up to? Still saving maidens, then?"

The patient next to him smiles but doesn't move from the neck down. Aine thinks he must be paralyzed. His hands lie alongside him like two sunbaked fish. The rest of him is covered by a blanket.

"He did save us," Spenser says from behind Aine. "All three of us. Are you two all right? It smells like sick people in here."

"I suppose it does," the bandaged man says. "But you can't see it? A blind boy, eh? That's a shame." He turns to the still man next to him, a word on his lips, and then suddenly snaps his gaze to Aine. She doesn't have time to hide her hands. His single eye rests on the symbols, blazing. "And a girl with the Gort on the back of each hand." His voice is a dangerous growl.

The man next to him blinks and strains painfully to see Aine. He is unable to raise his head and groans in frustration. Spenser quickly moves forward, feeling along the bed until he is touching the man. His little hand squeezes the large, motionless one.

Aine reaches out to pull Spenser back because the rage is growing in the bandaged man's face.

"You!" He points at her, his voice building into a roar. "You and your blind brother are the reason my wife and son lie murdered! Biblos tortured them to find out where you were hidden. Of course they didn't know, and so he drank their blood to get their power. You two are the cause of this!"

The room has gone deathly quiet. All eyes turn toward them. Those who are lying down struggle into a sitting position. Aine pulls Spenser and Tru behind her as the room begins to buzz angrily. People glare at the three of them with raw anger in their eyes.

"Stop right now!" The female healer speaks in a commanding voice, directing her comments at the entire room. "They are little more than children themselves. You all know the story. None of this is their fault, and if they're here, they've experienced a loss just like the rest of us." She points to the bandaged man. "You ought to be ashamed of yourself, Chiasmus."

He falls back into his bed, weary, though his voice is laced with sarcasm. "You're right, of course. Forgive me. The bell tolls for all of us."

The healer ignores him and shuttles the trio into the hallway. The conversation in the refugee room escalates to a fevered pitch.

"Don't take that to heart," the woman says, pushing them away from the doorway hurriedly. "We're not ourselves these days. We're all rooting for you to succeed, you must be certain of that. Everyone in that room has had their temporary homes destroyed by Biblos, and many of them have lost a loved one at the hands of the Bookworm. It has them understandably agitated, but they don't hate you like it seems. Not a one of us can return to Tir Na Nog until you open the doorway, after all. Now, keep walking in this direction, and you won't be able to miss the kitchen or the storage room off of it." She transfers the blankets to a single arm so she can give each child a quick hug with the other before returning to the refugee room, moving so fast down the hallway that she is almost running.

"What was that about?" Tru asks.

"Your guess is as good as mine," Aine responds, shaking. "Come on."

They locate the kitchen easily. The space is utilitarian, all cupboards and wood countertops except for the far wall, which is composed entirely of glass. On the other side is the same inky blue-purple Aine saw through the ceiling of the library. It is unbroken by stars or light. She imagines Ellipses to be something of a twisting castle floating in space, lengthy hallways joining rooms of books before turning back on themselves.

She goes to the cupboards, and it quickly becomes apparent that Ellipses barely has enough food for the refugees, let alone extra for the three of them. "Spenser, why don't you sit at this table? Tru, you gather cheese, meat, and bread but just a little of each, enough for a day or so. I'm going to look for water and bandages."

She enters the pantry hurriedly, still thinking of the bizarre encounter with the refugees. Their anger at her and the boys was both palpable and terrifying. She wants to move quickly so they can return to the relative safety of Kenning and the library. She locates empty water skins hanging on the wall, basics like flour and sugar lining the mostly-bare shelves, and a cupboard filled with medical supplies. She throws two of the skins over her shoulder and stuffs bandages and scissors into her book bag. She is about to return to the kitchen when at the last minute she grabs a small pot of ointment. Kenning said to take what they'd need, and Spenser's arm and her foot require attention.

She is tucking the pot into her pocket and closing the cupboard door when a glowing globe glides into the storage room. It floats to the rear of the small space, and then hovers over an oddly shaded section of the wall. As Aine walks toward the globe, she realizes that it's illuminating a small opening, not even as high as her waist, disguised by angles and darkness until the globe arrived. She touches the rough wood of the doorjamb, then puts her hand into the empty space beyond. A warm breeze flows past her, and it smells like caramel. She realizes there is another room hidden back here, possibly one with more supplies, and she steps through.

She plummets down, down into darkness.

Chapter 11

She is on some sort of sliding incline, hurtling forward and down. Panicked, she throws out her arms and legs to slow herself, but not until she hits the floor with an "oof" can she stop the forward momentum. The globe has followed her, twinkling merrily the whole way. She stands up and rubs her bruised tailbone.

She's landed in a small room, no larger than her bedroom back at the farmhouse. It is lined with books just like every other inch of wall space in Ellipses besides the kitchen. These books are different, though. They glow faintly, like gold, blue, and purple fireflies, and they're neatly arranged. A work desk below the raised shelves takes up nearly half the floor space. It's covered in bottles of paint and ink and clean sheets of parchment. In a corner stands a tub of brushes. Aine walks over and touches the paper. It touches her back, and she jumps.

She steps away from the desk and turns to the nearest bookshelf. *Fairies through the Ages. The Life of Fairies. Fairy Tales. Fairy Engineering.* Every title she sees is about fairies, and even more interestingly,

Kenning's name appears as the author of each one. She pulls out a book, a thin, grape-colored volume titled *The Secrets of the Fairies.* It is no larger than her hand. She flips it open to a random page. It's the beginning of a chapter titled "Ravin":

Fairies are each born with one of three ravin: Water, Earth, or Wind. Some lucky fairies have more than one ravin, and those of royal blood possess all three. The powers that the fairy wields run parallel to their ravin and allow them dominion over the characteristics of their ravin. So an Earth ravin has power over the soil, rocks, and plants, for example. The most powerful ravin is commonly agreed to be Earth, though a Wind or Water ravin might take a different view. Of course the fourth ravin, Fire, was bred out of the fairies during the time of Queen Mab and is never spoken of, though the Prophecy of the End of Times states that...

The page ends abruptly. She turns it. The next page opens a new chapter titled "Weapons and Elements Harmful to Fairies." She flips back. The previous page ends mid-sentence with the Prophecy of the End of Times. She flips back to the "Weapons and Elements" chapter and peers closer. Running her fingers down the crease, she feels the nubs: a page has been torn out, the page explaining the prophecy.

"Aine!"

Her brother's voice is distant but worried. She squeezes the book shut and slides it back into its space on the shelf. She turns to face the slide, but it's disappeared. In its place is a gigantic wooden door. She pulls it open and finds, impossibly, that she is stepping into the kitchen as if she hadn't just left a room several floors below. She turns to look behind her, and the door is gone. Replacing it is a wooden cupboard holding cups and plates.

"There you are!" Tru says. "Thought you'd leave all the work for us? Well, we showed you! We got all the food packed." He points proudly at a small stack of paper-wrapped squares, each large enough to hold a hunk of cheese and cinched with a piece of twine.

"Good work," Aine says absently. She puts her hands against the cupboard and pushes. It's solid. Shaking her head, she turns and tosses a roll of bandage to Tru. "Wrap this around your hands and Spenser's, like Kenning said, and I'll fill the water skins."

She goes to the hand-pump near the wall of glass and fills the skins before bandaging her hands. She wraps the bindings around both sides of her thumbs before tying it across the back. It is enough to hide her markings but not enough to inhibit movement. Hands disguised and water skins full, Aine gathers the groceries and the boys.

"Slinking away?"

She stops in her tracks. The one-legged refugee emerges from the shadowed hallway. He is leaning against a rough crutch and fresh blood stains the bandage over his stump. His smile is wicked, pained. "My son was only eight, you know. Almost as old as your brother. He wanted to be a musician, like his father." He holds up his hand, his laughter cold. "At least like I used to be, before Biblos got to me."

Aine notices for the first time that the fingers of the man's right hand have been broken and lie at twisted angles. She swallows hard. "I'm sorry, sorry for what has happened to you and your family. We are after the keys, and when we get them, I'm sure Biblos can be stopped."

The man limps a step closer. "You don't have any idea of his power. Neither does Gilgamesh. It grows, you see. When he tastes the blood of those he slays, he absorbs their aura. It's not much when it's just a single death, but he's killed hundreds. He's unstoppable, so why not give him what he wants, eh? You and your brother. What are two children in exchange for hundreds of us?"

He reaches for Aine, but his wound prevents him from moving quickly. She drops the groceries and grabs both boys. They skirt the wounded man and dart toward the hallway. The eyes stop her, glittering and animal-like in the dimly-lit corridor. She counts ten sets, all of them wounded refugees. Their expressions are not kind. She backs into the kitchen and toward the pantry, still holding tight to the boys. The refugees, including the man on the crutch, follow, trapping them. The three of them back into the deep supply closet.

"Aine?" Spenser asks. His voice is tiny.

She squeezes his hand, and Tru's. "There's a secret doorway back here. Find it!"

All three of them turn, feeling across the wall. Spenser locates the doorway first. Aine pushes him gently down the slide, and then Tru. She follows, just a breath ahead of one of the refugees. The man on crutches yells at her to stop, but she slips down the slide and hurtles into the darkness.

At the bottom, the office she'd originally entered has been replaced by a long corridor. Archibald sits calmly at the entrance to it. He meows once then pads rapidly down the hallway. The three of them follow quickly, hyper-aware of the pounding in the closet above. The refugees are yelling for them, demanding they return and give themselves over to Biblos. Surely, one of them will soon try the slide, and the rest will follow.

In a matter of minutes, they come out at the library. All three are winded from the quick pace. Kenning and Gilgamesh are in the middle of the room, normal-sized, with the toadhouse resting on a table in front of them. They are speaking urgently, but stop and turn upon the arrival of Archibald, Aine, and the boys.

"What is it?" Kennings asks.

"The refugees," Aine says. "They're after us."

Gilgamesh's jaw tightens, though he nods approvingly at their bandaged hands. When he speaks, his voice is tense. "I had hoped they would understand. Blasted! That means we must go. Now."

"Is the toadhouse working?" Spenser asks.

"Not the way I would like. I should be able to enter the name of the story and *swish*! That is where we land. But Biblos' word curse inflicted deep damage. I don't understand how. It struck high of its target, yet it has affected the entire machinery."

"What do you need to fix it?"

Gilgamesh shakes his head. "Mondegreen. In fact, he tuned her up just before we left. I should have asked him to create a shield for it. It's too late now. There's no getting to any other qualified engineer, not with the plotter off and you three to watch out for. We were lucky to land here. No, Kenning and I have agreed. We've decided that our best gamble is to retrieve the three keys. Then I'll have all the time in the world to fix her. Now that those who have lost their stories have turned against us, we must leave earlier than planned."

Spenser steps closer to Gilgamesh. "But how can we get the keys that will bring us to our mom if we can't reach the stories?"

Gilgamesh glances grimly at Kenning, who nods. "I think we have her rigged for manual entry. Instead of entering the title of the story, I can instead use a description. I only have so many letters allowed, however, and it's an inexact science. But it's the best we can do for now."

Aine clears her throat. "We've been talking, and we think we know what story we want to try first."

Both Tru and Spenser nod. She continues. "Grandma Glori's rhyme said—"

In a gesture that would be comical if not for the horror on his face, Kenning covers both ears. "No! Don't utter the rhyme. Please. I don't want Biblos to be able to torture it out of me."

"He could never find you here," Gilgamesh says.

"I might not always be here. This mission is too important, Gilgamesh. You know I'm right. Even Gloriana herself wasn't entrusted with more than the first clue. No, only you three, and for now, your stowaway, must know of it. It's time to say our goodbyes. Fate awaits you."

Aine thinks of her home with Glori, no longer safe, and now their small refuge here in Ellipses has been destroyed by the anger of the refugees.

"No place is safe, young lady," Kenning says as if reading her mind, "until you finish your mission. We'll have all the time we could want, then."

He pulls Aine into an embrace. His beard is scratchy, and he smells a little of mothballs, and she wants to stay exactly in this spot forever. He lets her go too soon and kisses the top of Spenser's head. He even gives Tru a hug. "Archibald is quite taken with you," he says.

Tru glances down at his ankles. He reaches down to pet the cat, his face looking as though he's about to swallow a spoonful of medicine. He continues gamely, though, and when he finally touches her back, he smiles in relief. "Why, he's soft! Not like a lizard at all."

Kenning smiles back then shakes Gilgamesh's hand. "I know you'll take care of them. There's no better man. Now, time's wasting. Off you go."

An angry noise bubbles from the hallway. The pack of refugees must have broken through the secret door, and they are bearing down on the library. Kenning waves all four of them into the toadhouse. Aine is the last to enter, and she feels Kenning slip something into her hand. She looks down. It's the little purple book, *The Secrets of the Fairies.* She looks at him in surprise. He winks before ushering her into the toadhouse.

She welcomes the electric shiver of shrinking, and slides the book into her bag before joining the boys at the doorway to wave goodbye. Kenning waves back, his eyes unreadable, and then bends down to scoop up Archibald before disappearing into the corridor to face the angry mob.

Aine quickly turns away. Her voice is hoarse. "We've decided to look for the first key in The Time Machine, Gilgamesh. What information do you need to get us there?"

The pilot is watching them from the shadows with his arms crossed. "A description of the story no more than five words long, each of those words not more than ten letters."

"Hmm," Aine muses, her mind now fully focused on this puzzle. "Can you use the author's name?"

"Won't help. Those aren't real. All stories are crafted by fairies."

Aine's hand goes to her book bag. The purple volume Kenning slipped her is there.

"What?" Tru exclaims. "Now we have fairies?"

"Always have. In fact, Kenning and everyone else in Ellipses is a fairy."

"What? The refugees too? They looked just like humans."

Gilgamesh rubs his hands over his drawn face, pausing to rub the scar. "I assure you that fairies are as real as humans. Some are engineers like Mondegreen. Still others are messengers like Tone. The fairy royalty of Tir Na Nog are the writers. They are the only ones who can hear the Word Tree, and they translate what they hear into stories for the entertainment of all."

"Tir Na Nog." Aine steps nearer to Gilgamesh. "That's where Glori said Helen is. You're saying our mother is a fairy?"

Gilgamesh shakes his head. "She is not. But she is in Tir Na Nog, and that's where we must go. It can't be found or accessed without the three keys."

"But why is she in Tir Na Nog? And why does Biblos want to storm the fairy kingdom, and where do we come in?"

Gilgamesh's face hardens to steel. He turns to the plotter and begins rearranging the symbols. "Let's find the keys and you can ask Helen yourself."

Aine crosses her arms. "You're as bad as Glori, only telling me what you want. I deserve to know! Spenser deserves to know! I saw my grandmother killed today, if that's even who she is, and I was chased by a monster into a tiny toadhouse where I now supposedly can fly in and out of books, and then I was yelled at by a man without a leg who thinks I'm responsible for the murder of his wife and son. You have to explain things. You have to!"

She suddenly finds herself crying. Spenser rushes over and pats her back. "Don't be sad, Aine."

She looks down at him. He's smiling at her even though a tear quivers on the edge of his eyelid. She knows if she doesn't calm herself, he'll collapse again. She takes a deep breath and rubs her eyes, ashamed of her childish outburst. "I'll be fine. I'm just tired. Let's go find mom."

She speaks in Gilgamesh's direction but is too embarrassed to look at him. "Okay, you need a description of the story no more than five words long, each of those words not more than ten letters. How about 'Time Traveler Eloi white Sphinx?' That should get us to the right location in the story." She shepherds Spenser and Tru over to the cot and gestures for them to sit down.

Gilgamesh is looking appraisingly at her. "I will try it."

"Hey," Spenser interrupts, "how does the toadhouse know where in the story to land?"

Gilgamesh turns to the plotter and appears to begin typing. "She goes for the nearest forest or garden, naturally. If there is one. Otherwise, a cupboard. She finds the best hiding spot she can, but it can't be the same location as the story's own toadhouse."

The toadhouse begins to quiver, and then spin. The books and smells of Ellipses begin to blur before they disappear into blackness.

"Wait, what?" Aine asks. "There's more than one toadhouse?"

"Yes. There's one hidden in every book, assigned to that specific story and destined to always return to it. That's how Biblos is traveling around. It slows him down because after he lands in one book, the toadhouse he rode in snaps back to its original story as soon as he steps outside of it. It's a one-way trip. Then, when he wants to leave that book, it takes him time to locate that story's toadhouse. That is why, with any luck, we'll always stay ahead of him." He pats the wall proudly. "This is the only toadhouse that isn't storybound and so can travel wherever it's directed."

Aine's head feels full of cotton. She glances at Spenser, who has lain down and fallen asleep before his question was even answered. His mouth is open, his hands wide on his lap, his soft pale neck exposed. She wants to hug him, or scream at him for being able to sleep at such a time, or maybe even race out into that evil black nothingness where she'll never need to think about anything again. Instead, she covers him with a blanket and gets as comfortable as she can.

Chapter 12

When she awakes, her stomach cries with hunger. Outside the window, she hears the sweet chirp of birds and smells blooming flowers. *What an amazing dream,* she thinks to herself. The bed is too comfortable to leave, but she forces her eyes open.

She's inside the toadhouse. And she's alone, on the floor.

Aine shoots up so fast her head spins. She rushes outside, where she's greeted by birdsong and a swarm of brilliant sapphire and tangerine butterflies, each one larger than the toadhouse. They flutter just overhead, huge as pterodactyls to her, with golden threads illuminating the undersides of their wings. She backs away and trips over what seems to be an enormous root poking out of the earth, until it raises its lazy head and she realizes she is facing an earthworm, grotesque in its vastness. It burrows into the ground with a loud scraping. She smells fresh-dug earth and acacias. The world is terrifying at this level, alone.

"Spenser! Tru! Gilgamesh!" Her voice is tiny, a scraping of sound drowned out by a sparrow's song. Her throat constricts. She walks around the toadhouse looking for signs of a struggle but sees none. She's torn between going off to search for them and staying put in case they return. Panic clutches her. What if Biblos has captured them, is torturing them right now? She yells for them again, her voice cracking. She is paralyzed by inaction. The world is closing in on her. Her heart races and threatens to rip itself out of her chest. Breathing is difficult. Her thoughts are ragged. She wants to run but can't move her feet. Twenty-four hours of loss and confusion threaten to bury her.

A diving bird finally breaks the horrible spell.

It starts out plummeting toward the worm's hole, but when its original prey disappears, it transfers its beady-eyed attention to Aine. She is nearly as tall as the sparrow, but she has moved her arm, and its pinkness against the stillness of her body has attracted the hungry bird. It veers toward her, screeching. She rolls away at the last minute, barely avoiding the scrape of its clawed feet. Fear for her life replaces her mental agony. "Shoo! Go away!" she shouts.

The sparrow is confused by her sudden movements. It lands a few feet away, cocking its head at her, hopping closer then back, closer then back. The sun glints off its sharp black beak. She steps toward the toadhouse, never taking her eyes off the hungry bird. Her instinct screams at her to run inside, but her thinking is once again clear. If she hides in the toadhouse, she'll have to wait another full nine minutes and eleven seconds to resize, time she can't waste if she's going to find the others.

To her right, she spots a branch that'd be no larger than a match-stick if she were normal size. It's hidden among grass that looms as tall as trees in her current state. She lunges for the branch then charges at the bird, frantically waving the stick and screaming as loud as she can. The bird spreads its wings wide and shrieks, raising eddies of dirt. Holding her twig like a sword, Aine charges again. The bird, sensing easier prey elsewhere, takes to the air.

"And don't come back!" Aine yells. She hurries toward the toadhouse on high alert, her heart hammering. Keeping one eye on the forest, she reaches inside for her book bag just around the door, careful to keep the rest of her body outside. Gilgamesh shoved Spenser into the toadhouse without resizing himself back in Grandma Glori's woods, so she knows it can be done. Looping the book bag over her shoulder, she steps cautiously toward the base of an enormous tree. She digs her fingers into the rough bark, clambers to a protective nook and backs into it. Scanning the area for threats and finding none, she pulls her pocketknife out of her book bag. She unsheathes the blade. Its silver edge catches the sunlight. She's going to make a vow.

"Never again," she whispers to the knife. She pushes aside the bandages and lets the blade kiss the palm of her hand before hesitating. She's never hurt herself before, but she needs to prove something. She draws a breath and slices quickly, wincing as she opens the zipper of skin. A thin red trail leads across her palm. "Never again will I get lost looking backward."

A new memory sideswipes her, this one so clear she feels like she's standing in the middle of it. It's her mother, and her beautiful face is contorted with anger. She's talking to a man, his back to Aine. Helen's voice is low and angry. *Never again.*

As quickly as it arrived, the memory vanishes, leaving her tense and confused. She wipes the blade on her skirt and snaps it shut, tosses it into her bag, and pulls the bandage back over the fresh wound. In the end, it hadn't been hard to cut herself. It was the first real thing she'd felt since she'd seen Glori murdered, a satisfying exchange of crystal pain for suffocating fear and confusion. Her oath sealed and her heart hammering, she crawls out of the nook and begins to claw her way up the tree, slowly, agonizingly, focusing on the pain in her hand and the unhealed wound on her foot.

She's aware as she climbs that a cat could carry her off for dinner, or a hawk could use her to feed its babies. She keeps one eye on the grooved bark in front of her and another toward the skies. Then…curiosity lays its hooks into her. Could she really be in *The Time Machine*? If so, no predators remain. There are only butterflies and songbirds, earthworms and gentle Elois, and that last bit of evil lurking underground. She shudders. She won't think about those creatures. But Gilgamesh will surely have warned the boys about the lone but sizeable nighttime threat remaining on planet Earth in H.G. Wells' future world. If he hasn't seen a need to worry them, then neither will she. There's plenty of daylight left.

Aine's ears pop, and she becomes aware of a tingle and adjusts her toe and handholds to move away from a low-hanging tree branch. She has only time to pull off her tiny book bag before she shoots up to her full five feet, two inches, every molecule in her body expanding until it is ready to burst and then stopping just short of explosion, prickling exquisitely, leaving her momentarily breathless. She steadies herself and takes stock of her surroundings. The egg-yolk sun is directly overhead and the day is as hot as any August in the South. From this angle she notes that the toadhouse is tucked in a natural bower at the base of a fruit tree. Her stomach is growling fiercely, but she won't eat until she's sure the others are safe.

Clutching her book bag until it catches up to her resize, she scrambles to the highest point in the tree. She spots a scattering of grand but decrepit buildings rising above the leaf cover, a rotting, empty city that stretches for miles. Two sights leave her cold. Fifty yards ahead and to her right is a white marble sphinx lording over a forest of rhododendron and poised as if ready for flight. Miles beyond that, a brilliant, green jade palace glitters in the sun. Her breath catches and the world shifts underneath her.

It's true, then.

She is in *The Time Machine*. She is sitting, breathing, living inside a fictional world, a book that lies dusty on her bookshelf between *Murder on the Orient Express* and *Anne of Green Gables*.

She leans back on her heels on the topmost branch of the fruit tree, its bark digging into her knees. Her head spins and her pulse races with a combination of joy and fear. She's in an actual book, inside of a story, living a dream. Despite herself, she smiles. But what is reality then, and what is fiction? The smile disappears. Are she and Spenser merely characters in a story? Tru? Gilgamesh, even? She mentally rifles through all the books she's read. She remembers the storylines and characters from most, but what about the millions of books she has never read, never even heard of? And how can books have books within them, and those, books within them? The possibilities leave her head aching. As she contemplates this new reality, her book bag resizes and she slings it over her shoulder.

Her attention is drawn to a rustling at the edge of a rhododendron forest just below and to her left. One loud set of footsteps are accompanied by two soft sets, one of those so quiet it's almost not there. She drops from the tree as graceful as a monkey and dashes toward them, sticking to the shadowed spots out of habit.

"Spenser!" she calls.

"Aine!" Her brother appears, leading the pack with his cane.

Behind him follows Tru, then Gilgamesh, his expression sour. "We checked out the area. It looks safe!"

She plants her hands on her hips. "Why didn't you wake me?"

Spenser sets his mouth in a serious line. "I figured you needed your rest. You'd do the same for me."

"Please don't do that again, Spense. I need to look out for you."

His face falls. "Sorry. But we got food!"

Tru marches forward, his arms laden with plump, ruby-colored fruit. His face is stained with juice. "You were right about all the easy stuff to eat here," he says. "Gilgamesh says we should fit as much as we can into the toadhouse so we're ready for a quick escape."

"Aye." Gilgamesh's shoulders are tense, and his eyes regularly sweep the surrounding forest. "We should retrieve the metal rod and go. Always assume Biblos could arrive at any time."

Spenser walks to the toadhouse, Tru in tow, and stacks the fruit just inside the door. Gilgamesh must have explained what Aine has observed, that a person has to fully enter the toadhouse to shrink.

"I meant to ask you about that, Gilgamesh. How could Biblos know which story we've gone to? He wasn't close enough to hear when Grandma Glori told us the rhyme."

"He didn't need to hear the exact words," Gilgamesh says darkly. "He can follow this toadhouse into any book. Each toadhouse leaves a trail, you see, a unique pattern in its wake, and he's one of the few who's mastered the art of decoding them. He knows you are with me, and he recognizes my toadhouse trail."

"So we led him straight to Ellipses?" Aine asks, alarmed.

Gilgamesh shakes his head. "Ellipses is hidden between the pages of various books, always moving, and it's only accessible by invitation. Even if Biblos could locate it, he wouldn't be able to enter.

Kenning created it as an underground railroad for injured fairies and a place to house dead stories until Tir Na Nog is reopened. Even Gloriana doesn't know about Ellipses. Biblos could never have followed us there but he will follow us here."

Tru stops in mid-gesture, his hand comically stretched toward a beautiful yellow globe of sweetness hanging from the overhead tree. "You mean that gorilla knows where we are right now?"

"I didn't say that. Once he locates the toadhouse in the story he is currently in, he can follow us here. After that, he'd still need to pinpoint exactly where we are in this book, both our geographic location and the place in the storyline. That takes time."

"How much?"

"That depends on how long it takes him to locate the toadhouse in his present story and the parameters of the book we're presently in. Could be minutes, could be weeks." He marches to the golden box on the outside of the toadhouse and uses a fingernail to force it open. "Still, it's best to not waste time."

Aine studies him. He's a temperamental, arrogant young man with a lot of secrets. Something about him sets her on edge, and she's always had good instincts. He might have told the truth about entering stories, but he's hiding something important, she's sure of it. But she's equally certain he knows where her mom is, and that means she needs to work with him. "Agreed," she says.

The fruit unloaded, a flush of excitement climbs Spenser's face. "Won't that be great to find the key in this story, Aine, so we're closer to finding mom? And think of what other stories we might get to visit for the other keys! This place seems fine, but what if we get to go into *Mary Poppins* or *The Hobbit* or *Tarzan*, or—"

"*The Turn of the Screw*?" Aine interrupts, reminding him of the story that had given him nightmares for three nights in a row. She needs him to be more cautious and not think of this as an adventure. "Watch what you wish for. This isn't fun and games. There's a monster after us, remember?"

"About that," Tru begins, scraping the dirt with his shoe. "If we know he's after us, and we know he's gonna be small when he lands, can't we just wait for him and squash him like a bug?"

"He's dangerous at any size," Gilgamesh warns. "Besides that, I'm pledged to not kill any living creature, no matter how vile."

"That doesn't seem fair," Tru says. "He can torture us and slice us in two but you can't kill him? What about the agents you said are in all the stories?"

"The fairy folk? To them, it's more than a pledge. They are unable to kill another living creature, just like a fish can't breathe out of water."

Tru tips his head, puzzled. "So how're they gonna stop Biblos?"

"If they catch him, by changing the outcome of whatever story they find him in. If they alter the story line so it is different than what was written, everyone in it becomes eternally booktrapped and the story dies. That's why it's so important not to remove characters from their books." He nods at Tru, but the boy is reaching for the yellow fruit again, unaware of the gesture.

"That's suicide!" Spenser exclaims.

The whites around Gilgamesh's eyes blaze momentarily, then clear. "There's no other way. If we don't stop him, he will destroy Tir Na Nog. He'll stop at nothing to get the keys, and you and your sister."

"And I suppose you won't tell us why he wants us, or why he wants to destroy this fairy land where our mother, who is not a fairy, currently lives," Aine says.

Gilgamesh stares at her stonily.

She throws up her hands. "Let's just get the cylinder we came for."

Gilgamesh is suddenly in front of her, holding her arm. His scar is the color of a plum up close, and it makes him appear fierce. He points at the blood staining the bandage covering the palm of her hand. "What happened?"

"Nothing." She meets his gaze defiantly despite the speed rap of her heart. His nearness makes her flush. "I scraped it on a branch when I was resizing."

He holds her eyes, searching, then abruptly releases her arm before returning to the side of the toadhouse.

Heart still beating unevenly, she picks up where she left off. "So here's what I know about *The Time Machine.*" She frowns, backtracking through her memory of the book. "The story is about a British inventor in the late 1800s who creates a time machine and comes to this future time."

"How future?" Tru asks.

"We're in the year 800,000 and something."

"How do you remember all that?" Tru asks, shaking his head wonderingly.

"She's smart," Spenser says proudly. "Her brain is like a spiderweb for stories."

Aine is embarrassed. "It doesn't take much. Besides, I read this one more than once. So, we're very far in the future."

Tru interrupts. "Are there outer space monsters here?"

"No, just...descendants of humans."

"Tigers?" Spenser asks. Gilgamesh moves behind him, wiping his hands on an oily bit of cloth.

"No big animals. Now please be quiet, you two. The Time

Traveler arrives in the future. He's not here very long, eight days if I remember. While he's here, he…" She pauses again and shoots Gilgamesh a look. She doesn't know how much the toadhouse captain has told the boys, if he's revealed that the underground menaces in this book actually stole the traveler's time machine and hid it in the white marble sphinx near their camp. She doesn't want to scare them if she doesn't have to. "Um, he stores his time machine in a little structure underneath the white sphinx."

"We saw that statue!" Tru sings. "I can you lead you right to it."

Aine nods. "The traveler's machine has two levers that control its passage through time. One lever starts the machine and the other stops it. They're both metal. One of them has to be the rod, the tool that makes the Time Traveler believe that men can move as freely as a god. We just grab it and the next clue will be revealed, right?"

Gilgamesh says, "Once you hold the first key, the next clue will be revealed instantaneously." He holds up a cautionary finger. "But you have to be gentle and thoughtful when you interact with anything here. Remember that you can't do anything that will change the outcome of the story, not without a good reason, or you sentence everyone in it to death for no gain."

Aine shoots him a look. "Piss on the outcome of the story." Spenser gasps, but she continues, her heart beating fast. She's never cursed out loud in her life, never said anything so cruel, but she's scared of everything right now and it's easier to be angry. "I want to get what we came for and get out."

Without warning, Gilgamesh lunges in front of her. She is surprised by the sudden, desperate strength in his eyes. "Please," he says. "If we rampage through stories, erasing them, we are no better than Biblos, killing worlds and murdering thousands of innocents.

If we return *him* before the end of his tale," he tosses his chin at Tru, "we'll not have harmed anything. But to deliberately destory a world is unforgivable."

She drops her eyes, ashamed of her outburst and humbled by his unexpected compassion.

Tru scratches his head. "I can't help but notice that's not the first time you've referred to me as a fairy tale character, sir." He offers an arm. "Here, pinch me. I'm as real as you are."

"Of course you are," Gilgamesh says brusquely. He steps back from Aine, leaving her light-headed. "All humans are. You are simply of your book. That's your world, and if you are outside it when the story finishes, the whole creation teeters off balance and is tossed forever into that black nothing we travel through to get from one story to another. The only memory of it will be a dry old book in Kenning's library, if he's lucky enough to save it. That's exactly how the fairies intend to capture Biblos—by snatching a character out, or adding one, so the story is forever dead and he is booktrapped."

"What happens to me in that situation? If my story is destroyed because I'm not there, I mean."

Gilgamesh pats his head. "With any luck, you won't find that out." He turns back to Aine, who's watching the exchange with owl eyes. "Now, is there a way to borrow the rod without altering the story?"

She considers. "I think so. We should be able to sneak in and out of the sphinx with no one seeing us. There's one problem, though. In the story, the structure is locked so the Time Traveler can't enter it right away."

"Gilgamesh could probably find a way in," Spenser says, aiming a shy smile nowhere in particular. "He's clever at fixing things. He's been telling me all about his toadhouse and how he keeps it running."

Aine kneels down to watch their young pilot, who has dipped into the toadhouse to work on the plotter. "And he can't fix it now?" she asks.

Gilgamesh steps outside, now only slightly taller than a plastic cowboy. He shakes his head. "This is different," he squeaks. "It's not just broken. It's destroyed. We need a new part. I can string it together enough for us to bump along, but I can't get her shipshape without an engineer."

Aine raises an eyebrow. "Why can't you just take the part from the other toadhouse in this story?"

A hint of a smile flashes across Gilgamesh's face. "No one has ever called you stupid, have they?"

She blushes at the faint praise and ducks her chin so he can't see the coloring. Oblivious, his focus returns to the toadhouse.

"Unfortunately, it is not that easy. Each toadhouse is protected. They have to be. Wouldn't want a child to stumble upon them and end up shrunk and inside another world. Part of that protection means only a person who believes in the toadhouse or who has been invited may enter it. The other part is that each toadhouse has a secret password needed to access its workings. Without it, the box outside might as well be a solid block of gold."

"Whose idea was that?" Aine asks.

"The fairy king, of cou—" Gilgamesh catches himself. "Enough. You can ask your mother these questions when you see her." He ducks into the toadhouse to maintain his size and returns to continue to toy with the golden watchworks.

Aine stores away the newly acquired knowledge with the other scraps she's collected over the last day. There's a fairy king, and why not? In fact, animals probably speak and goats fly. When she collects enough information, she'll sew it all together into a complete picture. In the meantime, she needs to speak to Spenser and Tru away from Gilgamesh. Talking about the time machine has hatched a back-up plan in case Gilgamesh can't fix his toadhouse.

"The boys and I will go check out the sphinx," she says.

"Boy!" Tru exclaims. "I'm nearly ten."

"And I'm nine," Spenser adds.

"Sorry. The little *men*"—Tru instantly pouts and Spenser giggles—"and I are going to check out the sphinx."

Gilgamesh shakes his tiny head. "You can't go alone to retrieve the rod. If it's truly the first key, releasing it will echo across stories, and Biblos will pinpoint your exact location in this story. I need to be near you."

Aine hides the unexpected warmth she feels at his words. "To do what? Make faces at him? Poke him with a stick? You said you're pledged not to kill any living creature."

"Do not underestimate me," Gilgamesh squeaks darkly.

Aine draws a deep breath. "Sorry. But we're going. We'll be back soon." She pushes both boys ahead of her. Although they allow her to, they keep glancing back.

When they have walked several paces, Spenser stops. "You were rude to him, Aine." His voice isn't accusing. He's simply stating a fact.

"Keep moving. Remember what I told you yesterday? I think he's hiding something from us. Besides, I'm not sure he can even fix that toadhouse of his enough to get us through all this. I'm going to sneak away tomorrow and find the other toadhouse in this story. We might need it. You two will have to cover for me."

"Hmm," Tru says, pushing through an overgrown violet rhododendron. Overhead, the sparrows dive and sing prettily, harmless to full-sized people. "Where would you look?"

"I haven't figured that out yet." Her attention is caught by a nearby fruit tree. The trunk is beautifully curved, as shapely as a woman's hips where the branches spread. Below the spreading is a knot, and if Aine tilts her head, she recognizes the outline of a face. It's an ability she's always had, the capacity to see small faces in the whorls of bark and weavings of wood. Once a face is in focus, shifting her eyes will change its expression; the forehead will become the nose, and she'll realize there is another set of eyes to the right, these laughing where the others were serious, or a mouth that was the chin in the previous face. It's a child's game but a familiar one, and soothing.

She squeezes her eyes, and as sure as the sun, a new face appears in the tree, this one clever-eyed and smirking. Aine smiles back, then her mouth drops open as the face emerges from the tree, followed by a neck and a body, and advances on the three of them in a quick, gliding motion.

Chapter 13

Aine plants herself between the approaching dryad and the boys. She holds up a shaking hand. "Stop!"

"Is it really you?" the woman asks, her voice as smooth and solid as heartwood. Away from the tree, she appears to be flesh and blood. Her skin is a beautiful mahogany brown and her eyes sparkle like green topaz. She smells of cloves. She reaches toward Aine as if to pet her hair.

"Stop, I said!" Aine leans so far backward she almost tips over. "Who are you?"

The woman pulls back her hand, startled, then chuckles. It's a rich, chocolate sound. "Sorry. I didn't mean to be so forward. Caesura is my name, though I'm called Sura. You came with Gilgamesh, didn't you? That man couldn't explain his way out of a milk pod."

Aine is suspicious. "How do you know Gilgamesh?"

"And where are your clothes?" Tru inquires, his head popping up from behind Aine. Next to him, a blind Spenser blushes.

"Oh!" Sura flicks her wrist and is instantly clothed in a flowing white dress. "Sorry. Haven't been around humans for a while. Been in this damn story for seven ages, it seems."

Spenser clears his throat, turning subtly toward Aine. "We don't curse."

"You might want to start, Spenser," Sura says, smiling. "It's as much fun as it seems." Overhead, the sun beats relentlessly, stunning the lazy bumblebees who careen off cherries as big as baby melons. Sura reaches up to pluck one of the succulent fruits and places it in his hands. "Have you tried one of these? You've never experienced a cherry until you've tasted a *Time Machine* cherry."

Aine sees that her brother is unsure, but he doesn't want to make Sura feel bad. He takes a tentative bite. Sweet, dark red juice runs down his cheek, and he swipes at it, smiling appreciatively. "How do you know my name?"

"Every fairy knows of Spenser and Aine." She bows. "I'm at your service."

"*You're* a fairy?" Aine tries to cover her surprise. Kenning and the refugees were the only fairies she'd ever met, besides Mondegreen and Tone, and she assumed because she hadn't known their true identity at the time, they'd all seemed so normal. This woman is several inches taller than Aine, stunning, lean and muscular with arms as sculpted as the tree from which she emerged. Aine surreptitiously flexes her own muscles; they barely crease her sleeves. "You must be one of the agents that Gilgamesh said are in every story. Why does every fairy know about us?"

"I'll leave that to Gilgamesh to explain," Sura says mischievously. "I deserve to have some fun with him, as bored as I've been here. Where is he, anyhow?"

"Back a ways," Aine says vaguely. The leaves overhead rustle at her omission, or at least that's how it feels. "Do you know him well?"

"Well enough."

Aine clenches her jaw. She'd pay $100 for a straight answer, if she had it. "We don't even really know who he is."

A sad smile settles on Sura's face. "He'll do his best to keep you safe, I give you my word, but he's never been one to talk too much about himself. Let's say he's an example of what happens to a young man when he defines himself by his mistakes. And one enormous mistake in particular."

Aine wants to know more, but Spenser interrupts. "Do you have wings?" he asks bashfully.

Sura cranes her elegant neck and reaches for his curved cheek. She caresses it gently. "Beautiful child. I forgot about your eye blindness. No, I'm sorry to disappoint. I am much like your sister, only taller and darker."

It's Aine's turn to flush, but she doesn't look away when Sura steps away from her brother and her piercing glance settles on Aine, studying her from top to bottom with such intensity that Aine suddenly feels as naked as the fairy was. Sura grabs Aine's unsliced hand and pushes back the bandages, rubbing her thumb over the scar in an intimate gesture as her soft smile grows into a grin. After several moments, she seems to reach a satisfactory conclusion and drops Aine's hand, but not before rebinding the Gort.

"My turn for questions," she says. "What are you doing here in *The Time Machine*?"

"Biblos chased us from our book!" Tru says, planting himself in front of Aine. "But before we left we got the clue for the key, and we're here searching for it. Once we have all three objects, we'll be the winners!" He puffs out his chest.

"Indeed," Sura replies, a troubled expression on her face. "Biblos is close, then."

"Gilgamesh isn't sure, though he said we should always be careful," Aine says, finding she trusts the fairy in a way that she doesn't the young pilot. "How long have you been in that tree?"

"As long as I needed to, I suppose. Can I ask where you're going presently, and why Gilgamesh isn't with you? You should not be alone with Biblos on your trail."

"We're headed to the white sphinx," Aine says, pointing through the rhododendron forest. "We think the first object we need is hidden in there. Gilgamesh is back working on the toadhouse. The plotter is broken."

"And he let you go alone?"

"Well," Tru says, scratching the back of his head, "I wouldn't exactly say that. Say, would you mind reaching me one those gargantuan cherries, too? They look delicious."

The fairy does not allow for Tru's distraction. "Your life is in danger as long as the Bookworm is free."

"That's why it's important we retrieve the key as soon as possible." Aine forgets for a moment her plan to leave Gilgamesh in the dust if he interferes with her retrieving the objects or protecting Spenser and Tru. "If we have it, the next clue will be revealed and we can get far ahead of Biblos."

"Very well," Sura says, her mouth set but her eyes twinkling. "I see you have your mother's logic. Besides, I am bound to do your will even if I don't agree. I will take you to the sphinx. We're almost there, in fact. If we can quickly and safely recover the first key, we will. If not, we'll return to Gilgamesh to come up with a plan under less dangerous conditions. Agreed?"

Aine nods. She can't look for *The Time Machine*'s toadhouse when the fairy is near, but there's nothing she can do about that right now. The soft, green thickness of the futuristic forest suddenly feels too close, the thick perfumes of giant flowers cloying. She isn't used to interacting with so many people, or to so many puzzles. For the moment, all she can do is follow Sura until another plan presents itself.

"Splendid. Come along." Sura takes the lead, skipping through the lush, butterfly-dotted jungle plants, peppered with questions from the boys.

Can you do tricks?

Depends what you call a trick.

Can you make a fairy ring like Gilgamesh did?

Of course.

Can you fly?

No.

Why aren't you tiny?

The fairy writers fashioned their characters after themselves. We are more similar than we are different, you and I.

Do fairies live forever?

If they don't die.

Can you cast spells?

After a fashion.

This last question jars a memory from Aine, a horrible recollection but one that feels too important to keep to herself. She squeezes her wounded hand. "Sura, Grandma Glori said something about summoning the four shadows before Biblos killed her. What are—"

Before the question leaves Aine's mouth, Sura crumples into a ball. Her knees crush orange and lemon-colored blossoms, releasing a honeyed scent. Spenser hears her fall and is the first at her side, grabbing clumsily for her arm.

"Are you all right? Did you trip?"

Aine reaches the fairy's side next and sees the fat tears in Sura's eyes. "Are you hurt?"

Sura's speaks painfully, as if voicing her question will make what wasn't true come to pass. "Gloriana is dead?"

"You knew our grandma?" Spenser's eyes are wide.

Sura nods, her shoulders bowed. "Every fairy does. Did. She was a great fairy queen. One of the greatest. Her sacrifice makes mine look like a silly game."

"Grandma Glori? A fairy queen?" Spenser asks, puzzled. Aine elbows him, and he adjusts his face. "She did make good fried chicken." He struggles for more positive memories. "And she smelled really nice, like—"

"Lilies."

"How'd you know?"

"They were her talisman." Sura runs her hand across her close-cropped mane. "Look at me, acting as foolish as a sprite." She pushes herself off the ground. "I'll mourn her properly after my job here is done. Mark my words."

A strong breeze bothers the trees, and stops as quickly as it started. Sura continues forward, but her shoulders have lost their set and her walk some of its confidence. Aine marvels at this, what might have been the biggest mystery of the last forty-eight hours: her grandmother had been a queen, respected by fairies and toadhouse captains alike, who ultimately gave her life to protect Aine and Spenser. What other surprises were to come?

Before she can explore the thought further, they break into a clearing. The marble sphinx with its half-spread wings soars majestically above them, perched on a mammoth brass dais gone green and soft-looking with moisture. Inside lies the first object prophesied by Grandma Glori, the path to the future and their mother. Aine is sure of it.

Chapter 14

The base of the sphinx covers roughly the area of Aine's bedroom back at the farmhouse. This thought makes her throat tight. She'll probably never see her room again with her books, her favorite amber bracelet, and the single photograph of her mom, a woman stunning in her beauty and even more attractive than Sura. Helen had a heart-shaped face, intelligent green eyes, and an aquiline nose over full lips. Her hair was cascading blonde curls. Aine believed her to be the most beautiful woman in the world. And, apparently, she knew—*knows*—fairies. Aine has given up the idea that Gilgamesh or even Sura will tell her much more about her mother, but it doesn't matter. She and Spenser are going to see her soon, and that knowledge fills her heart.

"Who carved that?" Tru asks, pointing up at the sphinx.

The creature is nearly as large as a pick-up truck and is carved out of vibrant white stone, decorated here and there with vines and pocked with age. The sphinx possesses the face of a woman, her eyes staring blindly and her mouth curved in a secret smile. She has the body of a lion, muscled haunches poised to pounce, and wings partially spread as if she is about to spring off her metal palanquin and take to the sky.

"I suppose, within this story, the previous civilization carved it," Sura says. "The key you seek is inside?"

"Yes. Look!" Aine says, calling attention to the base of the giant pedestal. The grass is trampled, as if flattened in a panic, and two deep ruts are forged into the soft earth leading to the ominous brass doors of the structure. The doors themselves appear battered, as if they have been hammered with large rocks. "The Time Traveler has already tried to get his machine back."

"What's it look like?" Tru asks. "The time machine, I mean. Like a sleigh? With lightning bolts?"

Aine permits herself a tight smile. "I suppose that description is as good as any. It's a story, so you get to use your imagination. Let's try the doors."

They put their shoulders into it, pushing and grunting against the immovable entrance. Their fingers glide along the seams searching for purchase or a secret latch. They walk the perimeter countless times but spy no entrance or egress. Disheartened, all three of them lean against the doors.

A few feet away, Sura studies the structure. "That's about right," she muses. "I think I can open it, but it'll take me some time and a little bit of fairy magic."

"How?" Spenser asks eagerly.

"And no offense," Tru says, as sweat drips down his cheeks, "but why didn't you tell us that earlier?"

"I wasn't sure. Do you see that star-shaped indent at the front foot of the sphinx? By the white flower? I believe it's a keyhole, and the old jade museum has an object that'll fit in there perfectly."

"I don't remember the key or the keyhole from the book," Aine says doubtfully.

"A writer can't put every detail in the story, Aine. It would bog it down. But it's here, if you look." She pitches her voice firmly. "So, you three are returning to Gilgamesh. I'll meet you there with the key. Yes?"

"We'll meet you back at the toadhouse," Aine agrees, disappointed. She'd so hoped they'd have the rod by now. "Thank you for your help."

"You've been very kind," Spenser adds.

"Yes, thank you," Tru seconds. "Do you think it will take you long to return?"

Aine rolls her eyes. The boys have been jockeying for Sura's attention since they met her, but now that she's leaving, they're batting their eyelashes at her so loudly that it's embarrassing. "Come on. The sooner we get back to Gilgamesh, the less angry he'll be. We'll see you in a bit, Sura."

They hurry back, winding along the faint trail they've left in the wildness. Since he has already trod this ground once, Spenser doesn't need his cane, though he keeps his hand out to protect himself from slapping branches. They are halfway to the toadhouse when Aine hears the trampling of something large moving through the brush. She instinctively shoves Spenser and Tru into a thicket then joins them.

Just as she ducks her head into the shadow, a brightly clothed pack of tiny, chattering albinos skip past. They appear to be nearly identical, genderless little adult humans, none of them more than four feet tall, wide-eyed, with close-cropped hair and wearing mono-colored tunics. They smile as innocently as babies, wrestling and teasing each as they patter along the trail.

Tru begins to speak, but Aine clamps her hand over his mouth. When they have passed, he removes her hand. "Are those the Elbows you talked about?"

"Elois."

"That's what I said. What language were they speaking?"

"Their own, I suppose. Does it matter?"

Tru shrugs. "I just wondered what they were saying."

"Not much, I'm guessing. The Time Traveler described them as no smarter than little children. They're innocent and harmless."

Spenser swallows. "They sounded nice, though they didn't smell too good, like herd animals."

Aine shoots him a glance, worried that he might somehow have happened upon the truth of the Eloi's purpose on this planet. Spenser, however, is gazing guilelessly into the blue sky, awaiting instruction. "You don't smell too good, either," she says, ruffling his hair. "Now let's get going. We've already wasted too much time."

They step out of the brush and hurry back to camp. Spenser and Tru joke with one another along the way, and Spenser manages to uncover a little more about Tru's past. The boy seems inclined to exaggeration, but when he talks about his parents as if they were pet owners and he a puppy they'd had second thoughts about, there is a strong vibration of truth to it. This seems to deeply sadden Spenser, and he brings the conversation back around to the more comfortable ground of hermit crabs, frog-catching, and the wonderful games that can be played with sticks.

The nearer to the toadhouse they get, the quieter both boys become. If they are conscious of Gilgamesh's command not to leave and are worried about the consequences, they keep these thoughts to themselves. Aine's prophecy about hurrying back to keep Gilgamesh from getting too upset proves to be strangely true, however, because as they return, they find him not angry at all. He is full-sized and sits in the shade of the fruit tree, a glass bottle of eggplant-colored liquid resting on a stone in front of him in the full sun.

"Hello, Gilgamesh," Tru says tentatively.

"Hello. You should have waited for me," he says reasonably. Too reasonably.

"We're fine," Aine says. She studies him critically, the tiny toad-house, the immediate area. Why isn't he raging mad?

"I see that. You got some help, then?"

"Yes we did!" Spenser makes his way to Gilgamesh's side and plops next to him on the ground. "Her name is Sura. You should hear her voice, Gilgamesh. It sounds like candy, and leaves in the trees, and smoke. And she smelled like cookies."

"Aye, Caesura could talk the ice off an igloo," Gilgamesh concedes. "I knew she'd found you the minute all the honeybees left." He eyes Aine peculiarly and speaks directly to her. "Don't run off again."

"I'll go where I please," she says. She doesn't like the way his voice changed when he talked about Sura.

"Then you'll die as someone else pleases."

"I'm as alive as you are."

"For now."

"Is it that you're scared to be alone?"

At this, Gilgamesh throws his head back and laughs, a full-throated belly guffaw that startles her. "Helen doesn't know what she's spawned, does she? Well, so be it, then. I'll do my best to protect you three, but I'm not your warden. You choose to listen, or not."

Tru is smiling, though he seems uncertain why. "What's in the bottle, sir?"

"If I'm able to wait long enough, sweet relief from you three. If not, sour grape juice. Now tell me what you found. I'm guessing it wasn't the rod we're after, or we wouldn't be in this story any longer."

Spenser and Tru fill him in, tumbling over each other in their effort to describe Sura but just barely grazing a mention of the Sphinx and their failed effort to reach the time machine. Gilgamesh listens attentively while Aine tends to her and Spenser's wounds, rinsing them with water, covering them with ointment, and then bandaging them.

When the boys finish their story, Gilgamesh absently scratches the scar on his face. "Nothing to do but wait for Sura to return, then."

Chapter 15

Spenser and Tru occupy themselves with weaving strong grass into a questionable fort and enacting an epic battle between the Cherokee Indians and the Egyptians, whom Tru swears crossed swords at least once in history. Aine spends the rest of the day filling her belly with sweet fruit and idly thumbing through the fairy book Kenning slipped her, though she finds herself repeatedly examining Gilgamesh from under her eyelashes, trying to pin down his age once and for all. If he dressed normally, didn't open his mouth, and got a haircut, she would swear he looked no more than seventeen or eighteen, yet he didn't act like any of the farm-scented, slow boys she'd gone to school with. Plus, he'd told Spenser he'd kept the toadhouse running for years, which meant he must be older than he looked. Or was he?

He is finely-muscled and compact, with brown hair brushing his shoulders. His eyes are also brown, his nose strong, and the deep red scar adds character to his boyish features. The silver necklace hangs around his neck, the chain visible but the amulet it holds always just out of sight. *Who are you,* Aine thinks to herself, *and what aren't you telling me?* He catches her staring and holds her gaze. She quickly looks down, flushed, but not before wondering what it would feel like to run her fingers down the scar on his face.

If he can read minds, he doesn't let on, hypnotized as he appears by his fermenting fruit juice. Aine thinks it ridiculous. Fruit juice takes far more than a day to turn into wine, but she isn't spending her time any more wisely, she supposes. She decides instead to devote her full attention to *The Secrets of the Fairies.*

The End of Times Prophecy section is still missing, so she reads the chapter titled "Weapons and Elements Harmful to Fairies." The first interesting fact she discovers is that fairies cannot stand to be around iron or ash trees. That explains why Glori had them dig up all the ash on her property, and throw away Spenser's metal jacks. She continues on to a chapter on careers for fairies and finds them to be mundane, reflecting what Gilgamesh had already told them: fairies can be musicians, engineers, carpenters, anything except a writer. That was saved for royalty.

She greedily reads the chapter on Tir Na Nog and its ancillary land, the home of the great Ogham, the tree of words from whence all power springs. She wishes for pictures. The rest of the book offers only miscellaneous facts, none of which help her in her present situation. When Gilgamesh shifts across from her, she glances guiltily at him and shoves the book into her book bag.

She pulls out her notebook. She's not a great artist but can create passable faces, and she's suddenly consumed by the need to create a lasting image of the mysterious Gilgamesh. As her pencil scratches on the paper, she wonders what his mistakes have been. Sura said they were giant. He doesn't have the face of a murderer, she's pretty sure of that, but the lines pulling down the corners of his mouth and his eyes suggest a deep sadness.

The portrait is nearly complete when Sura appears. The heavy sun is dipping toward the horizon and lighting the jungle sky with glorious lavenders and mauves. The air is cool and the honeysuckle scents of flowers perfume the night. When Sura arrives, it's as if she's always been standing there, and Aine observes an amazing thing: the moment Gilgamesh notices the fairy, his cheeks burn a fiery red. Is every male as deep as a bathtub? She slams her notebook closed.

"Caesura." He stands so quickly that he bumps a hanging globe of fruit above his head before executing an awkward half-bow.

There is laughter in her eyes. "And you haven't changed a bit either." She walks over and envelops him in a hug with arms as muscled as his. "It's good to see you."

"And you."

She leans back but keeps her hands on his biceps. "Your charges tell me Gloriana is dead at Biblos' hands. You have begun the journey back to Tir Na Nog?"

"We seek the first object." He indicates Aine with a tip of his head. "You helped her look for it today."

"Without much luck, I'm afraid, but I have retrieved the key to the dais. I checked that it fits, though I didn't rotate it."

She turns to Aine, who is again struck by the fairy's majesty. Her white dress of earlier has transformed into a short tunic of the same color, sensible for running through a forest. Around her waist is twined a belt of gold, and a red satchel hangs from that. Sura reaches into the satchel and pulls out a heavy cylinder about the size of Aine's forearm with a star shape soldered on the end. It resembles a branding iron more than a key, and as Aine reaches for it, she has the fleeting thought that this might be the rod they came for. She curls her fingers around the cool metal, and her hand drops with the weight. She pauses, holding her breath.

Nothing. She feels only the chill of the iron and the heft of it. No magic. Whatever that would feel like. "Thank you," she says.

Sura nods, training her eyes intently on Aine's face. "But it'll be dark within the hour so we can't use it tonight. You understand?"

Aine's glance swings to the boys. Of course Sura would know about the Morlocks. Nightfall is an hour away, and already she imagines she can hear the chuckling, snuffling, evil sounds of the only predator left on this planet, the nocturnal creatures that live underground and surface at night to harvest Eloi like cattle. It would have been better to have come and gone in the course of a single day, while it remained light, but that wasn't their luck. "I understand. We should probably move into the toadhouse soon."

"Why?" Spenser gives up his fort game to join the conversation. A grass hat sits askew on his head. Aine isn't sure if it's meant to be an Indian or a Pharaoh headdress. "And hello, Sura." He smiles broadly.

Sura's eyes light up. "Hello, sweet child. Your sister is just being wise. It's always better to be in shelter at night in a strange land. If Gilgamesh pushes the house back just a bit farther and invokes a fairy ring, you'll be as snug as bugs in a rug. But don't go in yet. It's been so long since I've had company. Sit and visit with old Sura for a few minutes, yes?"

"Ma'am, if you're old, then I'm the queen of England," Tru says, adjusting his grass hat like a crown and sending Spenser into a riot of giggles with his posh accent.

"At your service," Sura says, mimicking the royal British brogue and curtsying. She settles herself on the ground where Gilgamesh had been sitting and follows his sight path. "You're making wine?"

Gilgamesh nods.

"Want help?"

He shakes his head, and Aine imagines some anger in his gesture.

"Stop being such a donkey, Mesh. Here, it's no trouble at all." She stands, advances on the bottle of thick grape juice, and touches it gently. She whispers something too quietly for Aine to hear. The bottle darkens then clears to a light amethyst shade. "There. The finest of the fairy liquor, at your disposal. And who would say you haven't earned it?"

Gilgamesh walks over and kicks the bottle fiercely. The liquid spills like blood into the earth. The sweet-sour smell of wine fills the air. "But I haven't earned it, have I, or I wouldn't need your help to turn it into wine."

He stalks toward the darkening jungle. Spenser clutches at Aine's hand. "What happened? Why is he mad?"

"Shh. I don't know. Sura turned Gilgamesh's juice into wine, and it upset him."

Spenser affects an expression of deep wisdom, as if speaking from hard-earned experience. "He wanted to do it himself."

Aine is surprised at her brother's perceptiveness and squeezes his arm.

Sura is chasing Gilgamesh across the clearing. "I'm sorry. I shouldn't have done that." She glances at her audience, who is listening but pretending not to. "Now come back, and let's not ruin this beautiful evening. Tell me what you can of the other fairies, at least before the sun sets."

Gilgamesh stops at the edge of their camp and scowls. "I'm not a storyteller."

"Please." Her voice, for the first time, sounds weak. "It's been so long."

Gilgamesh grunts, but he returns to his spot. Sura stands as still as glass and the other three wait expectantly. After several uncomfortable minutes of silence, he finally speaks. At first he parses out bits of abstract details while the fireflies warm up, cautiously speckling the fading sky with tender bits of light. But soon, he becomes more animated than Aine has ever seen him, hands waving as he recalls rescuing a queen's dragonfly in *The Secret Garden* or ferrying messages to agents living near the third post from the sidewalk in Dr. Henry Higgins' fence, even chuckling as he recounts how he initially scared Black Beauty but was able to blend in without upsetting the story.

The brilliance of his rare smile shocks Aine. She has to look away, returning her gaze only when he switches to a new story. Gilgamesh begins to talk about the fairy Periphrasis who was required to defend King Arthur to save the tale at the cost of Periphrasis' life. Gilgamesh's face twists, and Aine is almost certain he's going to weep. The heady perfume of the jungle and the sweetly blowing wind seem to be in harmony with him, and Aine finds her opinion of the mysterious young man shifting under the light of the nearly full moon.

"The moon! We must get inside!" she cries. She scours the edges of the clearing for any sign of the night-hunting Morlocks, cursing herself for not grabbing matches when they fled her grandmother's cottage. Fire is the only defense against the creatures.

Sura's head snaps up as if slapped. "Sweet Elfame! How could we have let the time slip? Gilgamesh, I swear that sometimes you are a siren. Get these charges inside and set your protections."

Spenser is caught up in the urgency of the moment. "You'll come with us, Sura?"

She is scrutinizing the forest, her steely gaze jerking into the darkest corners, but she weaves a smile into her voice for Spenser. "Your concern is appreciated, child, but every tree here is my home. I'll be fine, and I'll return first thing in the morning. Now, duck into the toadhouse so I can see you all safe with my own eyes before I leave."

Gilgamesh tucks the toadhouse deep into the thicket until it is nearly invisible to even those who know where to look. He salutes a pensive Sura then shepherds Tru and Spenser inside. He steps back to offer Aine a small bow indicating she should enter before him. Once all four are indoors, he whispers quietly. The mushrooms pop up immediately around the house, so close they're almost touching it.

"Why don't they make us sleep?" Tru asks.

Gilgamesh starts as if pinched and steps away from the door. "Don't sneak up on me. And if we're inside the fairy ring when it's cast, we're not affected by it. Now go to sleep."

"I'm not tired," Tru says.

"Me neither, really," Spenser says quietly. "But if it's better for everyone, I can go to bed."

"I don't like it here," Tru mutters, his bravado erased under the heavy tide of sleepiness, unfamiliar food, and a strange bed. "I want to go home, to my friends."

Before Aine can object that they are also his friends, he dissolves into a puddle of tears, far closer to nine than eleven years old. Spenser is by his side. He wraps his arm over Tru's shoulder and leads him to the cot. Now both boys are crying.

"I miss my grandma," Spenser offers. "A lot. I miss Mondegreen and my mom."

"I thought you said you didn't know her," Tru says through his tears.

Aine watches her brother carefully. That's what he'd always told her.

"I was little," he says haltingly. "I only remember how she smelled, and that she cried a lot at night."

"That's not true!" Aine says, the vehemence in her voice surprising her. Across the room, Gilgamesh contemplates her, his eyes glittering. "She was always happy when she was with us. At least…I think she was."

Spenser shrugs. "It's just what I remember. Mom crying at night when she'd come into my room to check on me." He wipes his hand across his wet face. "I miss my room, too, back at Grandma Glori's, and my rock collection."

Tru snuffles loudly. "At least you have your sister. And hermit crabs."

Spenser reaches under the bed to assure himself they're still there. His face relaxes when he touches the terrarium. Aine knows exactly what he's about to do. Sure enough, he drags the terrarium out and proffers it to Tru, the tears still wet on his cheeks. "Here. Pick one. You can have Pinch or Shelly, and they'll be ours together."

"Really?" Tru starts rubbing his nose and ends up somewhere near his hair. "You'd give me one of your crabs?"

Spenser nods. "Yes."

"Can I have the bigger one, the one with the pink on its shell?" Tru asks warily.

"Shelly? Sure."

A tentative smile breaks through Tru's cloud. "Thanks."

"You're welcome." Spenser grabs Shelly and hands her to Tru.

Aine shakes her head and smiles. Spenser would give the shoe off of his foot if someone needed it. "Bedtime. Spenser and Tru can share the cot, if they put their heads at opposite ends. Gilgamesh can sleep by the plotter, and I'll rest over here, by the door."

Before she can finish, Gilgamesh tosses her one of the thin shirts from the coat rack. It morphs into a fluffy mattress, pillow, and blanket before it hits the floor.

"I'll be dipped!" Tru says.

"What happened?"

"The jacket. The one we wore in Ellipses? It just turned into a bed, all made up, right in the air!"

Aine makes a show of rearranging the bedding as Tru describes the blankets to Spenser. When he refers to them as "magic material," Gilgamesh corrects him.

"You're close. They're called comfort cloth. They change into any cloth-based object you need them to be in the moment."

"Handy," Aine says. She hears a tiny click over the door. She knows it's another page turning in Tru's archetyper. She checks on it regularly when she thinks no one else is looking and knows that over a quarter of the pages in the metal book have flipped. She points to the opposite wall at the single book on Gilgamesh's bookshelf to distract herself. "What is that book, anyway? I forgot to ask."

She walks toward it, but Gilgamesh yanks it off the shelf and locks it in a drawer in the base of the plotter before she can touch it. "That's mine."

"I figured," Aine says dryly. "I was wondering what its title is."

"It is mine," he repeats, "and it's not for anyone else's eyes."

More secrets.

"Nini, will you read me to sleep?"

Aine glances at Spenser and sees him, really sees him, for the first time all day. He is lying down, a hopeful smile on his face.

That hasn't changed. The rest of him, though, appears to have been erased at the edges. He has bald patches where he's twisted out his hair from nerves, deep gray pools under his eyes, and a pasty green pallor glistening on his face. His elegant fingers work nervously, continuously, at some unseen knot. The smile, even, slips quickly, leaving a too-small, too-thin boy who's lost nearly every bit of solace he's ever had, and even what's left, he's willing to share.

Her heart melts. She senses that Kenning wanted her to keep the purple fairy book a secret. She considers the only other reading material stuffed in her school bag. "I only brought *Dracula.*"

"Are you *serious*?" Gilgamesh says from his side of the toadhouse.

"It's what I was reading!" Aine says, blushing. She drops next to Spenser, rubbing his hair and editing the heck out of the story she reads aloud, until, as he dozes off, the nine-year-old is entirely convinced that Dracula is an avenging hero sent to Transylvania to save boys, hairless cats, and hermit crabs.

Chapter 16

Spenser's nightmares wake them repeatedly. He cries out for Grandma Glori, screams for Aine, pleads for a mother whose face he can't recall. Aine finally pulls him into bed with her. He nuzzles deep into the crook of her arm and sleeps soundly the last few hours until dawn. Aine does not.

She thinks of her grandmother. Glori kept food on the table and made sure they had two good sets of clothing, but most of her time had been spent shooing them away, either to school or the woods. And, Aine realizes painfully, if her grandma were here now, she'd take care of everything. Glori had been harsh, but she'd also been strong and devoted. Aine can't lie to herself any longer. She misses Glori terribly.

When she tries to remember her grandma existing at the same time as Helen, the thought grows slippery, a fish in her hands, and she's left fighting to recollect what she had been thinking about. Yes. Her grandmother. She has no memory of the woman before she and Spenser were dropped off on her front porch, and no awareness of her father, either. She believes her mother never mentioned either of them, but how could that be? Her head throbs with the effort of hanging onto the train of thought.

Spenser stirs softly in her arms, moaning, and she loses focus, landing back in the moment. Frustrated, she struggles to grab a single solid memory, but they flee. Then, suddenly, the recollection that's been worrying at her since she deliberately sliced her hand breaks through with such clarity that she gasps.

She's there, watching. A man speaks in a grave tone to her mother. His back is to Aine.

Never again, Helen tells him. She's not angry like Aine had thought. She's crying but determined.

Aine is certain that if she can just see the man's face, this memory will never escape her again. She walks forward, slowly, so close to him she can almost touch his white shirt. She smells lilac and clover. She steps around him, noting the back of his ear, the glide of his chin. There is something familiar about him. She is almost at his face. When she sees it, the memory will click home. It will be hers forever.

"No!" Spenser yells in his sleep, twitching again in her arms.

She's yanked from the recall, but she can't be angry with her brother. She knows he's remembering Grandma Glori's murder, the scent of fresh lightning and spilled blood, the scream, the emptiness. Suddenly the toadhouse is closing in and she can't stand it. The world is huge and strange, and she feels out of place. She gently tugs her arm from around Spenser, slips out of bed and darts outside, kicking at one of the circling mushrooms until her ears pop and she undergoes the intoxicating resize. All around her, the rising sun paints the sky a purplish gold.

"Rough night?"

She whirls. Sura is perched in a tree languorously eating a raspberry, each juicy seedpod the size of a plum. Aine stares at her feet. "I guess. Spenser had nightmares."

Sura hops to the ground. "I heard. I'd imagine both of you would. Biblos is a monstrosity of a man, and it was just two days ago that you lost Gloriana." She keeps her distance from Aine, examining her. "You want to ask me something?"

Aine hesitates, glancing toward the toadhouse. Soon, the other three will awake and the sun will be blinding. The tropical air is already heavy and redolent with sweet nectar. She has nothing to lose. She says it all, in a rush of words. "You know where the other toadhouse is? The one that always stays in this story?"

Sura takes a moment before responding. "Of course."

"You said yesterday that you were required to do my bidding. If so, I demand that you take me to that toadhouse. Now." Aine draws herself up, but she feels small, and like a traitor. She wants to trust Gilgamesh like Sura trusts him, but she's been responsible for Spenser for too long. She can't suddenly put that responsibility on the shoulders of a stranger. On top of that, she's confused by her feelings for the pilot, and it makes her crave a backup plan.

Sura's eyes gleam dangerously and she becomes still as ice. Then, instantly, she spins on her heels and races into the forest. Aine tenses in surprise. A quick glance at the toadhouse assures her that the others aren't awake. She follows Sura's trail, tentatively then picking up speed. At first, she is worried. Will Spenser be safe without her? Can she keep up with Sura, and even if she can, will the fairy really lead her to *The Time Machine* toadhouse? But the fears give way to exhilaration as the forest rushes past, a blur of greens and pollen-scented air. She has never run so fast or felt so alive.

That sensation soon gives way to smugness. If Sura thought she could lose her, this wasn't the way to go. Aine shoots under branches, over roots, slides around curves, and races so fast she becomes airborne. The colors become undifferentiated, the world around her quiet as she speeds faster than sound. Finally, she overtakes Sura, who is bent almost double, her breath expelling in deep pants.

"Well done," the fairy gasps, with no trace of rancor.

Aine can't wipe the triumphant smile off her face. "I didn't know I could run that fast!"

"Or so far." Sura indicates the green jade palace immediately in front of them, a once-grand structure now decrepit and aged. It's wreathed in vines, and flowering plants have taken up residence in every crack and crook, covering the building in sweetly scented living colors. The structure gives the impression of an immense, aged giant that is sleeping but alive.

"Why, this was miles from our camp!"

Sura nods wryly. "You'll find more of your memories and powers surfacing now that Gloriana has unbound you. She had a protection spell on you and Spenser both. So Biblos couldn't locate you, and so you wouldn't remember your past and become unbiddable."

Aine's eyes bug. "I have powers?"

Sura holds up a cautionary hand. "You don't think a normal girl could run that fast, do you? You'll have to ask your mother about the rest of your gifts."

"You sound like Gilgamesh."

Sura narrows her eyes. "Speaking of whom, do you want to tell me why you're after this toadhouse? You'll have no better pilot than Gilgamesh."

For some reason, Aine finds herself unable to lie to Sura. That doesn't mean she's compelled to reveal her backup plan to have the *Time Machine*'s toadhouse ready to go should Gilgamesh prove unreliable or his toadhouse fail. "I don't want to tell you."

Sura sighs. "Have it your way." She indicates the malachite stairs leading into the great green structure. The sunlight glints off it, and in spots where the stone is nearly transparent, light shines through like a lantern. "The toadhouse is under the stairs. It's on the western side, tucked inside a large fissure shaped like the letter 'Z.'"

Aine's heart leaps. Her fallback plan could work, and if they need it, wouldn't they all thank her, even Gilgamesh? She feels Sura's eyes on her as she struggles through the deep acacia to reach the side of the stairs. It is a patchwork of cracks and deeper shades of green, but if she squints as if looking for a face, she sees it: the deep, z-shaped fracture. She slips through the vegetation and peeks inside.

There it is, a version of Gilgamesh's toadhouse. At first glance they seem identical, down to the elfin curl on the top, but she soon spots the difference. It's the watchworks box on the outside, the one that powers the plotter. This one is silver, Gilgamesh's is gold. She calls to Sura over her shoulder. "Can it be moved?"

The fairy is perched on the great stone stairs and stares down at Aine. "The toadhouse? Certainly. Anyone can pick it up and move it, though you need to know what it is to enter it." She looks off into the distance thoughtfully. "I believe there are none safer in any story than this one. I am forbidden to transport it, as is Gilgamesh. The Eloi lack curiosity and the Morlocks aren't aware of its existence. Do you intend to take it with you?"

"No," Aine says, streamlining her plan. Given how fast she can travel on foot, this is as good a place as any to store the toadhouse until they have the rod in hand. "Not right now. I just wanted to see it. Thank you."

Sura opens her mouth as if to ask a question, and then shakes her head with a small movement like a bird ruffling its feathers. She retrieves a palm-sized glass marble from her pouch and begins to roll it between her fingers. "Anything else?"

Aine's eyes grow wide. "My grandmother had one of those."

"Every fairy does." Sura gracefully leaps from the stairs and lands in a crouch in front of Aine. The grapefruit-sized globe is perched on her pointer finger. "Would you like to see mine?"

Aine reaches for the clear glass marble, afraid to touch it yet drawn to it.

Sura chuckles. "It won't burn you. It's a know globe. See? It stores a fairy's memories. Child fairies love them, as do those of us on assignment in the books. Let me call up one of my favorites."

Exquisite diamond crystals glitter inside the globe, sparkling and then clearing. They are replaced by a vision of Sura, younger, maybe Spenser's age. She is sitting in a classroom but except for the desks, it isn't like any school Aine has visited. The teacher stands at the front of the room, unremarkable apart from his height and stark cheekbones. Aine's eyes widen as he demonstrates how to make a cat levitate, and then transform into a dog, and finally, duplicate itself. It is going wonderfully until Sura exchanges a mischievous glance with another student in the front row, a boy with big ears and a larger smile. They both stare intently at the stack of papers on the teacher's desk for several seconds. It bursts into a buzzing nest of bees.

The class squeals, the two dogs drop to the ground and revert to a single cat, and the teacher angrily orders everyone out of the room while he corrals the insects. The children scramble over each other in a mad dash to reach the outdoors, a countryside so magnificent that it steals Aine's breath. Rolling hills of green give way to thick hardwood forests, their edges freckled with perfumed white flowers. Birds sing a delicate melody, ignoring the children as they invade the woods to play hide and seek.

"It's Tir Na Nog," Sura said, her voice thick. "My home."

"It's beautiful," Aine says honestly. "I can even hear the laughter."

Sura nods. "The know globe will reveal any aspects of the memory you want."

Aine is reluctant to look away. The land seems so peaceful and welcoming. "Why would my grandma have pulled her know globe out when she was battling Biblos?"

"There's power in memories. Gloriana must have been calling on it to help her fight Biblos. He's the worst kind of monster, heartless. I've heard he's even turned fairies in stories he's visited, brought them to his side in this battle, though it's rare. Most fairies would choose death over betrayal, though Biblos' methods of torture are legendary in their cruelty."

Aine recalls the refugee camp at Ellipses. Then, in a horrible moment of clarity, she pictures all the floating glass globes that provided heat and light in the library. "What happens to a know globe when its owner dies?"

"It seeks out the next of kin, though just like fairies, it can't travel across stories without a toadhouse. If there aren't any relations nearby, the know globes in the past were transported to Tir Na Nog out of respect. With the homeland closed off, I don't know where they go."

Aine is overcome with deep sadness. Kenning must have retrieved all those know globes when he'd gone for survivors. Now they had nothing to do but hang in the air, all their families gone. "Was Gloriana really my grandmother?"

The fairy slips the globe back into her pouch. She takes her time cinching the drawstring and doesn't look at Aine when she's done. "No. But she really was the queen of the fairies once. She engendered such loyalty that Mondegreen, her ever-faithful servant, went with her to protect the two of you, even though it meant being separated from his beloved wife for many years."

The familiar confusion begins to boil in Aine. She feels a memory close by, but she can't bring it into focus. "Why would Glori and Mondegreen do that? Why would they leave their world to protect the children of a human, children not even from Tir Na Nog?"

Sura grabs Aine's shoulders fiercely. "Make no mistake. Tir Na Nog is your home. It always has been, and it always will be." Her passion leaves as quickly as it appeared. "We should return. I'll race you back!"

She darts off with Aine close on her heels. They speed over the ground as fast as color and light. Aine's head is full of visions of a great green land and worry that Sura will tell Gilgamesh of her strange request. Sura is silent in her swiftness. Aine eases up so as not to pass her.

Gilgamesh is outside but not yet resized when they return. Even in miniature, his tense movement and set jaw convey his mood. Aine watches him from the corner of her eyes as she kneels outside the toadhouse and calls for Spenser and Tru. Within minutes, both tousle-headed boys tumble out into the sunshine. Spenser hands her the school bag she requested containing the key to the sphinx's perch, her books, and her pad and paper. The cloth bag is tiny in her hands, a doll's accessory.

Both boys rub the sleep out of their eyes and share a bit of fruit and cheese before they resize. When they're at their normal height, Tru stretches like a cat before throwing Spenser into a playful headlock.

Spenser's eyes widen in surprise, then a smile lights his features. He twists his head slightly and slides out before returning the favor.

"Hey, how'd you do that?" Tru asks, grinning even though his head is pinched in Spenser's thin arms. "You're as quick as a flash!"

Sura claps her hands to distract the boys from their horseplay. "On to the sphinx!" she declares grandly, but Aine thinks she catches an odd hitch in the fairy's voice. She chalks it up to her forcing Sura to take her to the toadhouse. She's sorry, but she's not willing to share her backup plan and risk being talked out of it. If they need the other toadhouse to escape, they'll have it. If they don't need it, nobody will be the wiser.

"Yes," she says. "Let's follow Sura."

They take to the path in an orderly row. The boys chatter in excited voices about discovering the rod and taking off for a new story as Gilgamesh brings up the rear. The jungle is glorious, with saucer-sized forget-me-nots and elegant orchids fighting to be the most beautiful and the most deliciously scented. The only danger lay in entangling themselves in the thick vines littering the forest floor. Far off in the distance they can hear the babbling giggles of the Eloi, which blend harmoniously with the sparrow song.

They make quick time and are soon at the brass dais. Sura walks them around to the keyhole. Aine suddenly feels a jittery panic. Inside is the time machine. She also knows a tunnel exists inside which leads to the Morlocks' underground lair. They didn't encounter the hungry creatures last night, but that was luck as much as anything. For the millionth time, she is grateful neither Spenser nor Tru has read *The Time Machine*.

"Gilgamesh, do you mind?" Aine hands him the key. She wants to be as near as possible when the doors slide open.

He nods and accepts the heavy metal cylinder. Stepping to the side, he inserts it into the hole. The key slides in with a rusty click. He rotates it. The movement produces a ratcheting sound, as if he's winding a clock. The doors slide open with industrial ease, releasing the scents of steam engines and musty earth.

"What's that noise?" Spenser asks, cocking his head.

"Machines," Aine answers quickly. "They power an underground ventilation system."

She intends to make something up to distract from questions about why there would be an underground air system in this book, but she is captivated by the brilliant, primitive, gaudy machine just inside the brass doors. It is a futuristic sled crafted of dark, slender metal soldered at the joints and ringed by a thin ribbon of brass. At the rear of this cage, crystal and ivory tubes spring up like organ pipes, each pulsating with reflected light from the angled rays of the rising sun. A single bar in the center of this bouquet of tubes wavers as if not entirely real. Toward the front of the contraption is the chair, a dour, wooden affair among so much quartz and ivory and nickel. The feet of the chair are screwed to the base of the sleigh and a leather strap lies over the seat for extra security.

The propulsion mechanism is also simple. A column in front of the seat is supposed to contain a rod for accelerating and another for decelerating, or going forward and backward in time. Aine is certain that Glori's rhyme referred to one of these two rods. Last night she'd decided it must be the one that makes the machine go forward in time, which seemed more in line with her grandmother's admonition to "remember that man is not god."

Except the rods in the column are missing.

Chapter 17

Spenser appears at her side. "Can you see the rod, Aine?"

"No." Her stomach is leaden with disappointment. She imagines she can hear the click of another page in Tru's archetyper turning and feel her mother slipping farther away.

"I'm sure it's there," he says, ducking his head. He steps away from her and feels toward the opening, his cane swishing back and forth. "I can help you find it. What does the time machine look like?"

"Like a million bucks!" Tru says, dashing in to duck under the brass guardrail and sit in the chair before Aine can object. "Toot toot! Outta my way! I'm going to the few-cher!"

Aine charges in and yanks him out of the chair, almost slicing his ear off on a brass strip in the process. She throws him down outside the dais doors, guarding the time machine with her disgrace.

"Ow! Hey, what's that about?"

Sura kneels to tend to his ear. She speaks to Aine without looking at her. "What's wrong?"

"They're not here. The rods." She puts her hands to her cheeks as anger and shame fight in her brain. "I forgot. I forgot that the Time Traveler unscrews them and puts them in his pocket so no one could steal his machine. How could I have been so stupid?"

She kicks at the time machine. Behind her, down the tunnel, she hears a shuffling in the darkness. Icy fear licks at her spine, and she whips around to stare into the inky channel leading down to the Morlocks' nest. It's a narrow black mouth carved into the stone, sloping toward the machines huffing away underground. She observes only darkness but imagines that the Morlocks are nearing her, smelling her blood and flesh, and for a tiny moment, she wants them to come. She feels she could burn them all with her shame alone and still have fire left over.

Ignoring the faint smell of fresh blood emanating from the dark, unwilling to admit that she has botched things entirely, she grabs the organ pipes that decorate the rear of the time machine, grasping one after the other in the thin hope that it might be *the* rod. With each, she feels nothing. Even consumed by her momentary madness, she notices the darkness shift behind her and red eyes blinking, but she can't drag herself out of the cave. One of these rods has to be the one. She is frenzied when she touches the last pipe, the shimmering ghost rod that powers the whole mechanism. It burns her so sharply that she cries out.

"Come." Sura, who has been watching with concern, jerks her out unceremoniously. She exchanges a glance with Gilgamesh, who quickly removes the key with a scraping pull. The brass doors slide shut, but not before Aine catches sight of a filthy, yellow-clawed paw feeling toward her from the pitch-black tunnel. The Morlocks really were near.

Sura holds Aine's face in her hands. "It wasn't any of those rods on the machine," she tells her. "You touched every one."

"But I didn't pull them out!" Aine protests, cradling her burnt hand, the same hand she'd deliberately sliced. The size of her failure feels epic. She sighs deeply. "I'm sorry."

Her voice gentler, Sura reaches for Aine's hand and moves aside the bandage. One cool touch, and the burn eases and the cut Aine had inflicted on herself heals. "There's no point in mourning mistakes when you can fix them," she says. "The rods are in the Time Traveler's pocket, you say? Then what is the best way to retrieve them?"

Aine peers at the group hesitantly. She expects reproach but sees only expectancy. "Um, the Time Traveler sleeps deeply in the story. At least…that's what I remember."

"Then we retrieve the rods tonight while he rests," Gilgamesh says with finality. A look of concern clouds his face as he studies Aine. "What building?"

Aine's voice gains strength. Maybe it would be better to focus on the solution. "The one the Eloi congregate in. It looks like a French mansion only shabby and covered in vines. You can see it off in the distance when you climb the fruit tree the toadhouse is hidden next to."

Tru jumps up, his wounded ear forgotten. "Can we sneak in on him while he's sleeping and just slip 'em out of his pocket?" he asks eagerly. "I'm a real good pickpocket if I have to be."

Aine, for once, is grateful for his enthusiasm. She runs through the details of the story in her mind, though she is reluctant to share them. What if she's wrong again? "That should work, as long as we're early enough in the story."

Spenser turns toward his sister, his face screwed up like he smells something bad. The Morlocks, just on the other side of the metal door? "Aine, who else is in this book? Besides the Eloi and the traveler, I mean."

Of course her brother and his miraculous senses would pick up the scent of the Morlocks. She doesn't want to add to his fears, though. "The traveler sleeps at night among the Eloi. If we stick together and we're quiet when we capture the rods, it should all go fine." She shoots a look at Gilgamesh and Sura, daring them to fill in the blanks she's left.

"Can we wait until tonight?" Tru asks. "What about Biblos?"

"We don't have a choice. We can't leave without the rod," Gilgamesh says matter-of-factly.

"Where did you last see Biblos?" Sura asks, making the three-fingered motion over her heart.

"The book where I retrieved Aine and the children."

It's the second time Gilgamesh has referred to Aine as an adult. She stands up a little straighter, controlling the warmth in her cheeks.

"And then you came straight here?"

"No," Spenser offers, "we stopped in Ellipses."

"Ah." A shadow crosses her face. "Were you there long?"

"Long enough to throw him off the trail," Gilgamesh says, picking up her train of thought. "He'd need to leave the toadhouse he arrived in and find the one in Tru's story before coming here."

Sura smiles. "You did well, even if it was thanks to a plotter that needed tuning. Sometimes we have to trust the Fates, yes? You bought yourself time, and there's no book safer in the daylight than *The Time Machine*," she repeats. "None."

"What about at night?" Tru asks.

"Speaking of this book being safe in the daylight," Aine says quickly. "I was thinking it'd be a good idea to take the boys to the river. They're both growing a little ripe, and it'd give you two more time to talk." She concentrates on keeping her face smooth. She is trying to change the subject, but even more than that, she hopes the water will wash away some of the sadness around Spenser's face, that expression of being absolutely lost that he allows himself when he thinks no one is looking.

Gilgamesh shakes his head vehemently, apparently forgetting that only yesterday he'd agreed he wasn't going to serve as their warden. "I won't have it. There's danger around every corner."

"Hush," Sura says. "You can't leave the story until you have the rod, and we've already decided that can't happen until tonight. As long as they stay out of sight of the Time Traveler, their luck will hold."

"And if he sees them?"

Sura taps her chin, then abruptly faces Aine. "I'm going to teach you a simple trick, one I don't think even your mother would begrudge me."

Aine's heart hammers at this announcement, and she freezes, afraid that if she moves, Sura will retract her offer.

"You know what the Eloi look like?"

Aine nods.

"Hold that image in your head. Then visualize a clean white light covering you, Spenser, and Tru. You had movies in the book you were in, didn't you?"

Aine nods.

"Then pretend your brain is the camera and your bodies are the screen. Understand? What you picture is what others will see, or at least think they see. It's a simple version of something we call mind clouding."

For a moment, Sura becomes blurry, and then she morphs into Tru, only taller. "See? I'm picturing Tru and projecting his form onto mine. It's more difficult to change height and weight, too much to learn at this point, but you're all approximately the same size as an Eloi, so this will be simple."

Aine's pulse flutters with excitement. She's actually going to learn fairy magic. "What if I lose my train of thought?"

"Get it back. The Eloi are undemanding and the Time Traveler not so observant, so there is no better training ground. And with practice, you'll find you don't need to hold the image in the forefront of your mind. You can hang it in the back, like a song that you're not really listening to. Try it."

At first, Aine feels ridiculous imagining an Eloi, then a shimmery light around her, with everyone looking. She idly wonders if this is some fairy prank, or if they will all discover that she's an imposter who possesses no powers other than speed. Then Tru gasps.

"Wow, Aine, you're doing it!"

She breaks into a grin despite her best efforts. "What do I look like?"

"Just now, you went back to Aine, all angles and curves. Before that, though, you were like one of them real petite, super-white Elbows. Dead ringer, in fact." Tru whistles in appreciation.

Gilgamesh still doesn't appear convinced. He crosses his arms and cocks an eyebrow. "I don't like letting them out of my sight one bit, and I don't expect their mother will, either."

"The three of them have been through a lot and deserve some carefree moments," Sura wheedles, her eyes twinkling. "Aine will have the trick mastered by the time they reach the river. It'll give you time to tell me more stories, Mesh, and for me to finish stocking your toadhouse." She winks at him.

"One hour. That's what you have," Gilgamesh relents gruffly, before turning his back on them and marching toward the toadhouse.

Aine wants nothing more than to practice her trick in a mirror but their time is limited. Besides, she has no idea where she could find a mirror even if they had all day. She nods her thanks to Sura and leads the boys through the thick brush toward the flowing water, all the while thinking Eloi thoughts.

"What is hiding underground here, Aine?" Spenser pleads, surprising her. "Tell us really."

Aine loses her focus, and her hands waver between Eloi and human. She'd thought she'd distracted her brother from this question. She weighs her words. She wants to protect him from the sinister truth of this book, but she won't lie to him. She sighs deeply. "The Eloi aren't the only race on this planet. There's also the Morlocks. They both descended from humans. Eloi live above ground, happy and brainless like toddlers, eating fruit and playing their lives away. The Morlocks live underground."

"What do they eat?" Spenser asks. "Worms?"

"Eloi." She holds her breath and waits for the boys' reaction. She doesn't have long.

"They're cannibals?" Tru asks, spitting into the ground. "I say no thanks to that."

"But they can only come out when it's dark," Aine assures them. "Any sort of light terrifies them."

Spenser reaches for her shirt. "Why didn't you tell us earlier? You didn't want to scare me, did you?"

"I suppose."

"Don't worry so much about me." His voice is faint but stretches for boldness. "I'm stronger than you think."

She is sure he's imagining the horrors underground, needle-jawed mutated humans rending the flesh of the chattering, terrified Eloi, but she's proud of him for keeping his voice steady. "You had nightmares all last night, sweet little brother," Aine responds. "Pardon me for thinking you need protecting."

Tru isn't done with the subject. "So tonight, we're going to steal the rods when the Morlocks are out? Why can't we just cloud ourselves as Elois now and go grab 'em out of the Time Traveler's pocket?"

Aine considers. "I think it might change the story. Besides, he'd struggle if he was awake, and we might not be strong enough. If he saw the Eloi as a threat, he'll sleep somewhere we can't get him tonight, and we'll never have another chance. Our best bet is to stick with our current plan, get the rod, and bring you back to your book." She changes the subject. "I have good news. Sura showed me the *Time Machine* toadhouse this morning."

"She did?" Tru asks breathlessly. "Was it close? What'd it look like? Why didn't you take us? When'd you go?"

"If you woke up a little earlier, you'd know. It looks just like our toadhouse. If for some reason we can't get to Gilgamesh's, we have a fallback. I'm going to make sure we get to mom if it's the last thing I do."

"I can hear it," Spenser says unexpectedly, halting. "The river."

"Hold on." Aine stops them behind a blueberry bush as large as an apple tree with fruit its equal. She also hears the music of the water now. She peeks through the mountainous shrub. Ahead, the main group of Eloi is congregating around the river, frolicking, giggling, and chattering in their chirpy language. There must be at least fifty of them. She refreshes the Eloi image in her head and concentrates on a white light around her and the boys. "Tru, how do I look?"

"Why don't you look at me and see?" Tru asks.

Aine swivels and her jaw drops. Both Tru and Spenser are clad in matching orange tunics and their features are soft, white, and without gender or age. Exactly the image she was holding in her head. She looks down and sees the same orange tunic, the same soft, unworked hands. "We're triplets!" she frets.

"I don't think they'll notice," Tru says, indicating a group of five Eloi chasing butterflies like lazy kittens, laughing and bumping into each other, then rolling on the ground. A pair begins to make mud angels on the river's sloppy bank.

"Hey Tru," Spenser says. "Remember? Before we go into the river." He begins to remove an impressive rock collection from his pockets: gray ones, agates, quartz, most as large as or larger than a peach pit.

"Oh yeah!" Tru follows suit, and Aine counts. Thirty-two rocks between their four pockets.

"Those to keep Biblos away?" she asks, fighting a smile. It must have been uncomfortable to walk with that extra weight and chafe.

Tru nods happily. "We figured if one would throw him off our trail, a couple dozen would send him into a tailspin."

"Yup. Can we go to the water now?" Spenser pleads.

Aine gives in to the smile tugging at her lips. The nearness of the water and the certain proximity of the cylinder have put her in a good mood. "I suppose," she says, though she isn't in a great hurry to leave the protection of the bush. She might look like Eloi but she feels like Aine. The boys have no such worries. Tru streaks ahead, screaming like a maniac, and cannonballs into a cluster of Eloi, who giggle and twitter like happy birds. Spenser is slower but no less enthusiastic, his laughter like a sweet calliope when his body is finally immersed in the cool liquid.

Aine submits to the pull of the river and dives in behind her brother, surfacing next to him. The river is so clean that she can see her Eloi toes spread out beneath her on the sandy bottom. The sun glistens off the surface, and the air smells like fresh-washed sheets drying on a clothesline. "It's perfect!"

Spenser is beaming and doesn't respond. Instead he dives down for minutes. If she didn't know how long he could hold his breath, she'd be worried. When he finally surfaces, it's with a confused look on his face. "Aine, there's no fish."

She is floating lazily on her back, concentrating on the Eloi image but also on letting some of her fear and worry float downstream. "How do you know?"

"I can't feel any."

She flips over and eyeballs Tru on the other side of the river in his orange tunic. The boy is perched on a rock and mimicking a dive to a real Eloi in a white and gold shift. She appears different than the other Elois, and it's not just her clothing. Her face has a particular innocence, with round cheeks and red lips that make her resemble a China doll. Aine wonders if it's Weena, the Time Traveler's special companion. "Maybe they're scared of all the commotion."

"No. They're nowhere. Whoever wrote this book must not have thought to put fish into it." His face pinches in concentration, his dark eyes wide. "Aine, do you think that this book is flat? Like we could walk off the end of it if we went farther than the author wrote?"

She looks at her brother paddling innocently but quickly glances away. It's hard to converse with him when he looks like an Eloi. "I dunno, Spense. It seems like a good question. We'll have to ask mom when we find her."

"You think we will?"

"I know it." She creates a little whirlpool between them by twirl-ing her hands. "Just make sure to always follow me, okay? Just like we're running in the woods at home."

"K. And Aine?"

"What?"

"I know I'm slow and stupid, and if it weren't for me you'd prob-ably have all three objects and be to mom by now. I wish you didn't always have to be slowed down by me." His clear brown eyes stare straight ahead, his Eloi face washed clean of everything but inno-cence and regret.

Aine knows what to say. She should tell him that he's wrong, that taking care of him is all that keeps her going, that he's the nicest person she's ever met, that she's lucky he's her brother and wishes she could be half the person he is. Instead, overcome with emotion, she dives deep toward the river bottom. When she pops up she finds herself nearer Tru, who is trying to coax the doll-faced Eloi to jump into the water after him. The Eloi has a different idea, shaking her head and chattering insensibly at the water's edge, repeating little three-syllable bursts. She sounds agitated.

Aine turns away. If anyone can coax an Eloi to play with him, it's Tru. She searches the water for Spenser, who breaks the surface with his hands full of rocks and sand. Aine decides she can tell him tonight how much he really means to her and how amazing he is. By then, they'll have the rod. More importantly, she'll have her emotions in check and won't be so close to another embarrassing round of crying.

She dives back underwater and scrubs her hair, washing the roots with her fingertips and swishing it out underwater. She's surprised that her hair still feels like her own, even though she can see it's Eloi blonde and shoulder-length. When she's as clean as she's going to get, she herds the boys back to shore.

They are making their way back to camp when they hear the scream. It's the Eloi Tru was trying to sweet-talk into the water. It appears as though she jumped in on her own and is now drowning, waving her hands and taking in water. The other Elois glance at her with little interest before quickly returning to their laughter and games. Aine, Spenser, and Tru are all poised to dive in after her when a flash of movement catches Aine's eye.

"Look," she says breathlessly, pointing downstream and toward the opposite bank. "There he is. The Time Traveler."

He's not a large man, though he appears a giant among the Eloi. His hair is dark, and he's wearing an old-fashioned, three-piece suit without the tie and with the shirt collar undone. He's shouting, though Aine can't make out the words. He gestures angrily at the unconcerned Eloi before tearing off his coat and diving in. He reaches the drowning Eloi and pulls her out, both of them worse for wear. Her legs and head are bloody from the rocks, and he has a gash on his arm. He lays her on the shore, and she's crying. He rubs her hair then crumples her close to his chest, as if they're reunited lovers. The rest of the Eloi ignore this display.

"Does he know her?" Tru asks curiously.

Aine's nose curls. The Eloi is definitely Weena. "No, this is their first meeting."

"He's being a little forward, don't you think? Hugging her like that?"

"Is she okay?" Spenser asks.

"She will be, for a couple more days anyways," Aine mutters. The healing spell of the river is broken. "We should go back. I need to check on something alone. I'll bring you two back to your rocks then point you toward the original toadhouse. Tru, you think you can find it okay?"

"Does a country boy like cornbread?"

"Yes or no."

"Yes, ma'am! But where are you going?"

"To store some fruit in *The Time Machine*'s toadhouse. Shouldn't take me more than a few minutes but that's time we might not have if we need to escape in a hurry."

The boys nod and follow her to the blueberry bush. They load up on their talismans and start back toward camp with Spenser leading the way, his shoulders thin but assured as he retraces his steps. She would never let on, but when he is navigating the woods, she feels a deep admiration, a warm glow that feels exactly like pride. If she couldn't use her eyes, her life would be over. He simply heightens different senses in their place.

It's almost like magic, she thinks, as she plunges into the forest's shadow and launches herself toward the jade palace. She feels alive with absolute freedom, feet barely touching the ground. She wonders if she can only race this fast in a forest, when she can repel off one knotted trunk to another, whooshing through leaves and using roots like launching pads, or if she could also fly up a mountain or across a desert. For a moment, she considers Spenser's question, whether they could walk off the edge of this story, and she realizes she could find out in a matter of minutes. But now isn't the time. She slows enough to make out the majestic shape of the jade castle, its monolithic form still solid even as it rots.

She darts with human speed to the nearest fruit tree, plucking bananas as large as watermelons, before moving to the next and harvesting apple-colored, cinnamon-scented globes. She is whistling, her heart not light but focused for the first time in days. She is going to fix this. They're going to get the rod, get the boys, and get to her mother, whether in Gilgamesh's toadhouse or this one.

She makes her way around the emerald stairs and leans into the z-shaped crevice, her arms laden with fruit. She sneaks her head in and takes a moment to adjust to the darkness before peering around. At first, she thinks she is the wrong spot because she doesn't spy the toadhouse hidden in its shadow.

She pulls back, sets down the fruit, and surveys the area, a worm of worry nesting in her brain. Had she misremembered the spot like she'd forgotten where the Time Traveler kept the rods? Her cheeks flush with heat and she's glad there is no one to see her. She circles the jade palace searching for another set of stairs. There is only one. She returns to where she started. This is definitely the place. She leans her upper body into the crevice. The toadhouse must be in shadow. She reaches in and feels the entire space, her heart clutching: the toadhouse has vanished.

This can mean only one thing: Biblos has arrived.

Chapter 18

It doesn't change their plan. It can't. They need to retrieve the rod before Biblos locates them, which could take him hours. That realization, however, doesn't stop her from jumping at shadows and sniffing for Biblos' scent of rotting fruit combined with burning tar as she races back to camp. Once there, she is brusquer than usual with everyone, and even Spenser avoids her. She spends the rest of the day looking over her shoulder and trying to erase the vivid picture of her grandmother's face as she was sliced in half. She decides not to scare the others with information that would change nothing.

When dark finally falls, Sura is on the other side of the camp teaching the boys a gambling game involving rocks and twigs. Aine argues in harsh tones with a miniature Gilgamesh as he works on the golden box of the toadhouse. "I don't think Tru or Spenser should come along," she says, on her knees and leaning in close. "They can hide in the toadhouse until we get back."

"I'm afraid not." Gilgamesh shoves a hook-shaped tool into his belt and tugs out a thin strip of metal curved into an infinity loop.

This he draws over the surface of the watchworks. Tiny purple lights flash when the loop gets near them. The pattern seems to disappoint Gilgamesh, and he shoves the tool back into its harness. "We can't leave them for Biblos to find. He could appear at any time."

She swallows the lump of lead in her throat. There is no way he could know the toadhouse has been moved. He hasn't been out of her sight since she returned to camp.

"That's all the more reason to hide them here. Besides, the carnivores will come out of their wells soon."

Gilgamesh raises an eyebrow and is silent for a time. When he speaks, his voice is low and gruff. "Biblos and the carnivores can find the boys here as well as with us at their side, can't they?"

"I suppose," Aine admits. "But can't Sura stay here and protect them?"

"We have strength in numbers. Better we're together. Biblos is far worse than any flesh-eater. He acts out of cruelty rather than need." Gilgamesh draws a deep breath and closes the tiny golden door on the watchworks. "Besides, I'm bringing the toadhouse along. It's risky to move it in its delicate state, but it's too dangerous for us to travel all the way back here. I will hide it outside the stone mansion. Our escape will be much quicker."

"Thank you," Aine says. For the first time, she wonders if she can actually count on him to protect Spenser as Glori and Sura had advised. It's a peculiar thought, the idea of trusting this strange young man. "But we should go right now."

Gilgamesh nods. "Five minutes. I have business inside the toadhouse."

Gilgamesh darts in and out in a matter of seconds. The moon is heavy in the sky, a day or two past full. It's time to seek out the sleeping Time Traveler, but Gilgamesh refuses to leave until he has returned to his normal size. Aine uses the time to deliver clipped instructions to Tru and her brother: no talking, they must walk single file, and they need to remain absolutely quiet. She wants to emphasize that this could be life and death but figures she's said enough. Sura scrutinizes her with sharp eyes, has in fact been watching her since she returned from her second visit to the green porcelain castle. It makes Aine jittery.

Gilgamesh resizes and allows Aine to lead the way through the rustling jungle. The knowledge that Morlocks are prowling and Biblos is in the story is a tangible force, like scorpions crawling over her flesh. She rubs absently at the markings on her hands, shoves down her dark thoughts, and pads silently toward the mansion.

Though the night is as sweetly perfumed as ever and only soft flowers and feathery ferns touch them, she feels the danger in every gentle breeze. She winds under tree branches heavy with fruit, around acacia bushes and rhododendrons, skirting grand, rotting buildings, all five of them as silent as stars under the waxing gibbous moon. The only sounds are the sighing wind and the gentle brush of greenery against their bodies.

Within half an hour, they are in the clearing surrounding the massive building where the Eloi sleep every night. The structure is drooping with neglect under vines, moss, and time. Aine cocks her ear but hears only the sounds of sleep coming from inside. She escorts her group toward the chipped stairs. Tru follows immediately behind her, then Spenser, Sura, and lastly, Gilgamesh, who catches up after secreting the toadhouse under a thornless rose bush near the stairs.

Aine is conscious of her own breathing, and their mission to capture the rod.

Chapter 19

From the outside, the decaying mansion plays perfectly the part of the ancient haunted house, with its gaping windows and rotting exterior. Aine tries to blink away the thought, but the lattice-work of veiny, climbing vines, the sag of the massive roof, and the soulless stare of the empty windows send a warning that quickens her blood. She shivers away the ominous sensation and tiptoes up the tumbling stairs, her gang of four behind her.

Because the glass is long gone from the windows of the crumbling structure, enough moonlight filters in for her to discern massive green tables laden with fruit in the first room they enter. Hugging the wall, Aine avoids the furniture and is careful where she steps. She glances back and catches Tru reaching for a waxen globe of fruit. Her glare pierces the moonlight and him. He jerks his hand back and has the decency to redden in the evening light.

Soft snoring and burbling sounds float out from the next room. Aine creeps to the doorway and peers into the great hall. Inside is a luscious marbled floor supporting an army of mildewed couches and overstuffed pillows, all of them littered with tiny, white bodies curled together like sleeping puppies. Aine's heart pumps so loudly she fears it will wake an Eloi.

They are nearing the rod.

Her eyes travel hungrily over all the bodies, seeking the Time Traveler's form. She does not spot him amid the sleeping masses. Her stomach tightens, and she wonders if she has again made a terrible mistake. Then she remembers. The traveler sleeps apart from the population, but nearby. The Eloi make him uneasy even as he seeks out their company.

She continues into the next room, which is as empty as a dungeon, and the next, and finds it the same. It is in the fourth room off of the dining hall that she spots him, spread wide on a large couch, the female he rescued from the river curved against his body. Aine knows Weena will meet a gruesome fate in this story and feels a pang of pity for her. Why would the writer consign his characters to such awful fates? It makes no sense. She blinks away the thought and checks out the rest of the room. Besides the Time Traveler and his companion, the space is empty and smells of age.

Aine glances quickly behind her—her companions still trailing, watching her expectantly—and ahead at the only other entrance or exit from this room, a lonely door that leads into blackness. Aine signals for the others to stop. She tiptoes to the Time Traveler's side, imagining herself as quiet as the night air. He is snoring obnoxiously, his mouth wide, Weena tight against the warmth of his body. His utter commitment to sleep is a gift, along with the fact that his dress coat is open, allowing the moon to glint off the edges of the rods peeking out of an interior pocket. She feels like laughing. She's found them!

She reaches toward the rods, her pulse racing. Just as she can almost feel the cool metal against her fingertips, the Time Traveler stirs, grumbling in his sleep. Weena adjusts with him so she is still pillowed in his arms. The rods clink softly against one another but remain visible.

Ahead, through the threshold they have not yet crossed, comes a cold, shuffling sound. Something is awake. The Morlocks. Aine's heart locks. She snatches the rods, sliding them out like a sword from its sheath. She holds them aloft and clenches in anticipation of the next clue being revealed.

She expects light, dazzling sound, the words written on the air in electric neon pulses.

She stares.

The group waits.

The moon flashes off of the rods.

Nothing.

No second clue.

No enlightenment.

The rods lay cold and dead against her palms. She stares at Gilgamesh in a panic. He shakes his head, pity and something like fear in his eyes. These are not the rods Grandma Glori was referring to. Aine not only chose the wrong location in this book to hunt for the rods. She has led them to the wrong story entirely.

Aine feels sick. Hopelessness stuffs itself in her nose, her mouth, her eyes. She has risked their lives for nothing. Gilgamesh removes the rods from her hand, gently, and returns them to the Time Traveler's pocket. He grips her shoulders and steers her out, through all four rooms. The others follow. They make it down the stairs and to the rose bush. The sweet, slightly salty smell of the pink blooms makes Aine nauseous. She wonders how she could have been so wrong, how she has never realized before how worthlessly stupid she is. The rod was never in *The Time Machine*. She made them all come here because she liked the story, which is exactly what she'd accused Spenser of.

That's when Spenser shrieks. It is nearly soundless, a high-pitched animal cry of pure terror.

Her head whips. He is in the grip of an ape-like creature, bleached and profane, its lidless pink eyes staring at nothing as it clutches its juicy sweet prey. Behind it stand several other Morlocks, one of them already slithering toward Tru. The boy is swinging his fists like a boxer, but they are small hits and bounce off the hideous mutant like butterfly wings. The reek of putrefying blood and unwashed hair is suffocating.

Sura appears to be a spectator to the horror, neither running nor fighting, but then there is a flicker. Suddenly both Spenser and Tru transform into Morlocks. The captors loosen their grips in confusion but only for a moment because the boys still smell like meat. The creatures drag them toward the edge of the forest.

Aine and Gilgamesh lunge into the fray. Aine leaps straight at the creature abducting Spenser, howling a banshee's war cry. Her hands dig deep into the matted fur, hitting, biting, pulling at the monster that has her brother. She hears Gilgamesh growling to her left, where two sinewy Morlocks are fighting over Tru. The creature she is attacking snarls at her, flashing pointed yellow teeth, and tries to wave her off without letting go of its food. The Morlock is filthy. He smells like death and sweat, and he's solid muscle under the scraggly hair. She is stabbing her fingers into the only weak spot she sees, his eyes, when she smells a new horror, more primordially terrifying than the stink of old blood: rotting, lonely fruit mixed with decaying, burnt matter.

Biblos.

His hand at her neck is so hot it burns her. Biblos rips her off of the Morlock and tosses her several feet in the air as if she is a bag of rubbish.

"Not doing a bang-up job protecting your charges, are you, Gilgamesh? Then again, you're renowned for losing your cargo. Well, good news, then. I'm here to help."

The laugh is as Aine remembers, bone-scraping, chilling, huge and black, the accent a mocking Mediterranean song. Biblos isn't as large as he was in the forest near her grandmother's, but he is still sparking with some dark energy, his scarred jester face contorted into a wicked grin under that thick black hair. Even the gang of Morlocks is stilled by his power and light, temporarily frozen with their arms locked around Spenser, Tru, and Gilgamesh. Sura is free on the perimeter and races toward Biblos. Aine watches in horror as he swings at her. The fairy ducks, but instead of fighting him, she steps back.

Why? Fight! Aine struggles to her feet, dazed. The world spins under her. The Morlocks have recovered. Her brother is being dragged into the woods by the sharp-toothed beasts. The small boy's eyes are wide with shock, and his graceful fingers twist weakly at the fur of the carnivore gripping him. She sees his lips moving, knows he is begging, pleading for the terror to end, to just please let him go and he won't tell anybody. Tru is fighting but is just as surely being hauled into the woods. Biblos is stalking toward Sura with a grim smile exposing his horrifically beautiful pointed teeth. Gilgamesh is nowhere to be seen.

Aine clenches her fists. She hears a snap, and it comes from inside of her. She feels a surge like a river coursing through her, a tsunami of fury that swells, increases her size, powers her, screams for release. She holds her hands up. The tip of every finger has become a liquid knife, a blade of water molecules so charged and tight that they reflect the moonlight. She is going to kill, rend, tear, destroy the Morlocks. End Biblos.

Save Spenser.

Save Spenser.

Save Spenser.

She is flying forward, intoxicated with the majesty of power, growing even larger in the air, when she is struck from behind. She falls, and in her confusion feels the power ebb like water from a cracked vase. She lands on her back. The wind is knocked out of her and she is gasping for breath. Gilgamesh is standing over her, the whites of his eyes completely erased. The toadhouse is at his feet. He tosses her into it, follows her, and strikes her again. The world goes dark.

Chapter 20

Aine wakes up on the bank of a river. No lag. She was unconscious and now she is alert, with a pounding headache. It's daylight. Birds sing in the trees, and a tiger's growl rends the air. Gilgamesh, his expression sorrowful, is rinsing her head with cool river water. He is full-sized, as is she.

He notices her open eyes. "I'm sorry. I had to—"

She punches him in the face before his sentence is out. Jumping to her feet with her forest speed, she seizes a river rock as large as a baseball and swings it at the base of his skull in one smooth movement. He falls into the soft mud, face down. He is still. She notices blood on his shirt and wonders briefly if it is hers or his. Then she smells something new, and her attention is drawn away from the man who lies motionless: fire.

Delicious, roasting, almighty fire. The only element the Morlocks fear. She's going to burn every one of them alive. She's going to save Spenser.

Her eyes narrow. She focuses. Peacocks. Squawking parrots.

Caramel-barked trees draped in velvet flowers. Flowing under the smell of smoke is the scent of ocean and under that, jasmine and sandalwood. Pearlescent lotuses float on the surface of the river.

Gilgamesh has carried her into to a different book.

His toadhouse is just ahead, nestled in the nook of a eucalyptus tree. She races to it, reaches in for her school bag, dumps the contents onto the toadhouse floor. She jerks out the now-empty book bag, clutching the tiny bit of cloth in her hand. The surprisingly light toadhouse she tucks under her arm. When the bag has resized, she will stuff the toadhouse into it.

Size.

She is her full five feet, two inches. That means she's been away from Spenser for at least nine minutes and eleven seconds, plus however long it took to reach this book. Her mind threatens to veer into the darkness, to imagine the terrors her brother is enduring. That is, if he is still alive. She disciplines her thoughts. Fire.

Spenser, I'm coming.

Aine flies toward the smell of smoke. The soles of her feet barely touch the earth. The world flickers past in a watercolor smear of greens, whites, and browns with an occasional splash of red or pink. At this speed there is no smell, no sound except the cheering of the wind. She wants to run forever, to never stop, to not think. Because if she thinks, she remembers promising Spenser she'd never leave him, and later, him apologizing to her in the river for not being good enough, and her not telling him that he was the best thing in any world. And finally, his sweet, terrified face as the dank, profane Morlocks slobbered and dragged him away.

So she shuts off her thoughts and races, sensing rather than seeing when the walls loom in front of her many miles from where she started. She halts and plants her feet into the ground, the abrupt change in motion reigniting her headache. She ignores it. A city soars in front of her, magnificent, surrounded by a stone wall that dwarfs the trees encircling it. Jeweled, gilded minarets peek over the top of the enclosure. But fire has recently visited. Many of the rooftops peering above the wall are scorched, and the poor thatch houses and plants outside and nearest the wall are charred. No person, no animal moves out here. Aine's heart drops. Has the fire destroyed the population then burnt itself out?

But then she hears it, the distant clang of battle. Men yelling, rocks exploding against a far wall, the remote steel clash of sword-fighting. Surely there will be fire there, if she can locate the fight. She'll grab a bit of burning wood, step inside Gilgamesh's toadhouse, enter "Time Traveler Morlock capture boys" into the plotter to reach the correct time and place in The Time Machine, then set their foul fur and flesh ablaze. Biblos, too, if she gets her hands on him.

She follows the wall to the right, stepping quickly but not at full speed so she can search for an entrance. She quickly spots an opening, broad and tall enough to admit a walking tree. She wants to charge into the city, grab what she needs and leave, but she won't save Spenser by endangering herself. She must practice stealth and speed.

She slips into the city, sticking close to the wall. The metropolis is even grander from within. Many of the stone buildings soar to the sky, and even the plainest among them glitters with emeralds, rubies, and gold. The vegetation has all been recently burnt away by the looks of it, but a miraculous rebuilding is underway. New wood structures grow from the ashes, the mellow amber color of their wood like fresh skin against the blackened ground.

She soon finds herself in a garden where she hears voices. She darts behind a tree. This entire grove on the city's edge is whole and lush, at stark contrast to the charred city behind it. The school bag resizes. She stuffs the toadhouse into it, freeing her hands. She climbs to the top of the tree and peers through the branches. What she sees leaves her cold.

A hundred feet ahead of her, a handful of giant, terrible demonesses torment a woman lying on the ground. They are each as big as her grandmother's house, some with several arms, hunched backs, sagging breasts barely covered by putrid cloth, and blistered skin. Their faces are even more horrible, many eyes blinking and weeping yellow fluid alongside hooked noses, mouths full of sharpened, blood-dipped teeth screeching and laughing at the woman in their center. Their voices sound like knives being sharpened.

At first, Aine can't make out the features of the woman on the ground because of the fury and motion of the colossal hags. The victim appears ragged, dusty, her dark hair matted. But then she turns to plead for mercy, and Aine is momentarily dazzled. The woman is stunning, a vision of absolute beauty even in her tortured state, nearly as breathtaking as her own mother.

Aine would have wasted more moments spellbound by her exquisiteness if not for one of the hags slamming four of her fists into the ground. The violent motion knocks an incense holder off a nearby table. The demonesses scream and scramble like children, warning of another fire, and hurry to replace the censer before it catches the straw littering the ground.

Fire.

Aine scrambles out of the tree and drops to the earth behind some brush. Once on the ground, she realizes that the creatures are taller than she expected, at least thirty feet tall. They have regained their composure and again torture their beautiful victim with threats and insults.

Before she becomes too terrified to act, Aine imagines an enormous, mutated hag of a woman with three eyes, no nose, rusty knives for teeth, hissing, writhing snakes for hair, clawed fingers on all eight hands, looming, threatening. Holding that image in her head, she concentrates on a white light around her, focusing, building, hoping. Sura hadn't taught her how to alter her size to match her appearance, so she guesses at the process, envisioning the monster in her head stretched large over a tree.

She steps into the clearing in full sight of the ravenous mob.

Chapter 21

Aine just needs to grab the incense burner and make it back to the tree. That's all. She feels terrible about the woman being tormented by the demonesses, but she must save Spenser, tell him that she's sorry, that he's a far better brother than she deserves, prove that she hasn't left him like mom and Glori. She strides resolutely forward, noting with satisfaction that her feet have transformed into trunk-like, hairy appendages. She is halfway to the censer and can smell the sandalwood smoke it eases into the air. She nearly has it in her grasp when the hags notice her.

"Trijata?" The meanest-looking of the hags places herself between Aine and the small metal fire-holder. "Where have you been?"

The blood-thumping of Aine's heart nearly drowns out the question. The creature speaking has the breath of a thousand dead rats, and clicking beetles crawl in her teeth and slipping out the sides of her mouth. Aine grunts, hoping that it's enough. She steps around the demoness and reaches for the censer.

"Trijata, I'm talking to you. You don't look well. What is it?"

Aine pitches her voice low. "I'm fine. I came for some incense."

Another hag steps up, this one smaller, with bones woven in her scraggly hair. The bones make a hollow ticking sound when she shakes her gourd-shaped head. "For who?"

Aine is cornered. She has no idea what book she has entered, no names to guess at. The demonesses have given up harassing the beautiful woman to fasten on her for the moment. She has no choice but to meet their aggressiveness and hope none of them comes close enough to touch her and feel her true shape. "Back away!" she growls. "I don't answer to any of you! Who are you to question me?"

To her surprise, they inch back, all but the one who first questioned her. This one chuckles, spitting out a mouthful of beetles. "I am Tryakshi, and I will ask what I wish. Is the incense for Ravana?"

The name strikes a note in Aine's brain, but she can't place it. "Yes."

Tryakshi bows, revealing blinking eyes on her shoulders. "Then it is yours."

Aine seizes it, her throat still constricted. These hags eat human flesh, she can smell it on her breath, and she feels a distant sorrow for their captive. She must be someone's mother, sister, or daughter. The sadness, however, can't compete with her fear for her Spenser's life. She must save him. If there is time afterward, she can return to this story to help the beautiful woman.

Spenser, I'm coming!

She is about to leap out of the garden to a quiet spot in the woods when the sun is blotted out. Overhead, a demon so large he makes the females look like toddlers appears, his eyes blazing. He rides atop a huge, glorious chariot that casts night below him. He descends with noise and wrath, cracking a mighty whip. "Get into the chariot and bring the human!" he bellows.

For a second, Aine's heart seizes. Can he see through her disguise, smell her mortal blood? But then she realizes they mean the tormented prisoner. Tryakshi tosses the captive on her shoulder and indicates for Aine to lead the way onto the chariot. Aine's throat closes. *No! This is the wrong direction.* But underneath her magic, she is just a girl. She has no choice but to follow, or become another prisoner. She curses her hesitation. She should have run with the fire pot when she had a chance. *I must get to Spenser. Every second away is terror for him. Agony. He is in a slaughterhouse with no one to comfort him.* A tear slides down her cheek. She twists at the spot on her palm where she'd cut herself and feels the soft ridge of the healed scar.

The world flashes under them, and the city is quickly erased from view. A great, glittering ocean beckons in the distance. They near, hovering over tiny figures locked in an epic battle. Grunts, crashes, the acrid smell of smoke, screams of pain pierce the air around them and become more visceral as they drop closer.

"See there, Sita?" The demon charioteer picks up the beautiful woman as if she is a blade of grass, directing her attention below. On the ground, thousands of monkeys as large as giants are throwing stones across a great expanse. They are squealing and pounding their chests. Around them and in the same battalion, chiseled men sling arrows that blaze like bullets before raining down on an army of demons and other evil-eyed, screeching monsters.

The demons' roars are like a hundred souls dying. They slash off gigantic monkey limbs and bellow with delight, and more monkeys surge forward to replace the injured ones, slipping on the bloody war field only to regain their footing and charge again. The demons seem to be gaining ground despite the vast forces opposing them, however. They are raging toward a spot where the monkey soldiers stand in a protective ring around two golden warriors who lie as if dead, arrows shot through them in multiple points.

The charioteer points at them and chuckles wickedly. "It is over. Your husband and his brother are dead. Say goodbye to Rama."

Aine gasps but none of the creatures notice, as pleased as they are by Sita's reaction. The woman has crumpled to the floor of the chariot, wracked by pitiful sobs so powerful that they rip the cloth on her back.

Aine realizes she's in *The Ramayana*. Though it's been years since she read it, she remembers the story of Rama, who is the god Vishnu reborn, and who goes through the world slaying evil. He is unfairly denied his kingdom and cast into the wild forest because of a promise his father made before he was born. During this pilgrimage, a demon named Ravana captures Sita, his wife.

Rama finally tracks her down with the help of Hanuman and the other monkey warriors and kills Ravana and all the rakshasas in a terrible battle. That's what I'm seeing below me. Spenser would love to hear this story, to live through it.

The thought slices right through her heart. She must return to firm ground immediately. She has wasted too much time in this story. She kneels by Sita and pretends to torment her, speaking so quietly that the other demons can't hear. "Rama is fine. The arrows are just stunning him temporarily. He's not dead."

Sita turns her head slowly, and Aine feels certain the woman can see through her disguise to the girl underneath. "How do you know?" Sita whispers.

Aine makes up a reason. "I recognize the arrows. Those arrows just stun, they don't kill. The demons are trying to convince you Rama is dead so you'll give in to Ravana."

Sita smiles tremulously, and it's as if the sun has risen twice. "You are certain?"

"I promise. But you must act devastated so the demons think they've fooled you. Don't worry. Rama is going to save you. This story has a happy ending."

Sita nods, and reaches out to squeeze Aine's hand. Only a widening of her eyes gives her away: she has felt through Aine's disguise and squeezed her thin wrist rather than the thick, rough skin of a demoness. Quickly, Sita slips her hand inside her ragged sari, makes a tearing motion, and then sneaks something into Aine's hand before pretending to faint.

Aine lurches to the side as the chariot is steered around to fly back to the city many miles away. She takes advantage of her position to open her hand. Sita has placed a large diamond ring in it. Aine doesn't have time to consider the meaning of this gesture because a spray of flaming arrows has thunked into the side of the chariot, lodging itself deep in the wood but not harming the transport. Aine realizes this vehicle must be the Pushpaka, Ravana's legendary chariot that can travel any distance in a flash. She stores that fact, saving it to tell Spenser when she rescues him.

She shoves the diamond into her school bag. When the Pushpaka touches ground at the grove, Aine doesn't hesitate. She yanks a still-burning arrow from the side of the chariot, grabs the smoking censer, and rushes outside the city walls. She pauses only long enough to set the toadhouse down before she leaps inside, cursing the millisecond it takes to shrink. The normally joyful pleasure-pain of a resizing feels like a loss of control, a waste of precious time.

Spenser, please don't give up. I'm almost there.

She stabs the now-miniature arrow into the table so it can

continue to burn and rests the incense next to it. Turning to the plotter, she wishes she had paid more attention when Gilgamesh was running the vehicle. Gilgamesh. She feels a stab in her chest. His face when she'd regained consciousness on the riverbank had been etched with regret and sadness. She buries her doubt. Let the traitor wrestle with the demons in this land if he reaches this far.

The face of the plotter is a circle of whorls and runes carved into wood but no words she recognizes. She rests her hand on it, and English characters appear in the center, spelling out "Time Traveler Eastern."

These must be the words that brought the toadhouse to *The Ramayana*.

Gilgamesh must have punched in something quickly, changing only the last half of the phrase that had carried them to *The Time Machine*. But how to change them back? Aine sees no recognizable letters, no keys like on a typewriter, nothing to write with. She imagines she can hear Spenser weeping in pain and fear.

She slams her hand down in frustration. The gesture trips a switch and releases a small drawer on the underside of the plotter. Inside it are wooden squares the size of sugar cubes. Aine frantically feels along the plotter's surface until she releases another catch, and a tray slides out next to the drawer. It is the size of a book and contains 54 slots, enough for five words, each with no more than ten letters, and a space between each word. She's found the place to spell out the phrase.

Aine paws through the cubes, frantic, searching for the right ones. She hears a commotion outside the toadhouse and curses herself for not having hidden it better. Are the demonesses after her?

"Take me back!" she yells at the plotter. Instantly, twenty-seven cubes take to the air before settling themselves into the slots to spell "Time Traveler Eloi white Sphinx," the words that brought them to The Time Machine. She pushes down on the words with both hands, just as she'd seen Gilgamesh do, and releases the toadhouse into the universe with a flourish of darkness.

Chapter 22

The black nothingness of the in-between is so lonely it shrieks, calling to her like a wounded animal. She grips the plotter desperately, fighting the powerful urge to fling herself outside the door. Scents, noise, and finally sight are sucked out of the toadhouse until she is trapped in the darkness of her mind, rattling on her own cage, terrified she'll never find a way out. She hadn't experienced this when Gilgamesh controlled the toadhouse. Does a toadhouse pilot have to battle this every time?

She can't stand the agony of absolute isolation. Her hands begin to slip from the wood of the plotter, and she leans toward the gaping door. It would be so easy to let go and join the nothing, ease its aloneness, forget forever. All she has to do is release the plotter, and it's done. She lets go with her right hand. She relaxes her left, and feels a gratifying expunging of all guilt and fear as she slides toward the door.

Suddenly she hears the roar of wind in a tunnel and smells honeyed flowers. The skin of her neck prickles, but there is no time to prepare for the collision. The crash to earth jars the toadhouse and tips it on its side. The impact is violent, but she welcomes the plate and cup slamming into her, even the chair grazing her head, because they pull her away from the terrible, unfulfilled promise of the in-between. She pushes away the mess, noting that the table, coat rack, and plotter are screwed into the floor.

Aine tries to stand, stumbling, disoriented by the sideways room. She landed underneath the high cupboard. She is staring at the floor. Fortunately, the doorway is facing up rather than into the earth. She is still wearing her school bag with the censer inside it. Cautiously, she pulls out the fire pot. The latch has held but the tiny coals are no longer glowing orange. She flips open the catch and shoves her finger in. Cold.

Her heart plummets, and she yells her agony. At the noise, the arrow she'd forced into the table blazes to life then dims. The sight fills her with gratitude. She can still do this. Using the legs of the table like a ladder, she hoists herself to the middle of the room and removes the faintly burning arrow with a heave. By standing on the uppermost edge of the table and stretching her full length, she is able to touch the door jamb. Tru's chained archetyper sways over the door, grazing her head. Less than half of his book remains. Aine tosses out the arrow, grasps the door jamb, and heaves herself outside.

The air is cool, rose-scented, and dark. She leaps to the ground and seizes up the arrow before it burns itself out, if that is even possible. The four-armed lotus flower on the weapon's side suggests it was taken from Rama's quiver, meaning it is a representative of Vishnu. Aine doesn't have time to consider whether its powers extend to this story. She's just glad the arrow still burns.

Overhead, the moon is as she left it, glowing, just past full. The crumbling mansion where the Eloi sleep rises into the night behind her. Surprised, she notes that the toadhouse has returned to the same area. The dirt around her is scuffled, some of the gouges in the earth so deep that she could fall into them. She sees a bit of white cloth pierced by a branch. *Sura's comfort cloth.* She is in the exact spot where Gilgamesh knocked her out but has no way of knowing how much time has passed. She should wait to resize so she can take the toadhouse with her. That would be her best plan to escape once she has located the boys, but she can no more remain in this spot than she can stop her blood from pumping.

I'm almost there, Spenser. Please don't give up. Don't let them hurt you. Don't be scared!

She runs away from her hot tears, accelerating to a speed that allows her to pass through trees. The first time she enters one and emerges on the other side she is astonished. There was only a soft ripping sound to indicate her passage through solid matter. She smiles grimly and increases her pace. The arrow burns, more brightly, licking against her clenched fist but not harming her. Her tears are dry when she reaches the nearest well rising five feet out of the earth like an infected sore.

But she is still tiny. She wants to toss branches down the well, start a fire, smoke the Morlocks out, but she isn't large enough to move so much as a pebble. She can't wait. Using her speed, she scrambles up the outer wall of the well, drops over the side, negotiates the crevices one-handed, the arrow in her other. The industrial pumping reverberates through the walls like an ominous heartbeat, and the smell of freshly harvested meat is strong enough to gag her. A small sob escapes her but she continues down, painfully slowly, centimeter by centimeter.

At last she arrives at solid ground. She drops to the earth at the same instant her ears pop and she, the arrow, and her school bag zoom to their full size. She almost yells with the power of it. She feels a burst of strength but also a feverish anxiety. Which way to go? The passage runs two directions. To her left is darkness, the smell of mildew and mud, and silence. To her right, the clanking of the underground ventilation system is loud and the air smells of iron and rot.

She charges to the right, but not at full speed. The darkness is so deep that it feels like liquid. The only light emanates from the arrow, and she doesn't want to miss a turn. She clings to the moist dirt wall, straining her ears for the sound of Morlocks or the boys. But she should have been attuning to her nose. If she had, she might have smelled Biblos in time.

Chapter 23

Aine takes the corner fast, too fast, but she is nearing her brother, she senses it, and she's going to lose her mind if she doesn't find him alive. Because of her reckless speed, she is not aware of Biblos until she is almost upon him, stopping herself just sort of ramming into his back. She is so near that she feels the rough cloth of his vest scratch the tip of her nose. She halts her breath. Her skin tingles painfully. Slowly she draws back.

He hasn't noticed her. He is swearing. The language is unfamiliar but the heat of the words burns her ears. He holds his hand over his head. A dim blue light surrounds it, illuminating the area he points it at. Like her, he's searching, his focus absolute. Is it possible he's also seeking her brother? The thought gives her hope. It means Biblos hasn't killed him.

She melts into a crevice in the wall, worried the arrow's flame will give her away. The thought, like a command, extinguishes the burning missile. Panicked, she wonders how she will rescue Spenser without fire. The arrow blazes to life. Aine's eyes widen. She concentrates on the flame disappearing. *Wick!* It's out. Her mind somehow controls the fire. She thanks Vishnu from the tips of her toes, then wonders if it is Sita she should be praising. Surely the diamond the woman gave her, the plum-sized, glittering carbon rock, is what is keeping Biblos from sensing her nearness.

But how to sneak around him? She peeks out of the crevice and sees that he is at a three-way fork. Biblos fumbles at his belt and yanks out a pointed jewel on a chain, which he holds in the air. The gem begins to swing, slowly at first then faster and faster. *What is he doing?* At this proximity, the stink of him is overpowering. She is almost ready to dart past his considerable girth when they both hear it: Spenser's terror-soaked wail.

She soars with joy—he's alive!—but then her heart plummets. The pain in his voice is visceral. It's not misery or even fear. It's the appalling shriek of a dying rabbit. *What are they doing to him?*

The scream escalates, hurtling down the central corridor. She shoots past Biblos, who is also propelling himself down the middle tunnel at great speeds, though not as fast as Aine. In seconds she finds herself in a cavernous room blurrily lit by cloudy lights. They decorate the massive pump heaving in the center of the open space. The room is dense with Morlocks, the scent of their mangy, matted hair fouling the cavern. Tunnels lead out from all sides of the enormous chamber like arms off an octopus.

In a dim corner to her left, Aine spies the greatest concentration of Morlocks snapping and slurping over a pile of white and red. She blocks the sounds and image from her mind, frantically scouring the gigantic chamber for Spenser.

He screams again. He's to her right, laid out on a slab of rock. In the shadowy glow of the ventilation machinery, two Morlocks pin him to the rough table while a third twists his arm to an unnatural angle. Towheaded Tru lies on the ground nearby, dead or unconscious, on a pile of brightly-clothed Eloi in a similar state. Sura is nowhere to be seen.

Aine's arrow blazes so brightly that for a second, the chamber is lit as if by the sun. The glare settles to a sizzling orange but is still intense. The Morlocks hiss in fear and pain. They are scuttling into dark corners, shielding their rat eyes from the light.

Aine launches herself at the rock table, stabbing at the remaining Morlocks with the arrow. She is sickened by the popping sensation of the arrow sliding through the taut flesh of the nearest Morlock's thigh, but she doesn't slow. That Morlock falls, screeching in pain and exposing the one behind it. She stabs mercilessly at its back. This time, the arrow only grazes, but the monsters retreat, the wounded Morlock dragging his leg. She lets them scurry away so she can go to Spenser. He is limp, his arm broken, his skin clammy.

"Spenser! It's Aine. Please, Spenser. Please talk to me." Her voice cracks. She can plainly see the deathly paleness of his skin. Urgently, she places her ear on his chest searching for a beat, holding the arrow away from them.

"That is quite a toy, child."

Her head shoots up. Biblos has entered the chamber and stands on the far side, studying her, not more than two hundred yards away. His blue light is as weak as a firefly next to the blazing arrow.

"I'll kill you with it," she says.

His blue eyes blaze, and a grin cuts the scarred, lettered skin of his face. In a wave of tiny crumbling sounds, worms begin to break out of the cave floor and crawl toward him. His mutated hand squirms in response, whipping erratically at his side. "I recognize that spirit in you. Just like your mother, eh? I think you'll be my favorite. And since I only need one of you, I'll ask you to step away from what's left of your brother and come with me."

She shoves the arrow into her bag, gathers up Spenser and instinctively retreats, moving toward the wall with him in her arms. He's heavy. He doesn't stir but she hears it: a breath. He's alive. The arrow gives off a flash of light from within her bag, as powerful as a hundred camera bulbs. Underfoot, she feels a shift and hears a crunch. Branches, probably, washed to this low point by rain through the wells.

Behind Biblos, the Morlocks are seething against the wall like a nest of snakes exposed to the sun. They scrabble on the ground, seeking with their hands, but Biblos appears oblivious to them.

"I'm not leaving Spenser," she says forcefully. It's all she can do not to snarl like a wolf mother.

"Spenser, you say," Biblos stalks closer. "And what did your parents decide to name you, pretty one?"

The greedy curiosity in his voice turns her stomach, and she wishes she hadn't revealed her brother's name. "Jane." She moves along the wall slowly, hoping for an opening.

His laugh echoes off the ceiling. "Unlikely."

Aine has no plan. She stalls for time. "Where is Sura?"

"Who?"

"The fairy."

Biblos shrugs and moves to the middle of the chamber. "I'd check that pile of limbs in the corner. Haven't seen her since Gilgamesh betrayed you and tried to whisk you far, far away from me. But here you are again. I wonder how that happened? You'll have to tell me the story over a nice glass of ouzo, yes?"

He steps toward her, and Aine scrambles to escape with her brother. Her feet crunch again and a tiny scheme takes root. It pains her beyond words to set down Spenser, but she has no choice if she's to save him. She dashes to her left, back to the cold slab, and lays him down just as she hears the clatter of rocks. The Morlocks are pelting Biblos with stones, aiming for his light. They are momentarily successful, and the blue glow is extinguished. Aine yanks the arrow out of her bag and ignites the brittle brush at her feet.

Too soon, Biblos flicks his light back on, though it is pulsing. In the flashes of blue, Aine is only able to make out erratic pieces of his attack. He roars then surges in size, grows massive, fills the chamber. He swings his arm like a scythe, cutting down a swath of Morlocks as if they are ripe wheat. Aine turns her back on the fight to blow at the embers. They smoke, then take. The flame is at first tiny but as Aine gathers more brush, it begins to blaze.

She scuttles over to the pile of bodies near the slab. "Tru," she whispers urgently. Behind her, the squeals of the Morlocks are fewer and farther between, and she hears the crisp, awful sound of Morlock bones snapping. The sour scent of fear and sweat is stifling, and the brush fire she's started is growing, licking eagerly in her direction. She finds Tru and shakes him, swallowing hard against the feeling of cold Eloi bodies. He doesn't move, so she pinches his arm. Hard.

"Ow!" He tries to sit up. In the flashing light, his face is confused. "Aine?"

"Can you walk?"

He rubs his head. "Where am I? What's happening?"

"We're underground. In the Morlocks' lair. We need to get out of here now, and I need help carrying Spenser. Can you do it?" As she talks, she realizes Biblos' blue light is no longer erratic. It's a steady, vulgar hue. She sneaks a peek. Only a handful of Morlocks continue to battle him, their eyes so bloodied that his light no longer affects them.

Tru turns to dig through the pile of Eloi.

"What are you doing?" Aine yells. The fire is almost upon them.

"One of these is Sura! I'm looking for her. She's gonna feel taller than an Eloi."

Biblos is bellowing at the center of the cavern. He kicks at the remaining Morlocks. He is still huge, but some of the rocks have struck true, and his own blood trickles down his arms and face. A furious blue halo grows around his head, humming with power. He roars. The letters on his face and good hand stand out like etching against his scarred skin.

Aine drops to the ground next to Tru, moving aside the tiny, unconscious or dead natives captured tonight, their heads bashed in, their bodies waiting to become food. She digs until she feels a body that's heavier than the rest. She slaps at the face and is surprised that her hand comes away red and wet. The Eloi-figure stirs, shimmers, and becomes Sura. Her beautiful wiry hair is matted with blood from a large gash on her forehead.

"Aine," she croaks. "You're alive."

"So are you. We have to get out of here. You, me, Spenser, and Tru. Come on. We haven't much time."

Sura shakes her head and smiles. The gesture is heavy with finality. "My arms and legs are broken. The Morlocks wanted to make sure I couldn't go anywhere until they were ready to harvest me."

"No!" Aine cries. "I can carry you!"

"You cannot, I'm afraid." A paroxysm of coughing shakes the fairy, and a great spill of blood leaves her mouth. She appears devastatingly human despite all her magic. "It was an honor to meet you and your brother. Be kind to him."

"Aine!" Tru wails. "Look!"

She hasn't heard the sounds of fighting for several seconds. She feels sticky green breath on her neck. Tru stares over her shoulder, his eyes widening to dinner plates and his jaw slack.

"I told you to leave the boy," Biblos growls intimately, horribly, almost directly into her ear. He has felled the Morlocks and come to collect his reward. "You should have listened."

She turns. Biblos is bent over double, his face inches from hers, only it's swollen to horrible proportions. His mouth is so large she could walk into it. The letters in his eyes fly past and form words she can almost recognize. It's hypnotizing. She stands, every move slow and underwater. At her full height, she comes level to his eyes and finds herself unable to look away. This close, she sees the pulsing veins in the murky, tattooed whites, counts the hairs of his eyebrows. She hears muttering and realizes that the words in his eyes are whispering in her mind, confusing her.

She fights for clarity, speaking through clenched teeth. "And I told *you*, I'm not leaving my brother."

The fire she started is hungry and is devouring a pile of rags. She'd started it to burn the Morlocks, but now it is turning on them, filling the chamber with smoke.

"Don't leave me!" Sura yells.

Biblos looks over at the fairy, and his spell on Aine is broken.

When she follows Biblos' gaze, she sees that Sura has clouded her appearance. She looks exactly like Helen, Aine's mother, lying on a bed rather than on a pool of mangled bodies. Sura's beautiful, bruised flesh has been replaced by Helen's ivory skin, her brown hair by Helen's golden. Helen's mouth curves in an alluring smile tinged with sadness, and she reaches toward Biblos.

The image stops Aine's heart. It appears to have the same effect on Biblos, who drops to his knees. If not for the weak cough from Spenser, Aine would have been equally hypnotized. *Why Helen?* She rips her gaze away, shoves the arrow into her book bag, and grabs Tru's hand. They hurry over to hoist Spenser on their shoulders like a trussed pig. Aine leads them out the tunnel she entered through, her mind reeling. Sura was so perfectly Helen that it is all she can do to leave the chamber, but she refuses to waste Sura's sacrifice. She's grateful that Spenser isn't conscious to feel the pain of another loss.

The smoke clutches at her throat, gagging her, misleading her. She thinks she has taken a wrong turn. Her brother is heavy. Tru is panting but not complaining. A searing roar reverberates behind them followed by a ground-trembling smash. Rocks shake loose from the ceiling. Aine is certain Biblos has discovered Sura's deception, and she whispers goodbye to the brave fairy who has saved their life.

Biblos will be after them now. They must move faster, but which direction?

She chooses a left at the next fork, certain now that she is in new territory. Their only hope lies in finding another well to escape from. "Tru, you okay?"

His words stutter out through the huffing and puffing. "Better than dead. Where'd you go? We thought the Morlocks got you, but we didn't see you anywhere in the cave."

"Gilgamesh took me to another story. How long was I gone?"

"I dunno. I was fighting those mangy apes, watching Sura try to draw Biblos in to fight them, then one of 'em got me good on the head. I didn't wake up until you pinched me. I swanny I was gonna get ate." He shakes himself all over except for the shoulder that's holding Spenser. "What happened to Spenser?"

"He's hurt. We're going to get him to a doctor."

"Here?"

"We'll get back to the toadhouse, and we'll find a hospital in another story." The thought had been working like a mantra in her head. *Spenser is going to be okay. I'm going to get him to a doctor. Spenser is going to be okay.*

Tru adjusts Spenser on his shoulder, groaning under the weight. "Aine, why'd Gilgamesh take you to another story?"

She feels along the dark wall with her free hand, balancing her brother with her other. She doesn't want to risk using the arrow to light their way. If they can see, Biblos can see them. "I don't know," she says honestly.

She forces herself to relive the event: the seemingly impossible odds in *The Time Machine*, Gilgamesh forcing her to leave, his face sorrowful when she came to. "He didn't try to hurt me in the book he brought me to. He thought he was helping me, I think. As near as I can tell, Gilgamesh wants to get back to Tir Na Nog as badly I do, but I think he only needs one of us to do that. Same with Biblos. Back in the cavern just now, he said he'd take me, and we could leave Spenser. They need me *or* Spenser for something, not both of us."

Tru whistles softly. He shifts the load in his arms. "Like one of you is connected to the keys?"

"Exactly. Sura mentioned that Gilgamesh made a huge mistake. I think it was big enough to get him kicked out of Tir Na Nog. That's why he's got his own toadhouse to pilot, and why he's more interested in returning than in keeping both me and Spenser alive. I think his secret is in the book he locked away in his toadhouse. If we can get to that, we can find out who he is."

"Maybe, but I still don't understand why Glori and Sura trusted him if we're not supposed to." He smothers a cough. The smoke in the tunnel is thickening, mixing eerily with the damp cave walls.

"I didn't say I had it all figured out. I still—"

Those are the only words she is allowed before the club crushes her free shoulder and she recognizes the vile snuffling of a Morlock.

Chapter 24

Aine stumbles, nearly dropping Spenser, and a groan escapes her mouth. Her left shoulder blazes with pain so intense it blinds her. She kicks in the direction of the blow but is off balance and falls into the wall, grazing her wounded shoulder and causing sparks to dance in front of her eyes. She can't fight with her brother in her arms. "Tru, get Spenser out of here!"

"I can't carry him by myself!"

"You've got to."

She releases her brother as gently as possible and turns just as the Morlock kicks her in the stomach. She doubles over, the wind knocked out of her. Tru, hyperventilating, tucks his hands under Spenser's armpits and drags the unconscious boy, inches at a time. The smoke from the fire in the harvesting chamber fills their passageway.

Aine can make out the shape of only one Morlock in the shadowy, polluted darkness, but he's armed and swinging the club again. She's caught her breath but is now numb on her left side. Standing, she charges at the beast with her head down, using as much of her speed as she can in the cramped space. Her head connects with his stomach in a crunch and sends him flying into the far wall.

It's not enough. The white ape is back on his feet and charging. Aine shuffles to keep herself between the Morlock and Spenser, distantly aware that the boys have hardly moved. She hears a sad, soft singing, and realizes it's Tru.

"Pull faster!" she yells. "Follow the tunnel straight. Go up as soon as you come to a ladder." She knows it's futile, knows there is no way even the two of them could haul Spenser aboveground. They'll be buried down here.

The Morlock swings his club and misses, but follows the motion with his fist. He connects with Aine's arm just below the wounded shoulder. The pain forces her to her knees, and she hears a raspy chortle from the hideous, pink-eyed creature. He grabs her hair and begins dragging her back toward the carnage, through the smoke. She twists but his grip is tight. Behind her, Tru watches with a blank face while singing a high-voiced child's lullaby. *Hush little baby, don't say a word.* He is no longer pulling Spenser.

A blaze of orange from the tunnel casts stark shadows, distorting their figures and playing them against the far wall. The fresh light comes from the direction of the harvesting room, and Aine wonders if her fire has reached them. *Better to burn than be eaten.* She revives the feeling of the in-between and its promise of forgetfulness and imagines that is what death must be like. That doesn't seem so bad as long as they're all together.

It's the smell of burning hair, not her own, that finally brings the fight back into her, through the fog of pain and despair. The crisp odor is sickening, heavy, dirty, and she realizes it is coming from the

Morlock. He bellows in pain, momentarily loosening his grip, and Aine wrenches herself free. Using the nearest wall to pull herself up, she screams at Tru. "Go!"

He shakes his head and points behind her.

She turns.

Gilgamesh stands in the mouth of the tunnel, filling it. A torch blazes in his hand.

Chapter 25

Gilgamesh parries with the Morlock, his torch against the creature's club, but he retains the advantage of sight. He's also got a fighter's body and practice despite the wound he suffered at Aine's hands. The beast screams at the pain of the brilliant fire and disappears into a passage, clutching his wounded arm. Gilgamesh watches him go and then holds his torch high.

"All three of you? Alive?" His voice is stricken, his face contorted in an agony of discovery.

"No thanks to you," Aine manages to croak. The guilt pulling at his face is difficult to bear, but she dismisses empathy. Whatever he's suffering, he has brought on himself.

He nods in an acceptance so self-damning that she has to look away. He speaks quietly. "The fire is coming, and Biblos with it. We must get aboveground immediately."

"Sir?" Tru's voice is scratchy and high. "All of us?"

Gilgamesh's expression is wiped clean. It's as if the war that had just played out across the planes of his face never happened. "All of us." He thrusts the torch into Aine's hand. "You're hurt," he says matter-of-factly. "Take the fire. I'll carry your brother."

"And do what with him?"

Gilgamesh stops, turns, looks her in the eye. In his gaze she sees years of pain. "Bring him to my toadhouse, if you'll show me where it is."

A flare-up of the fire sends a fresh gust of contaminated smoke into their tunnel. She holds her hand over her mouth, her eyes burning. "What will you do with me? And Tru?"

"The same."

"You won't separate the three of us?"

His face is chipped from stone. "Never again."

She believes him. She doesn't trust him but she believes him. In any case, she has no choice but to accept his help. She grabs the torch with her right hand and stands over him as he cradles Spenser in his arms. The boy's head lolls back as if tied on by a string. Gilgamesh leans so he can tuck Spenser's head under his own chin.

"Go," he commands softly.

Aine obeys. She clutches Tru's hand and steps as quickly as she can while keeping her brother in view with frequent backward glimpses. The tunnels are byzantine, dank, endless, but they seem to be climbing upward, and the smoke and sounds of the killing room recede. Eventually they reach a ladder. Above, so far away it is a pinprick, they spot the worried face of the moon.

"Can you climb?" Gilgamesh asks.

Aine bites back a retort. "I'll follow you. Make sure Spenser gets up all right."

He indicates the torch in her right hand. Her left swings uselessly at her side. "You can't hold the torch and climb at the same time. There's no point in you going behind me. Spenser will be on my shoulder, freeing both my hands. I can kick if we're followed."

Aine glares but she doesn't argue. If she can't exit last, she'll lead to make sure they're safe coming out. She drops the torch and climbs. It's slow going with one arm, the pain piercing, and she bites the inside of her mouth until it bleeds to keep from crying out. But she continues, focusing only at the rung in front of her, conquering them one at a time. The hardest part comes at the top, when she has to maneuver her body over the lip of the well. Her left shoulder makes a grinding, ripping noise as it skids across the surface, and she momentarily loses consciousness. She comes to on the ground.

"Aine?" Tru's voice is feeble, far away. He pinches her, hard. "Sorry about that. But we're even now."

He attempts a smile, and the courage of this simple gesture is enough to pull her back into the moment. She takes his hand, allowing him to help her stand. Together with Gilgamesh, they ease Spenser out.

"Is that coming from one of the wells?" Tru asks, pointing to the east. In the distance the sky is blazing, day trespassing on night.

Aine sucks in a breath. "We must be near the end of the story. The Time Traveler burns the forest. You don't think that I started that—?"

Gilgamesh shakes his head, out of breath from the difficult climb. "We can't worry about that now. We need to escape this story. Biblos is close."

"This way." Aine leads them to the toadhouse half a mile from where they surfaced. The walk is fraught with potential danger, and the distant squeal of Morlocks being devoured by fire sets her teeth on edge. She wishes she could whisk Spenser to the house herself, but with her arm a useless hunk of flesh at her side, it isn't possible. Every moonlit shadow is a predator, every whisper of wind threatens to carry the scent of rotting pumpkins. They march grimly through the overgrown jungle.

When they reach the toadhouse, she's alarmed to see the state she left it in, out in the open, on its side, in full view of the debauched old mansion. She exchanges a glance with Tru, but neither says anything.

Gilgamesh uses his foot to flip the breadbox-sized toadhouse onto its base, then reaches in to set the cot into place while balancing Spenser against his chest. He follows with the still, clammy body of the child and places him on the bed as if he is made of glass. Aine and Tru follow, Aine rushing to her brother's side, ignoring the electricity of shrinking.

Gilgamesh enters last, a look of intense relief on his face. He runs his hands gratefully over the plotter. "I was wondering if I'd ever get back to her."

Aine watches him even as she tends to her brother. "We need to locate a doctor. We haven't time to search a whole book. Make sure we land in his office and that it's a human doctor, not a linguist or a veterinarian."

Gilgamesh nods and leans close to the plotter. She notices what she hadn't seen before, which is that he whispers into the mechanism rather than spelling out the guiding phrase. She hears the words "medical doctor," "equipment," and "hope," and a fifth that she can't make out. The vehicle begins to tremble. Tru sets the chairs upright and plops into one.

Once the toadhouse is in motion, she asks the question that's burning her brain. "Why'd you do it?" Her voice is lethal, her eyes needles through Gilgamesh's back.

Gilgamesh sways, holding onto the plotter so hard he appears to be praying. But he doesn't respond.

Her rage bubbles up with a ferocity that will not be ignored. "Why'd you kidnap me? Spenser couldn't fend for himself. He's blind and small. A defenseless child. You let the Morlocks take him!"

He glances over his shoulder but can't hold her stare. He says, simply, "I was told a moment would come where it seemed like the end. In that moment, I could only save one of you. If I tried to save both, both would die."

"You know Sura is dead? And my brother and Tru nearly so? It didn't have to be that way, Gilgamesh. You shouldn't believe everything you're told. You have to fight for what's important to you, not what's important to someone else."

He nods with terrible sadness and returns to his plotter. His lack of fight sparks Aine's anger, but the emotion unexpectedly dissipates, leaving only exhaustion.

"The hermit crabs!" Tru cries. Both Pinch and Shelly are scuttling dangerously close to the door. The terrarium must have been overturned in Aine's landing, releasing the tiny creatures. Tru dives for them, retrieves both, and settles them gently into their cage, which he wedges under the cot.

Aine arrests her full attention on Spenser, ignoring the throbbing, angry pain in her useless arm. He is breathing shallowly. His pallor has gone from white to a gray-green, and the tips of his fingers are ice-cold even as his body runs with sweat. Aine spies no open wounds on him, though he is decorated with bruises and his right arm lies at an unnatural angle. A deep red mars its surface at the elbow and below the shoulder.

She covers him with a blanket and guides her good hand gently through his damp, tufted hair. "Hang in there, sweet Spenser. Please. Please don't leave me like everyone else does. I need to tell you things about mom, and the best place in our woods to mushroom hunt, and how you used to follow me everywhere when you first learned to walk, and how sorry I am. Please, Spenser. Please."

Tru stands off a ways with his hands in his pockets, looking lost. Gilgamesh rocks back and forth in front of the plotter like a supplicant and outside, the nothingness calls.

There is a thump. They've landed.

Chapter 26

Aine is startled. The trip felt too quick. The sudden stillness and freckled light peeking through the toadhouse's orifices are unnerving. The air smells like dust and leather. From outside comes a soft thudding, like a muffled hammer hitting a table top. She can't see anything outside the toadhouse from the cot other than the indifferent light. "Tru, what's outside?"

He steps tentatively toward the door followed closely by Gilgamesh. "We're in some sort of closet, I think," he whispers. "Or a cupboard. It looks like morning out there, though."

"Can you see any people? Does it look like a doctor's office?"

"No people. And I can't tell what sort of room it is from here."

Spenser's shallow breathing has devolved into a rapid pant. Desperation claws at Aine. "We have to see what's out there. Spenser needs a doctor."

"I'll go," Gilgamesh says.

Aine is reluctant to leave her brother's side but is also aware she might be the only one who can identify the story or the doctor in it.

She's begun to realize that Gilgamesh's memory of stories is spotty at best. Spenser can't be left alone, though, and she doesn't trust Gilgamesh with him. The indecision is agony. "If we're in a cupboard or a closet, we can peek together to see where we're at," she finally says. "Tru, stay with Spenser. We'll be right back."

Ignoring the frightened look on Tru's face, she pads quickly out of the toadhouse and toward the sliver of light leaking in as if through a door that is slightly ajar. The ceiling of the structure they've landed in is only a few inches over the toadhouse, and a stack of linen shirts is piled next to them. The tight quarters give the illusion of safety, yet Gilgamesh stays close. "You need to get that arm looked at as well," he says.

"My brother first." She reaches the edge of the shelf and peers out. They're in some sort of armoire. Its door has come loose from its latch. The toadhouse rests at the rear of the top shelf. The drop is at least five feet, a death sentence at their present size.

Gilgamesh curses under his breath. "It's rare for the toadhouse to lodge itself this high up, in an enclosed space. It must have sensed the urgency of my directions. We'll have to rappel down."

"No need," Aine says, her voice leaden. She points at the source of the repetitive, small striking sound they've been hearing. There is a man, his hair a shock of mad scientist white, bent over a small wooden bench with his linen shirt open at the collar. He appears well-fed, yet his skin hangs loosely as if he was once larger. His posture is one of absolute absorption. He is at turns pounding on a bit of leather with a mallet and slicing at it with a dangerously hooked knife, his movements unhealthily repetitive.

"It's Dr. Manette," she says flatly.

The man lifts his head at the mention of his name even though

Aine's voice is as tiny as her body. It is impossible for him to have heard it. He glances around the room, confused, before dropping his head into his hands and rocking. After a moment, he fits the knuckle of one hand into the other then switches, twice and then three times, before returning to shoemaking.

"But if he's a doctor, that is good news," Gilgamesh says.

"No. This is *A Tale of Two Cities*. Dr. Manette, if he is making shoes, has gone insane. He's remembering a time when he was imprisoned." She looks around the rest of the room, as much as she can spy through the slit of the door. "We must be in his apartments in London, which means he'll recover, but no telling when."

The pulsating pain in her left arm makes it difficult to concentrate. Her eyes burn, and she's so tired that it's all she can do not to crawl back to the toadhouse. If she doesn't get her brother to a doctor soon, maybe within minutes, he will die. And they're wasting their time in the wrong book, just like she led them astray in *The Time Machine*. She's responsible for all that's gone wrong and this knowledge fills her like hardening cement.

"Please. We have to find a real doctor."

Gilgamesh nods. He makes as if to comfort her but pulls his hand back awkwardly before he touches her. "We'll get it this time. I promise."

Aine doesn't have the strength to acknowledge his words and doesn't know if she would if she could. They hurry back to the toadhouse.

Spenser is still, Tru by his side. He is still panting. The water in the skin is tepid, but Aine uses it to cool Spenser's forehead and wet his parched lips. His skin is so hot that the water evaporates quickly.

"He's going to be okay, isn't he?" Tru asks, standing over her.

She doesn't answer. She stares at her fragile little brother, remembering the shape of his smile and the bright farawayness of his eyes.

Tru shifts from foot to foot, apparently upset by the silence. "I heard you out there, back in that book. Why was that guy making shoes if he's a doctor?"

"Tragedy," Aine says absentmindedly. "He was imprisoned in the Bastille to cover up someone else's crime. He wasted there for eighteen years, and he only saved his mind by teaching himself to make shoes. When he's reminded of the past and at the edge of losing his sanity, he returns to shoemaking to soothe himself."

"Maybe we should *all* learn to make shoes," Tru says quietly.

Aine isn't listening. She is wishing she could take Spenser's place, and he could be the one who is alive and awake. She leans toward him and sings "Aspri Mera Key Ya Mas" quietly. He has the scent of sour fear and great illness on him, but he also smells like her brother, a cross between duckling and boy. Her eyes close tight, and she remembers the day he met his hermit crabs.

Two years ago, a classmate of his brought two of her own hermit crabs to school so the whole class could play with them. Most of the children lost interest after a few minutes, but the scrabbling creatures captivated Spenser. They tickled the palm of his hands and sent him into fits of giggles. Hermit crabs were all he talked about for weeks after, and Aine got it into her head that she'd buy him one for Christmas.

They didn't have any money to speak of at Grandma Glori's house and had never received presents, but after weeks of secret begging on behalf of her brother, Aine got Grandma Glori to relent. She said she'd be willing to give Aine a quarter to buy the crabs and their terrarium if Aine could go two weeks without butter. Aine had, then had gone another four just for spite.

Glori honored her deal but refused to let Aine shop for the crab. Mondegreen picked up two in town the week before Christmas. Aine discovered them on the counter one chilly morning when she came down for breakfast. She kept them fed and watered until Christmas Day. When Spenser came downstairs that morning, she placed them in the palm of his hand and told him Santa had finally found Grandma's house. His smile of absolute, trusting joy was so pure that it sang.

Aine keeps her eyes closed to hang onto that vision. Never once does she take her hand off of her brother's dripping forehead.

Chapter 27

"We've landed indoors again," Gilgamesh says thickly.

The toadhouse has come to rest in another dark space, distinct only by its scent of pungent chemicals and stale air. Unlike *A Tale of Two Cities*, it is nighttime here, though some faint light offers shadows. The silence is complete, almost as if they're still traveling the in-between.

"It doesn't matter!" Aine says. She is wrapping the blanket around Spenser to use as a sling to transport him. "I don't care what story we're in. We have to find the nearest doctor. His pulse is fading."

Gilgamesh hesitates. "It will be dangerous to move him."

The strain of keeping her voice even is too much. It cracks. "He's dying."

Gilgamesh opens then closes his mouth. Runs his hands through his hair. "All right. I'll carry him."

"I can come with, right?" Tru asks timidly.

Aine's acquiescence is terse. The wasted trip to Dr. Manette's chambers took more out of her than she knew. Her mind and body

quiver at a thousand different edges, threatening to shatter and separate in a great explosion. She imagines she can hear the shrill tension
pulling at her flesh, and she finds herself suddenly unable to look at
Spenser. Her smiling brother's image she holds firmly in her mind,
marveling at a person who sees the world with his heart instead of
his eyes, and in the meanwhile, she needs to find help for that sad
lump on the bed. She grabs her bag out of habit and slings it over
her good shoulder. She says only one word. "Hurry."

Outside the toadhouse, the harsh tang of chemicals curls the tender skin in her nostrils. Their feet leave tiny prints in the dusty floor
as they make their way single-file: Aine, Tru, and Gilgamesh, with
a limp Spenser held tightly in his arms. Their soft tread is the only
sound. The room they have entered is cavernous, a storage space of
some sort, full of tables and boxes and doors. Its shape is off-kilter,
unnatural, as if it is hiding a second level or was built where a room
was never meant to be. Moonlight sneaks past the cloudy hopper
windows set nearly level with the ceiling.

Aine points to a change in the pattern ahead. It is not quite light
so much as less darkness, and it possesses a shifting quality. She picks
up her pace, and they reach a point where the wood floor is heavily
trafficked. A skeleton key, giant to them, rusted and snapped in two,
rests ominously in the main pathway. To their left, the darkness
continues to lift. Aine moves in that direction.

"What story are we in?" Tru whispers.

"We'll find out soon."

They follow her quickly, silent soldiers. She passes a heap of
wheeled metal tables stacked one on the next and spots a monstrous
door ahead. Uneven light from a candle or a fire flickers underneath.
The pungent smell of scientific compounds is powerful. Tru draws

a sharp breath but doesn't comment. Gilgamesh is huffing quietly with his motionless bundle, his expression unreadable.

"I'm going under." Aine indicates the three-inch tall space beneath the warped door. The legs of furniture and a rug are visible on the other side. "Wait here."

"We're coming with you." Gilgamesh leaves no room for debate.

Aine says nothing. She slips under the door. She moves as quickly as she is able with her damaged arm, recollecting the handful of times she was irritated with Spenser, annoyed by stupid little things like how he breathed and chewed his food. How, to her great and eternal shame, she'd pretended on the first day of school that she didn't know the new blind boy, and how when he'd found out, he'd shrugged it off and told her it was okay. She recollected his smiling face with his heart in his eyes.

She enters a surreal laboratory space cluttered with operating tables, glass vials of scarlet liquid, tubes of white powder, a roaring fireplace, and in front of it, a man. She can't see his face but he is little, stooped, his clothes overlarge and hanging off his wiry figure. He's pacing. He turns.

"Biblos?" Her heart is in her mouth.

"You've mistaken me," he growls, chuckling, staring at the miniature girl.

The image passes. It must have been a trick of the firelight that for a moment put Biblos' horribly handsome jester face on the little man's body. It had been painfully vivid, so clear that Aine could hear the Mediterranean accent. The sensation leaves her scared then unexpectedly disgusted with the man. "My mistake. Sorry."

He is shuffling toward her, the odd half-smile still on his face. "What are you tiny creature, pray tell? Oh! And two more."

Tru clutches her wrist. His trembling threatens contagion.

"We need a doctor. Now." It's Gilgamesh. His voice is thin but weighted with revulsion that Aine recognizes from her own reaction to the odd, twisted man. She wonders what Gilgamesh sees as he looks at the stooped scientist, for that is what she assumes him to be.

"You're in luck." The man bends, a greedy expression burning up his eyes. "You have one right here."

"You're a doctor?" Tru asks incredulously.

The man throws back his head and laughs. "Not I. No. I am not a doctor, though my better half is. My name is Edward Hyde."

Chapter 28

A ine is the first to resize, the horrible awareness of which story they have entered growing with her. Tru is next, followed immediately by Gilgamesh and Spenser. The room is no less threatening at regular height. Aine catches sight of herself in a full-length, central-pivot mirror across the room. She looks like a wolf girl with snarled hair, wild eyes, and one arm hanging limply. There isn't time to escape to another story.

"We need to see Dr. Jekyll. Immediately."

Tru squeaks like a frightened mouse. "I *read* that story."

Hyde ignores their resizing and the outburst. If possible, the greed and slyness in his eyes increases. "I'm afraid he's not in. Could I offer you something to…drink?"

"Aine," Tru whispers hotly in her ear, "don't take food from strangers!"

Hyde's smile widens. "Wise advice indeed. But I'm no longer a stranger. I've introduced myself, you see?"

Aine never removes her eyes from the man as she barks orders. "Tru, clean off that table. Use a rag from near the door where we entered. Gilgamesh, put Spenser on it, but gently. And you." She strides close to Hyde and shoves her face to within inches of his. "I'm not afraid of you. You will allow Dr. Jekyll to return, or I'll open that door and bring in the police. The constables. Whatever you call them."

"But why would you do that?" Hyde asks, steepling his hairy, knotted fingers. "I'm simply a man in his own home."

"If you're Edward Hyde, you're wanted for murder."

"Can you prove it?"

Eyes blazing, Aine makes for the door. She remembers this story clearly because it had scared her. She knows Dr. Jekyll has a full staff of servants. They can help her fetch a doctor if Hyde won't, and she can worry about explaining their presence afterward. Too much time has already been wasted.

The hand on her good wrist is strong as a panther's. She whips around.

"I was just having some sport," Hyde says, holding her tight. "Here, be a good girl and have a seat."

"You'll bring Dr. Jekyll?"

Hyde's eyes are raging, petulant, but he stomps back to the chemist's table, where he snatches up one of the delicate glass bottles of crimson liquid. "If you insist." He pours the liquid into a beaker of white powder, and the mixture storms and froths. He glares as he swallows, but he takes the draught whole.

The metamorphosis begins immediately. His spine arches as if drawn up by a hook and his face contorts in agony, veins appearing, throbbing, pulsing with hot magenta blood until they're stretched to bursting. Hyde's shaggy hands clench then stretch, the hair melting into the skin and the fingers extending with painful cracking sounds. His body also swells, but unevenly, as if burrowing creatures swarm beneath, separating muscle from bone then skin from flesh. A haunted moan escapes his lips, but it is no longer the mouth of Hyde. The man who stands before them, panting and nearly doubled over, is a stranger.

"Dr. Jekyll?" Aine asks unevenly. Watching the transmogrification has left her feeling ill.

"Yes." He glances around the room shakily. His eyes settle on his reflection in the mirror, where he can also see his four guests. "Who are you?"

"Please. My brother needs a doctor." Aine leads him to the table where Gilgamesh is standing over Spenser with the expression of a junkyard dog protecting his pup.

"You trust him?" Gilgamesh asks, jabbing a finger at the doctor.

"No," Aine says, "but he's our only hope."

The declaration seems to revive the doctor somewhat. He runs his faltering hands through his hair, but when they come to rest on Spenser's cheek, they're firm. "He's had a great shock. What are his injuries?"

"I'm…I'm not sure. His right arm is broken, I think. But…" The confession is almost too painful to utter. "I wasn't with him when he was hurt. I didn't see it."

"How long ago did it happen?"

The question silences all three. "Four hours is my best guess," Gilgamesh finally responds.

The doctor leans in, entirely focused on his patient. After a long minute of gently tapping Spenser's still form, he issues instructions much as Aine had done moments earlier. "You," he indicates Tru. "Fetch me hot water from the kettle over the fire, please. Pour half of it into a bowl and leave the other half in the pot, but bring it nearer. You," he lifts a shoulder toward Gilgamesh. "Fourth drawer from the bottom, in that bureau behind you. Grab the bottle labeled 'carbolic acid.'"

Gilgamesh's reaction is immediate and vehement. "You'll not turn the boy into a monster like you."

Dr. Jekyll peers up sadly before returning to palpating the unconscious Spenser. "It's to sterilize my hands. I'll take the stethoscope, too." He strips Spenser to his underwear and examines him thoroughly. Finding no physical injuries other than the right arm broken in three places, he has no choice but to set the bones, trickle some cool water into the boy's throat, and declare him beyond further help.

"Is he gonna make it?" Tru asks, his brow furrowed. He has grown as pale as his hair.

Dr. Jekyll wipes his hands on a clean bit of cloth and glances at Aine. "It's hard to be certain without knowing what's happened to him. If he had a concussive injury, there'd be more bruising on his skull. If he was poisoned, at this point it's either going to work its way through him or kill him. If it's a mental shock," and here he raises his eyebrows at all three, inviting a further explanation, "he could come out of it at any time, or never."

A fat tear rolls down Tru's cheek. Gilgamesh coughs roughly.

He directs his next words at Aine. "Do you want to tell me what happened to you, or is that also a secret?"

The question startles her. She follows his gaze to her left shoulder. The swelling is so severe that the sleeve of her blouse is cutting into the flesh, and a purpling has begun to creep toward her elbow. It had gone numb over an hour ago. "I got hit."

"With a carriage?"

She shakes her head. "A club."

He is quickly by her side. She is surprised that he smells like peppery tobacco. His face bears no trace of Hyde, but still, his touch makes her jump.

"I'm just going to examine this area. I'll be gentle." His touch is light, pleasant. She can feel the pressure only, no pain. "Ah, just as I thought. Sir, Gilgamesh, is it? Will you lend me a hand here?"

Gilgamesh seems reluctant to leave Spenser's side, but he comes over. "What do you need?"

"Hold her undamaged shoulder, like this. That's a good chap."

Aine also shies from Gilgamesh's touch, but he clamps down tight with hands as strong as a vise. Dr. Jekyll is still holding her other arm, peering at it as if waiting for it to speak. She glances from one man to the next, travelling between panic and outrage. "What are you going to—"

Dr. Jekyll jolts her upper arm with enough force that he groans from the effort. The pop of ball returning to socket is louder than ten wine bottles being uncorked. A white sheet drops over Aine's body and she falls, drifts, plummets down, through the floor then the earth, past dirt and rock. She's distantly aware of her stomach twisting then emptying itself. With her belly clean, she has room for all the pain in the world. It consumes her, making it difficult to think.

But that's a luxury she can't allow herself. She concentrates on the blue-glass bottle a million miles above and crawls back toward it, scraping her fingernails and sweating as she goes. A voice guides her back. It sounds like her brother, so she hurries. The bottle is growing nearer and the voice louder, and the pain even more like a battering ram inside her head and melting away the flesh of her arm.

"Aine! Aine!" Tru's slapping her good hand frantically. "You fainted. Come on, Aine! Come back!"

She blinks. The room is hot. The blue glass bottle rests next to her head on the rough wooden table where she collapsed. Amazingly, she avoided vomiting on herself, though the rich Persian rug beneath her is not so lucky. "I'm sorry," she croaks.

"Nonsense," Dr. Jekyll declares. "I've seen grown men weep for their mothers when they've had a dislocated shoulder set. There's no shame in emptying your stomach. We're only human." To her surprise, he sets to work cleaning up the mess himself, speaking matter-of-factly as he does. "Your arm will be stiff for a while, so we'll need to bind it. Don't use it if it can be avoided. Should be no long-term damage. Your brother, as I said, I'm not sure of, though I would beg you to not move him for at least twelve hours if you're invested in his recovery."

They digest this information as he continues. "I assume the four of you are in difficulty with the law. You're welcome to stay here as long as you need, though you've met my...friend. I can't be sure when he'll return, nor responsible for what he'll do when he does."

Gilgamesh has returned to Spenser's side, though he watches Aine rather than the boy or the doctor. She meets his stare.

"Thank you," she tells the doctor. "We'll stay. For twelve hours."

Chapter 29

'you wanna hear something off the cob?" Tru sits cross-legged on the surgical table next to Spenser. His voice is hushed. Aine and Gilgamesh lean in to catch his words, all three shooting fleeting, preoccupied glances at the pacing Edward Hyde on the far side of the room. "That Hyde guy looked just like my dad when I first spotted him. Scared the pants clean offa me. Thought he was gonna yell at me for running away. Or even worse, yell at me for *not* running away."

Aine stops short of sharing that she'd thought Hyde was Biblos. "Gilgamesh, how did he appear to you?"

Gilgamesh clenches his jaw. "Like me. But younger."

"How can that be?" Tru asks. "He's the ugliest man I've ever seen, and you're not a bad-looking fellow."

"Is your dad hideous?" Aine asks the boy.

"No," Tru says. "I guess he isn't. He's the person I'd least like to see, I'll grant you that, but he's got his eyes, nose, and mouth right where they're supposed to be and a decent size, each of 'em. So how can one man look so different to each of us?"

"In the story, Hyde is a man without boundaries, living only for his own pleasure. He is also horrible to look at, but no one is quite sure why. Maybe he reflects what we're most afraid of. That would explain why he appears different to everyone." Aine's hand involuntarily seeks Spenser, as it has since she's had her shoulder set. If anything his condition has grown worse, a fever bubbling across his skin like a gas fire.

Jekyll had offered salicylate salts to reduce the fever but warned against overuse as it would cause internal bleeding. He'd reverted to Hyde shortly after without the necessity of a potion and in the same grisly, jerky manner in which he'd transformed into Jekyll. He'd been carving his footsteps into the wooden floor ever since, occasionally muttering to himself and tossing black glances at his company.

"The boy's fever has to break or his brain will be cooked," Gilgamesh offers darkly.

"Shut up!" Aine gathers herself around Spenser in a protective posture. She'd been thinking something similar but wants desperately to believe she is misreading the signs. "You're not a doctor. His arm just needs to mend, and he'll come to."

"I'm tired of standing here and watching him suffer. We need to keep him cool." Gilgamesh soaks a blanket in the remaining water. "We need to move him further away from the fire."

"Wait! Spenser is moving!"

His eyes twitch rapidly under his closed lids, and the fingers of his right hand shuffle at each other.

"Spenser? Can you hear me? It's Aine. I'm right here. Spenser?" She touches his forehead but yanks her hand back immediately. "He's burning up! Gilgamesh, you're right. We need to cool him off. Hyde, we need ice!"

Hyde's laugh is dry. "Godspeed."

"Call for your servants," Aine demands.

"They're not mine. They wouldn't answer to me even if they were still around for the night." He appears to occupy more space than when she last noticed him. His shirt doesn't hang so loosely, and he's standing taller. Is he feeding off their fear and anger? "As you pointed out, I am not free to roam the city, being an accused murderer. We'll have to spend a pleasant evening together watching, as your friend said, the boy's brain cook inside his head."

"I'll go," Tru says. "I can find ice."

"You can't!" Aine exclaims. "We're in late 1880s London and it's the middle of the night."

"It's true," Hyde confirms, chuckling. He has the air of the cat that has trapped the mouse. "Only a criminal could find ice at this hour."

"I have a diamond," Aine says desperately, digging in her school bag. She comes out with Sita's ring, set with its strawberry-sized jewel. "See! I'll give it to you if you get us ice."

"Money is nothing to me. I have plenty."

Spenser's left hand has begun the same scrabbling motion as his right, as if he's trying to dig his way out of a terrible deep hole. Shimmery waves of heat distort the space over his body.

"What about a magical conveyance," Gilgamesh says quietly, his voice picking up urgency, "that could free you from this building and take you anywhere you want, where no one would recognize you and you could live your life as you chose?"

"Gilgamesh!" Aine cries. "You can't inflict him on other stories."

His look silences her.

Hyde eagerly humps in close to Gilgamesh. "That would be quite something different than a diamond, wouldn't it? You say you'd let me have this magical conveyance in trade for enough ice to break the boy's fever?"

"I won't let you keep the vehicle, but I will transport you wherever you want to go and leave you there to live out your life."

Hyde scratches his bristled head, his eyes sly. "If the carriage can take you where you want to go, why don't you fetch some ice yourself?"

"It would take too long. We can get to a town and a period in time, but we would still have to locate the ice."

"I need to see this magical carriage."

"Stay." Gilgamesh moves swiftly out the door and returns in moments with the toadhouse in his hand. Hyde wants to hold it but Gilgamesh refuses.

"It's nothing more than a child's toy! How can I believe that this garden decoration will convey me to another land?"

"A test," Gilgamesh says. "Request an object, and I'll retrieve it."

Greed etches itself like acid onto Hyde's face. His answer, however, startles them. "Grapes. I want a fresh bunch of grapes, which are out of season and impossible to obtain on this continent." He is triumphant.

Aine shouts the first thing that comes to her mind, a short story where every scene is guaranteed to have the fruit. "Aesop, Fox and the Grapes."

Gilgamesh acts quickly, jumping into the toadhouse. It disappears immediately.

"A parlor trick," Hyde says, but he sounds unconvinced.

Within seconds, the toadhouse is back. Gilgamesh leaps out, tiny, his arms laden with purple fruit.

Hyde sucks in his breath in rage. "Why, he's been morphed into a homunculus! I won't risk my life to be alchemized thus."

"He'll grow bigger," Aine explains. "We were all that size when you first saw us, remember? The toadhouse brought us here, and as you can see, we've resized. It takes fewer than ten minutes to return to normal. By the time you've returned with the ice, he will be as large as you again."

Hyde seems unconvinced. "This arrangement appears to cost more than it provides."

"Fine," Aine says. "Then we leave immediately. Spenser needs the ice, and if you won't retrieve it for us, we'll try our luck elsewhere."

"But you said that it would take too long!" Tru exclaims.

Aine shoots him a look and pretends as though she is preparing Spenser to be moved.

"All right!" Hyde is unable to resist the temptation. "I'll get your ice. If the homunculus isn't his regular size when I return, *if* I return, I'll bludgeon you all to death and take the house for myself."

He leaves out the opposite door that they entered, and Tru takes up Hyde's position, pacing.

Chapter 30

The grandfather clock ticks loudly in the corner, counting out minutes, and then a half an hour, and then an hour. Every tick exacts a small slice of flesh. Aine watches over Spenser. Gilgamesh resizes and after much searching, hides the toadhouse underneath a worn velvet sofa. His task complete, he yells at Tru for pacing then takes over for him as the boy joins Aine.

"Hyde sure has been gone for a long time."

"I bet the iceman isn't awake," Aine says. "Even if he is, he probably won't give Hyde anything. He'll need to break into the icehouse."

Tru ponders this while chewing on the end of a fountain pen he'd picked up. "He seems the man for the job." He pauses. "Hey Aine?"

"Yeah."

"We're going to get clear of this, right?"

She sighs deeply, still concentrating on holding the pieces of herself together. She's always hated it when adults lie to kids. "I don't know."

He takes the pen out of his mouth and twists it with his fingers as words tumble out like spilled seeds. "I was thinking, I'd sure like to. Get out of this, I mean. And not only this story, but this whole job. Maybe my old life wasn't as bad as I thought. Sure, my parents didn't need me, but my other kin seemed to like me, and I had friends back in Monroe County. I knew where my next meal was coming from, and nobody died except in my imagination." He pauses for air. "You think I'll ever return home?"

The question squeezes Aine grievously tight. Her home, she'd thought, was her mother. Then it became the farmhouse with her grandmother. But really? It had always been her brother, and look at what a disaster she'd made of that. "I hope so, for your sake."

A scraping at the main entrance calls their attention. Gilgamesh is the first to reach it, and he yanks open the heavy wood door. Hyde is there, dragging two huge blocks of ice, his face bloody. Gilgamesh takes one and sets to chopping it with an axe that had been propped near the fireplace. Tru and Aine transport the chips onto the blanket covering Spenser, and soon, he is buried under a glistening crystal mountain with only his face visible.

No one asks Hyde if the blood belongs to him or someone else, and he makes no effort to explain or clean it. He only watches eagerly until they are done. "There. I held my end of the bargain. I brought the ice, and the boy is swimming in it. Now take me to Shanghai."

"Not until his fever breaks," Gilgamesh says harshly.

Hyde sneers but doesn't argue, returning instead to stalking the floorboards. Aine feels his eyes on her more and more frequently, and she pulls Gilgamesh aside.

"He'll destroy any story you bring him into, you know. He's unrepentant by design."

"I don't intend to take him anywhere."

"What will you do?" She notices Hyde is staring at her, so she leans in closer. "He's already killed a man, a stranger, for the joy of it. It happens earlier in the story."

"I'll detain him here. You and the boys will enter the toadhouse and travel to some other story. I'll find the toadhouse here and meet you in that book."

The fear that grips Aine surprises her. "We can all escape together."

"Possibly." He refuses to say more. Hours pass, and the murky sun tries to peer in through the strange, high windows. The dusty light doesn't know where to land in this room of dark corners and oppressive gloom so it halts just above the surfaces, creating a surreal wateriness. Spenser continues to burn beneath the ice, unresponsive.

There's a knock at the door. Hyde, who'd fallen into a fitful rest in a straightback chair, jumps to attention. "Who is it?" he snarls.

"Poole, sir. Dr. Jekyll, is that you? I have your breakfast."

"Leave it outside the door."

"Really, sir, I'd like to bring it in."

"I said leave it!" he roars.

The commotion wakes Tru, who'd drifted off on the floor. "Breakfast?"

"I've had enough foolishness!" Hyde storms over to where Gilgamesh and Aine are keeping watch over Spenser. "The boy is as good as dead, and it's not my fault. I brought the ice. Now release me from the bonds of this city."

The ice shifts. At first Aine believes it's the strength of Hyde's ire, but then Spenser's hand appears, his fingers tipped in blue. It's not the ghostly scratching motion from before but a deliberate reaching.

"Spenser?" She clasps his hand tentatively, afraid to move too quickly and shatter the beautiful dream. "Are you awake? Can you hear me?"

Her hand on his forehead reveals that he's warm but no longer on fire. "His fever's broken! Get the ice off of him. Now!"

Gilgamesh and Tru hurry to obey. In the commotion, Hyde slips unnoticed into the storage room.

"Is there a dry blanket to wrap him in?" Aine wants to gather him up and rock him, but she's conscious of his arm, recently set. She leans in close. Her voice is shaky. "Spenser, I know you're in there. We're all out here, Spense. It's safe to come out."

"Nini?" It's a scratchy, timid word.

"I'm right here." Tears salted with joy, guilt, and hope stream down her face. Spenser tips his head toward her. His eyes flicker, then focus on his sister's face. She realizes with a jolt that he is looking at her, actually seeing her, for the first time in his life. But then his eyes slide to the left, and she understands she must have imagined it, or misread the shock of awakening to great pain.

"You left me," he says. It's a sad, factual statement.

His words send her reeling. Of all her imaginings of this moment, none of them featured an accusation. The terrible finality of his statement extinguishes the last ray of the child inside Aine, the bit she'd been clinging to since she'd seen her grandmother and then Sura die. She thinks of protesting, of saying it wasn't her fault, but she knows that ultimately it doesn't matter. She wasn't there when he needed her the most. Her voice catches when she speaks. "I'm so sorry."

He turns away from her, though it obviously pains him, and cradles his loose arm near his chest. She wants to explain, to tell him that she's going to make everything right, but she knows that's a lie. Nothing is ever going to be right again. Her brother is alive, he'll make it through this, but she's lost him. Her shoulders slump and she retreats to the perimeter of the room to weep. She is no better than the adults in their life who disappear at a whim.

"You should come with me." The sinister voice startles her. "To Shanghai." Hyde has re-entered the room through a tiny door hidden behind the fireplace. His eyes are bloodshot and frantic. He keeps reaching for his belt then pulling back from it as if it's hot.

Aine recoils. "No thank you."

"It wasn't a request." He unexpectedly pivots so he is standing behind her, a dagger retrieved from his waistband now at her neck. The cold metal presses so deeply into her throat that she has difficulty breathing. "We'll take the conveyance!" he yells across the room.

Gilgamesh and Tru had turned their backs to allow Aine her privacy as she wept, or because they weren't sure what else to do. At the boom of Hyde's voice they swivel, and the blood drains from their faces.

"Bring me the carriage you fetched the grapes in. If you don't, I shall slit her jugular."

Gilgamesh retrieves the house from under the couch, his movements stiff. He sets it on the operating table next to Spenser.

"Bring it here, I said!"

"I made a promise never to separate the three of them again. If you take the female, you take the boys."

"What? I'll kill all three of them as surely as I'll kill one."

"So be it."

Tru stares bug-eyed at Gilgamesh but doesn't argue when he's ordered into the toadhouse.

"I warn you," says Hyde, pressing so hard on Aine's throat that a trickle of warm blood slides down, "if you take off now with that lad, I'll cut her through."

"I'm only putting the boys in, and then you can leave with Aine. She knows how to operate the house well enough."

He gingerly scoops up Spenser. The boy groans but doesn't resist. Gilgamesh leans forward to place him in the house then steps away from it, his hands in the air, still fully-sized. The scar on his face pulses. "I have an oath to not kill another living creature. If I break that oath, I can never return to Tir Na Nog. You have my word that I won't stop you. Just don't hurt them. You can let them go wherever you end up."

A yell outside the door interrupts their tense exchange. "Jekyll, I demand to see you!"

Hyde grimaces, relaxing the knife only slightly against Aine's neck. The man outside continues, his voice firm and resigned. "I give you fair warning, our suspicions are aroused, and I must and shall see you, if not by fair means, then by foul. If not of your consent, then by brute force!"

Hyde bellows in return. "Utterson, for God's sake have mercy!"

An axe through the door replies to Hyde's plea. He grunts and pushes Aine toward the toadhouse, never releasing his grip on her neck. The axe takes a second bite out of the heavy door, then a third, and the wood screams. Urgently, Hyde shoves her through the toadhouse entrance headfirst. Tru is waiting inside, butter knife in one hand and fork in the other, the only weapons available. He leaps at Hyde's tiny hand but seems afraid to stab while the man has a knife pressed to Aine's neck.

Unexpectedly, Hyde gives a throaty groan and his hand slides off of her. A mighty shove forces her the rest of the way into the toadhouse in an ungainly pile. She just manages to protect her wounded shoulder. Tru rushes to her side to help her up. She spins, ready to fight, but Hyde has not followed. They hear a fourth axe blow and the sound of metal hinges giving way.

"Gilgamesh!" She scrambles to the doorway and peers out. Gilgamesh is staring down at Hyde's still form, the fireplace blazing merrily at his back. He's clutching the hearth poker in his right hand and a beaker full of frothing liquid in his left.

"Gilgamesh!" she yells again.

He looks up, wearing a feral, satisfied expression before he kneels down to pour the liquid into Hyde's slack mouth. He works the throat of the unconscious mutant then pours in more. A man's shoulder breaks through the slivered door. Gilgamesh drops the beaker with a crash and leaps into the house.

"What happened?" Aine asks.

Gilgamesh races to the plotter. "I blindsided him with the fireplace poker then had him drink some of his own medicine."

"What about your oath?" Tru asks, incredulous.

"I'm not a foolish enough man to sacrifice a child for an oath." Gilgamesh powers up the plotter with an unsettling calmness. "At least," and here he looks at Aine, "not twice. Now, where are we off to?"

Two men charge into Jekyll's room. Their exclamations sound muffled in the toadhouse. They stampede toward the fire and the body.

"Sinbad," Aine says, thinking of Spenser and how she'd never followed his lead. She points at the archetyper over the door. Less than a quarter of the pages remain unturned. "I figure we have less than ten hours to retrieve the metal staff before we have to return Tru to his world."

Tru glances at the mechanism, his face hopeful. *Home*, it says. He meets Aine's eyes and drops the expression.

"It's okay," she says, thinking of the land of Tir Na Nog in Sura's know globe. The green hills and clear sky promised safety and familiarity. "I understand wanting to go home. I really do."

Gilgamesh leans forward and whispers into the plotter. The toadhouse trembles, spins, and takes off. The last image visible through the door is of two men leaning over Hyde's body, their expressions astonished. Then the world outside the toadhouse goes black, and the black gives way to sucking nothingness.

Aine checks on Spenser. He's asleep, still impossibly pale but breathing rhythmically. She thinks of his accusation that she left him and knows he's right. The sorrow settles into her chest, and she shuffles to the opposite wall and curls into it.

Chapter 31

Their time in Sinbad's second voyage is mercilessly brief. The toad-house alights in the forward corner of a mammoth cave, near the entrance. Through the tiny door, they can see the deepest part, where two red eyes as large as automobile tires glimmer at the newly-arrived object, taking its stock. Enough sunlight filters through the mouth of the cave for the tiny travelers to see that the enormous eyes belong to a gargantuan snake coiled on her nest of eggs.

The horrors outside the cave are no less forgiving. Scaled claws, sharp and large enough to scoop up a whale, crash to the ground and scissor around a colossal serpent. The snake's black, gold and green diamond-patterned back splits with the force. The roc takes to the air with a deafening screech and only half a serpent dangling from her claws. Diamonds that once glittered like the sea are now awash in blood.

Gilgamesh yells "Ether!" at the plotter, and the mechanism buzzes and whirrs. The mother snake, curious, slithers off her nest and approaches, her tongue seeking. The toadhouse trembles and begins to move, spinning the image of the approaching snake into a web of black. Aine is clutching her brother and the bed, retraining her heartbeat to normal rhythms.

"That was close enough to leave a mark," Tru says, the first to speak.

Spenser is sitting up and holding his arm. He's pale, but there's a fire in his eyes. "That was the wrong Sinbad."

"What do you mean?" Aine asks. When her brother had initially woken up, he'd been tentative, quiet, not mentioning his earlier accusation. He'd even hugged Aine, holding her tight and thanking her for saving him. He'd refused to talk any more about *The Time Machine* but he had accepted food and water.

Spenser brushes his hair out of his eyes. "Our teacher read all the Sinbad stories to us in class this year. Sinbad sailed on seven different voyages, and each one is like its own book. There's lots of gold in his stories, and I think lots of walking staffs, too."

Outside the toadhouse, the inky nothing vibrates with emptiness. Gilgamesh drops his head and grips the plotter, sweat beading along his neck. Aine glance at him worriedly and directs the question to her brother. "What voyage were we just in?"

Faint color shades the edges of Spenser's cheeks as he relays the tale. "I think the second."

"Which voyage contains the golden staff we seek?" Gilgamesh says through clenched teeth.

Aine knows the pain he is experiencing, the burning urge the toadhouse pilot feels to leap into the ether while commanding the ship. She rises to stand in front of the door. She doesn't know if it will help, but it's all she can offer.

Spenser seems to listen in Aine's direction, as if waiting for her to interrupt with the answer. When only silence meets him, he continues, more energized. "The seventh, I think. In that story, Sinbad builds a sandalwood raft and floats it down a river. He's starving and dying of thirst and too tired to get off his little boat. But then he hears a roar ahead and realizes he's going to go down rapids! He can't do anything about it. He goes over the falls, and his raft shatters. When he comes to, he's surrounded by a crowd. The man who runs the nearest town, a sheik I think, takes Sinbad in and showers him with riches and tells him to marry his daughter. Sinbad does.

"He lives happily for a while but notices that on the first day of every month, all the men of the town turn into bird people and fly up to the mountain. Sinbad convinces one of the bird men to take him with. In the air, Sinbad offers praise to his God, and fire rains down from the sky. The bird man drops Sinbad, and he lands near two men, each with a golden rod."

Tru sucks in his breath, leaning forward anxiously to catch every word. "That sounds like a grand time."

Spenser pauses for dramatic effect before continuing, his face flushing with pride at the interest in his story. Aine would give her right ear to have that color stay in his cheeks. "Sinbad is offered one of them and takes it. Then he starts walking and comes across a man being eaten by a giant snake and uses the rod to stun the snake. The man is grateful, and they walk back to town together and meet up with a crowd and set up camp for the night. While there, Sinbad spots the bird man who dropped him, so he gives the gold rod to the man he rescued from the snake and he leaves with the bird man the next morning."

"And we need to get that rod, right?" Tru asks.

"Exactly," Spenser says.

"No sense in talking about it anymore. Let's go," Gilgamesh says. Sweat is pouring down his face, staining the neck and arms of his shirt. "What words shall I enter?"

Aine watches in awe as Gilgamesh fights indescribable pain and manages to carry on a conversation at the same time. She knows how much the effort is costing him, sees him tremble and his muscles strain, and she relents to the grudging admiration.

"Sinbad fly birds burn," Spenser says with finality.

"These are dangerous stories," Gilgamesh warns after he whispers the phrase into the plotter. He sounds as if he's been running for hours. "We've got to be on guard."

After a journey measured in seconds, the toadhouse lands in the soft shade of a tropical plant. Its spiky green leaves offer perfect protection. It's early morning. The air carries the tang of the sea, and powdery white sand breaks up the tropical foliage.

"Now this is more like it," Tru says, skipping out the door.

"Be careful!" Gilgamesh yells, but Spenser has already followed his friend. He's walking slowly but steadily, and though his arm clearly pains him, he seems to be returning to himself by the minute. Aine lags behind.

"Are you all right?" she asks Gilgamesh.

The back-to-back trips have leeched the pilot's strength. His shoulders are bowed, and his eyes are held up by dark bags. His hand, when he runs it through his hair, shakes. "I'm fine. Tend to your brother."

Aine furrows her brows. "I'll be sure to do that." She grabs her school bag and stomps out of the toadhouse. The grains of sand are as large as pencil erasers in her current size and are difficult to walk on. A skittering bug, flat like a plate and nearly as tall as her waist, scrabbles toward her on six legs. Its eyes are perched on the ends of stalks and quiver in her direction. She waves her arms and yells, and the bug scuttles away. Her heart is beating fast, and she reminds herself of the dangers at this size even as the fresh salt air invigorates her. The humidity is thick enough to slice like pie, reminding her of the close heat of Alabama. "Tru, Spenser!"

"Over here." Tru's voice is accompanied by a giggle.

Aine follows their minute footprints around their protective plant and discovers a creek burbling. It's narrow enough that she could swim across it at her current size, clear, and lined with smooth river rocks. Tru and Spenser both have their shirts off, and Tru is splashing around like a seal. Spenser is at the bank, tentative.

"Don't do it!" Aine says. "Your arm has to heal."

Spenser grimaces, a gesture she's never seen on his face, and dips his feet in. "I wasn't going to swim."

Brushing off his peevishness, Aine walks to the bank of the creek and plunges her hands in. The water is cool and sparkling. She puts her mouth to it and drinks deeply of the sweet water. "Have you had some?" she asks Spenser. He lets her help him drink, but she senses a space between them that had never been there before.

Gilgamesh joins them at the water's edge, stripping down to his underwear without any embarrassment. Aine turns away, but not before witnessing the livid white scars carved across his back. Five, maybe more, split his rippling muscles directly across the spine. She gasps, and he turns.

"I need a bath," he says simply.

She covers her shock. "You've needed one since we first met. Still, you're wasting time that we don't have."

Tru shrugs. "Can't go anywhere until we're big again."

Aine scowls. "I'm going to check the area, make sure we're safe until we resize. Spenser, does this feel like the seventh voyage?"

"Hard to tell. I hope so."

Shaking her head, she stalks off and circles their landing spot. The toadhouse has done well. They are near a banana tree heavily laden with yellow fruit, they have the creek, and no footprints besides theirs mar the ground. For the moment, the area seems as free from predators as *The Time Machine* in the daylight.

She returns to share the good news, resizing on the way, now used to the familiar ear pop but still delighted by the impossible joy of her cells stretching almost to the point of no return. She takes a moment to recalibrate to the world from a different level, and then resumes her walk. She finds all three of her traveling companions scrubbed clean and returned to normal size.

"You're the only one who still stinks," Tru jokes.

She runs her fingers through her hair. They catch on a knot. "I wouldn't mind a comb, but I'd rather find the rod. We're down to about ten hours before we need to return Tru. Shall we search for the city?"

"Yes!" Spenser and Tru respond in unison. The adventure of Sinbad seems to be a healing balm to Spenser's trauma.

"Wonderful. I'll grab the toadhouse," Aine says.

"What?" Gilgamesh sputters.

"We're bringing it with, of course."

Gilgamesh smiles grimly. "Of course. But I'll be carrying it. Your last treatment of it left something to be desired." Aine's is about to protest when he holds up his hands, palms out. "I didn't say it was your fault. Just humor me. The toadhouse is mine to protect."

Aine can't argue. She leads the way toward the sea under the assumption that a city would be near a port. The going is easier at full size, but the shifting sand quickly tires their calves. None of their bodies have healed from *The Time Machine*, and they stop to rest often. The ocean seems always just beyond their sight, and they're forced to walk farther and farther.

Still, the landscape is beautiful, the island a paradise of purple-plumed birds, decadent fruit hanging heavy off of trees, and the sweetly-singing creek leading them to the ocean. The apparent lack of human habitation worries Aine, but the rhythm of the island soothes her. Behind her, she senses the other three also releasing some burdens. The sensation is so relaxing that she almost stumbles right into the sandy clearing where a man stands, his back to them, with something on his shoulders.

If not for Gilgamesh's hand over her mouth, she would have given them away. He pulls her into the tropical brush, where knife-like leaves scrape her arms. Tru leads Spenser. They all crouch down and inch forward through a new type of plant, one with thick, soft vines, to spy on the person ahead who seems to be arguing with himself.

Tru, being the smallest next to Spenser, is the first to find a peeping spot still out of sight. He grabs Spenser's arm and whispers madly in his ear. Aine pushes forward impatiently. The smell hits her first. It's the scent of the unwashed, and the pungent, sour odor of old urine dominates. It's not what she smells but what she sees that stops her cold, however.

About fifty yards ahead, next to a draw-bucket well fed by their sweet-running creek, a tall, dark-skinned man stands hunched over, now facing them, his expression completely forlorn but striking even under his scraggly beard and mustache. His ribs are showing, and he is speaking loudly, angrily. A raggedy old whip of a man perches on his back with both feet locked into his captive's armpits, his face a painting of cruelty and glee.

The old man wears only a skirt of palm fronds, and his waste is visible down his carrier's back. He acts the mute, beating the shoulders on which he rests or pulling his carrier's hair to direct him toward this tree or that. Neither says a word. The carrier's achingly bent posture testifies to weeks of living like this. Tru has described the scene to Spenser in rapid whispers.

"That means we're in the fifth voyage, not the seventh," Spenser says under his breath. "The old man in the sea has locked himself onto Sinbad's back."

"How does Sinbad get away?"

"He tricks him," Spenser says. "What are they doing right now?"

"Sinbad has just taken the man to a banana tree. Geez, he's eating a banana right on top of Sinbad's head, and bits are falling everywhere. I feel sorry for that guy. Wait, Sinbad grabbed a coconut just now, and he's beating it with a rock. There you go, you can do it. He's handing the white part up to the stinky old guy, but...wait... he's keeping the shell for himself. He's looking at it now, like he just thought of something. Now he's looking our direction, he's still looking over here, now he's...wait! He's coming this way!"

There isn't time to run. All four of them pull back into the vines, making themselves as unobtrusive as possible. Sinbad pauses feet from them and plucks something from the vines. Grapes. His hands full, he returns to the side of the well, where he makes hard work of balancing the man while pounding the fruit. The four of them breathe a sigh of relief.

"I guess we're hiding in some grape vines," Tru says belatedly. "Sinbad grabbed a bunch, and now he's squeezing them into the coconut shell. Maybe we should gather some juice for the toadhouse." He goes to punch playfully at Gilgamesh's shoulder but Spenser comes between them and lurches out into the clearing.

"Spenser!" Aine warns in a hiss.

It's too late. Spenser crashes out of the vines and walks straight toward the well, feeling the ground with his cane. The old man tightens his legs visibly around Sinbad's throat at the sight of the small, pale boy.

"What have we here?" Sinbad asks through choked breath. "A blind boy, on this island? Allah be praised, have you been saved from a shipwreck as well?"

Spenser doesn't slow. He walks straight to Sinbad, sniffs the air, then puts his hand out tentatively toward the half-gourd of grape juice.

"Are you thirsty, son? You're welcome to this. I can make more."

Spenser, one arm still in a sling, hooks his cane to his pocket so he can accept the juice with the other. He bears forward as if to drink, but instead whispers a single word and hands it back to Sinbad.

Sinbad sniffs it wonderingly, and a blinding grin lights his face. "Allah Almighty, the juice has become wine! Indeed, there is no one higher than Allah, and he be praised. Is this a trick you can do more than once, little Jinn?"

Spenser nods. From their hiding spot, Tru, Gilgamesh, and especially Aine watch, ready to pounce should Spenser need them. He has a plan, that's clear, but they have no idea what. Soon, Sinbad has a whole row of wine-sotted gourds lined up along the well, and he's offering one to Spenser.

"You've certainly earned it, little Jinn. No? Well, any other favor in my power to grant you, I will." The old man on his back is scowling mightily, his legs holding as tight as nails in wood.

Spenser nods with a pleased expression and backs up to the grapevines.

"Leaving already, Jinn? Well, may Allah bless your travels. If we should meet again, remember you'll always have a friend in Sinbad." He is drinking heartily of the wine, and begins to dance a hot-footed jig. When Spenser finally reaches the full cover of the vines, he's sporting a beaming smile.

"What was that all about?" Tru whispers.

"That's how he tricks the old man off his shoulders. He gets him drunk."

"How'd you know how to do that?" Aine asks.

"Sura."

The sudden memory of the fairy turning Gilgamesh's juice into wine is painfully vivid—Sura's beautiful mahogany face, her teasing, gentle nature. Aine also remembers the whisper of a word Sura spoke to the juice, too quietly for her to hear but not for her brother's finely tuned ears.

"Good work," Aine says, amazed at her brother's ingenuity.

He ducks his head, a secret smile on his face. "I had to help him, though I don't know what it got us."

"Sinbad's favor," Gilgamesh says, setting the toadhouse quietly on the ground. He indicates for the three of them to enter. "That's something we may be able to use if we ever make it to his seventh voyage."

Aine hears the lonely click of another page in the archetyper turning.

Chapter 32

"Do you think this is it?"

Ahead, a huge mountain soars so high its white-capped peaks nearly block out the sun. Rubber trees cascade down its side, their roots strong and seeking, gripping the ground like weathered hands. Glorious parrots try to outwarble plain brown nightingales among the thick canopy, and they lose. The lushness of the vegetation renders the air thick and green with health. An initial lungful refreshes, and repeated breaths strengthen. It smells sweet, like blooming fruit trees. It is late afternoon.

"I hope so," Tru responds. "I like it here."

All four of them stand outside the toadhouse, which has landed in the welcoming roots of a banyan tree. A dime-sized butterfly with translucent silver wings flutters close to his head, flirting, before drifting off to rest on the pollen-dusted petals of a giant violet flower.

"We can't be sure," Aine says, searching the sky. At this size, she is especially wary of predators.

By way of response, Gilgamesh points toward the mountain

top. An ugly cloud of grey maneuvers toward it erratically. Distant screeching reaches their ears, followed by a lightning strike of deep red flame. It targets the center of the inky cloud, which breaks up, revealing a flock of birds. They must be gigantic up close, each as least as large as a grown man. One beast breaks off from the rest and careens toward the earth. It's carrying a load on his back. When the bird creature is within two hundred yards of the top of a rubber tree, he releases his load with an accusatory caw.

"The birdman's just dropped Sinbad!" Tru yells, jumping into the air. "We did it! We're in the seventh voyage! I get to go home soon, and you'll have your rod."

Aine looks at her brother, her voice proud. "You did it, Spenser."

"We don't have the rods yet," he says with a quick smile.

"No, but soon." She feels in her bones that they are close to getting the metal rod that Glori prophesied, close to seeing Helen again and being wrapped in her lavender-scented embrace. "We should take the archetyper out so we can keep an eye on it."

Gilgamesh nods curtly. "I agree. Do you have room for it in your bag?" He reaches in and hands the mechanism to Aine.

It's surprisingly light. Aine studies it up close for the first time. She can almost make out the tiny letters dropping like grains of sand into their crucible. When five of them exit the crucible as a word, she reads it: *tears*. Only a tablespoon or so of letters remain. Thirteen pages are unturned.

"I don't think we have more than six hours, depending on how much time passes in these last pages."

"Maybe we could just go up and ask Sinbad for the rod," Tru suggests over her shoulder. "Would that change the story?"

Spenser tips his head. "I think so. Sinbad is gifted with one of the rods then needs it to strike the giant snake. Afterward, they run into a crowd and Sinbad gives it to the man he saved. That man disappears. If we take it from *him*, it shouldn't affect the outcome of the story because he sorta walks off the page."

"That sounds like our only option," Gilgamesh says. "Let's hope to High Elfame that this rod is the right one."

"If Sinbad's golden staff is the one we're after, will Biblos know as soon as we have it?" Spenser asks.

Gilgamesh's jaw tightens at mention of the name. "Yes. Collecting the correct object will resonate across every story. We'll keep the toadhouse close."

This time Gilgamesh leads the way, making slow time until they resize. It takes them three full minutes to scale a tree root that they could have stepped over without a second thought in their normal size. As they drop to the other side of the branch, a pained expression appears on Tru's face.

"I have to use the outhouse," he says.

Gilgamesh knits his brows then points toward a scrub plant as large as the toadhouse in their miniature state. Tru smiles gratefully then scurries off. They turn their backs.

"I really like this place," Tru jabbers as he walks away from them. "It's got a nice smell to it, almost like candy. Makes me hungry. Think we'll ever have candy again? I sure would—"

He stops in midsentence. Aine cocks her ear. No more words from Tru. She and Gilgamesh exchange a look. "Tru?" she says.

No answer.

She grabs Spenser's good hand with hers, and all three dash toward the scrub. They find Tru on the other side mashed face-first into a spider web three times his height. He is twisting, and the more he moves, the more the sticky white strands adhere to him.

"Hold still!" Aine commands. She pulls the pen knife out of her bag and slices at the gluey strings. Gilgamesh stands back and watches with Spenser at his side.

"Aren't you going to help?" Aine asks. She looks around for the hideous spider that surely lurks nearby.

Gilgamesh crosses his arms in lieu of an answer. Aine opens her mouth, ready to curse at him, when her ears pop. Her flesh tingles then stretches, and it feels like a million little butterflies are kissing her tenderest flesh. Instantly she is resized, as are Tru, Spenser, and Gilgamesh. Other than a face full of spider goo, Tru is none the worse for wear.

"Did I say I liked this place?" he asks, trying in vain to remove the sticky webbing from his clothes and face. "I've since changed my mind."

"No one goes off alone anymore. Ever." Gilgamesh turns to walk into the forest.

The three of them follow, and soon all four are sweating. The salty-hot clamminess of their skin attracts mosquitoes as loud as airplanes along with brambles, dropping spiders, and the blows from branches prematurely released by the person in front. The banyan roots seem particularly interested in bedeviling Tru, tripping him at every turn and taking a lick at his knees when he falls.

"Can we rest?" he asks. His arms and legs are welted, his knees bloody, and his hair decorated with bits of leaves and twigs.

The other three aren't faring any better. The mosquitoes and spiders seem to know better than to bother Gilgamesh, but as the front line of their troop, he's taking a special beating from the branches. Sweat drenches the back of his shirt in a V-pattern, and his long hair has come loose from its binding and clings to his face.

Spenser, his right arm still in a sling, has always been sweet meat to bugs despite Aine's best efforts to swat them away. One of his eyes is nearly swollen shut from bites, and a rip has appeared on the sleeve covering his good arm from repeatedly dragging it through branches to swat at himself. He doesn't complain. Aine sports only a few bug bites, but a permanent swarm of gnats buzz at her eyes. Her legs from the bottom of her skirt to the top of her socks are scratched by brambles, and she vows to get her hands on a sensible pair of pants at the next opportunity.

"The bugs'll find us quicker if we stop moving," she says. "Besides, we don't want the man who receives the golden staff from Sinbad to escape before we see what he looks like. We should keep going."

"Here." Gilgamesh at her side startles her. He offers her a fan-shaped palm frond. "It'll cut down on the bugs." He offers identical fronds to the boys, and they resume their trek, waving away the insects.

"Aine," Tru asks after countless strained footsteps, "what was your grandma like?"

She'd been daydreaming of swimming in the crystal clear creek she'd seen in Sura's Tir Na Nog. The question catches her off guard. "Grandma Glori? Why?"

"It's just that…" He coughs uncomfortably. "Well, everyone in town said she was a witch. Who ate children."

Aine snorts. "How'd they explain us?"

"Said you two were bait," he offers cheerfully. "Like, to draw other kids in so your grandma could cook 'em up in the oven."

"That's ridiculous. Did any children ever disappear that you're aware of?"

"That's not how it works," Gilgamesh says sadly, holding back a whip-taut bamboo branch so the children can pass. "Fairies try to help the stories, but they're different than everyone else in the book. They never quite blend in, and they're treated poorly for it. It's true across every story. The one who stands out is hurt by those around her."

"Why do people do it?" Tru asks.

"Why did you?" Gilgamesh asks sharply.

Tru snaps his mouth shut. Then he opens it. "I didn't say I *believed* she was a witch. I said that's what other people said."

"Not a witch but a fairy, and not just any fairy," Aine says proudly. "She was the queen of the fairies once. Sura told us."

"Gloriana was a grand leader, though a little too harsh for some right up until she stepped down from her throne to watch over you two," Gilgamesh agrees, resuming his position in the lead. "There was no one with a more generous heart, I'll tell you that. But she wasn't your true grandmother, and I'll wager Sura shared that with you also."

"Gilgamesh," Spenser asks, "you're a fairy, right?"

Gilgamesh picks up his pace and stops holding branches for those behind him. He speaks as if through a closed jaw. "You've tricked me again, haven't you? Gotten me to reveal information only your mother should tell you. I've already said too much."

All the coaxing in the world from Aine doesn't get as much as a grunt out of Gilgamesh. They're forced to trot to keep up with him. The only blessing is that their faster movement, plus the palm fronds, cuts down on the bugs. They stop once more, to drink water from a clear-flowing stream and eat plump mangoes plucked from a nearby tree. Other than that, they march. The jungle is full of noise—the shriek of exotic birds, the burbling of water, the maddening buzz of insects. The only sound with any cadence is their footstrikes on the damp earth or against the tough bark of a tree root.

Gradually the trees thin out, the terrain becomes rockier, and their steps take on a different rhythm. It's hypnotizing, at least for three of them. The fourth, the one without sight, relies heavily on his other senses, and he picks the alien noise first.

"A snake."

Tru jumps and glances at his feet. "Where?"

"A giant one."

Before Spenser can explain, they all hear it coming from a few hundred yards ahead, on the other side of a ridge: a hiss like a thousand marbles rolling down a metal roof and a man, hollering for his life.

Chapter 33

"Wait!" Gilgamesh holds out his arm to stop Aine from charging over the ridge. "If Sinbad isn't yet on the scene, we must let him rescue the man and give him the golden rod. It's the only way to retrieve it without altering the story."

They all nod in agreement. Renewed, they jog toward the sound. Gilgamesh waves them down as they reach the lip of the outcropping. Forty yards below, a black-with-white snake as long as a cargo train slithers toward a man dressed in robes. The man frantically backs away while screaming for Allah to release him. The snake dips its lazy head and tastes the air around the man with its forked tongue. The last rays of the setting sun highlight a faint checker pattern on its back. The man lets out a moan, and the snake rears up and flares its head, revealing a demonic hood.

"A cobra," Tru breathes. He explains what he's witnessing to Spenser by habit. "It's about to...oh! There it goes. The man tried to run away, and he tripped. The snake's got him in his mouth right up to his knees. Now to his belly button. But wait! Sinbad has just shown up! He's running down a path toward the man and the snake."

Sinbad is paunchier than when they'd last seen him, his body soft and his face growing jowly from an easy life. He still appears strong, however. He wears a Persian fighting knife thrust in a sash at his waist, and he carries a magnificent rod of red gold nearly a head taller than him. It glints warmly in the sun. The sight of it makes Aine tingle.

"Most High Allah, this cannot be!" Sinbad rushes at the snake, wielding the staff over his head. The first blow falls between the snake's beady brown eyes. The cobra, unable to react because of the heavy meal in its mouth, spits out its prey. The man falls to the ground, his robes soaked with thick, glistening saliva. The snake rears back as if to strike again, its hood wide and its tongue shivering with rage. Sinbad swings the rod a second time, striking below the head and drawing blood. The snake recoils and skids down the other side of the ridge.

The rescued man lies prostrate at Sinbad's feet. "You are God come to rescue me."

"No, I am not God. There is only one, and his name is Allah. But he has sent me to you, and I'm grateful for his care of my fellow creatures." Sinbad offers his hand. "We should leave the area before the snake returns."

The man seems loathe to stand in the presence of one he considers so great but Sinbad insists. The man rises. "Since you delivered me from the serpent, I will never leave your side as long as you desire."

It's all Aine can do not to tell them to hurry up already and exchange the golden staff.

"I welcome the company as we walk on this mountain," Sinbad says, clapping him on the back. Together, they return to the path leading downward as if nothing unusual had just happened.

"Did you see that?" Tru asks incredulously. "They act like they just played a game of hopscotch instead of wrestled a giant cobra. That's so weird."

Gilgamesh nods. "It depends on the fairy writing the story. Some of them craft action scenes very well but have difficulty with the connecting parts. The characters, for better or worse, have to live their stories as written."

"But Sura said a writer can't include everything," Aine interrupts, "and that even if we can't see it, it's in the world the book occupies."

"The book doesn't occupy the world," Gilgamesh corrects. "It *is* the world. But it's true that things happen outside of the dialogue and description set down on paper, things the reader never sees. Such is likely the case with Sinbad and his new friend as we speak. They must be conversing about topics never covered in the original story."

"So a book is Fate?" Aine asks.

"As long as you're in your own book it is." He indicates the two men. "They're getting away."

Aine holds out the archetyper. Five pages remain. "And we're running out of time."

They follow Sinbad and his companion for nearly an hour. The deepening night brings more bugs along with eerie jungle noises that are strange to them and so come with imagined teeth and claws. A low mist necklaces the tree trunks, giving the forest a mysterious, otherworldly feel. Soon Gilgamesh is carrying Spenser. Collapse is imminent for both when a commotion ahead signals that they don't have long to wait. They are reaching part of the story where Sinbad encounters a group of people before giving the staff to the man he rescued and taking off with the bird man who dropped him from the sky.

They hide behind a tree not far from the meeting spot, a cross-roads overlooking a cliff. One path goes up the mountain while the other continues down. Approximately twenty brightly clothed men stand at the intersection conversing loudly. Goats and camels, discombobulated by the darkness, push against each other and scare up dust. The men welcome Sinbad and his new friend, and then begin to set up camp. The animals are tied at the perimeter, and several small campfires are lit. The soothing smell of burning wood soon reaches the foursome.

"When is our man getting the rod?" Tru asks.

"Definitely before morning," Spenser says. "But I don't think the book was real clear on the exact time."

Tru's stomach rumbles. "I'm hungry."

Aine glances down at the archetyper as another page turns. "We have to move in close so we can retrieve the rod as soon as Sinbad hands it off."

"No," says Gilgamesh. "As soon as we leave cover and head into the clearing, we give ourselves away. It could change the whole story besides destroying our chance of getting the rod."

"Unless…" Spenser and Aine say the word at the same time, and Aine is delighted. He's thinking what she's thinking.

"I disguise us all," she finishes. "We can get in close, set up a fire, eat dinner, and be right there when the rod is exchanged. It's our best shot!"

Gilgamesh doesn't love the idea, but he can't come up with a better one. After studying the group of Arabian men for several seconds, Aine faces her companions and concentrates. First Spenser is altered, becoming a tall, dark-haired man wearing a turban, with a curved scimitar at his waist. After that is Tru, who becomes a near twin to Spenser, except where Spenser's pants are a midnight blue, Tru's are silky green.

She changes Gilgamesh next, modifying only his clothes so they become the flowing, comfortable tunics with balloon pants that she's seen on the other men and put on Spenser and Tru. She changes her shape last, becoming the tallest of the group. Her white shirt contrasts beautifully with her now-dark skin.

"We all look good?" she asks.

Gilgamesh nods, appearing a little startled as he studies the three of them, particularly Aine. "If I didn't know any better, I'd say we were travel-weary nomads."

They gather scraps of wood from the edge of the forest and walk cautiously toward the other travelers. Aine is uncomfortable with the bustle and chatter of the crowd, but she feigns confidence, which she finds easier now that she is disguised as a man. She files that away to think on later.

The nearer they get, the more she can smell the sour sweat of the goats mingled with the scents of smoke, travel, and a diet of meat and spices. She wrinkles her nose but says nothing. They choose a spot on the farthest edge of the camp, close enough to have a clear view of Sinbad and his companion yet far enough away that their conversation won't be overheard.

Aine reaches into the toadhouse for two water skins, a package of meat, and four of the plump *Time Machine* cherries. She divides it while Gilgamesh lights a fire from branches they'd gathered on the way. Soon they are seated comfortably around the crackling flames, eating in a companionable silence and periodically glancing over at Sinbad and his friend.

Tru breaks the silence. "We've been through quite a lot, haven't we?"

Aine stops chewing. The sweet bite of cherry becomes difficult to swallow. "Yes," she says.

They eat some more, but slowly, Aine now deep in her own thoughts. They're each worlds away from their homes, and safety, and comfort. This isn't the first moment of rest they've had since they've left their book, but being amongst other people, even if they're strangers, gives her a strange feeling of safety. Plus, she feels a little celebratory. Her brother is alive, and they're near to obtaining the first key.

Aine considers that it was just three days ago that she and Spenser were playing hide-and-go-seek in the woods, Aine having hardly a care in the world except for missing her mom and chafing against Glori's rules. What irony that now that she'd gotten her deepest wish—they were traveling to Helen—she wanted nothing more than for everything to be back as it was. Now books were worlds, monsters existed, friends died. She'd nearly lost her brother.

"Aine?"

Startled, she looks at Spenser to her right. She'd clouded him with an exotic height and coloring, but she'd left his dark eyes exactly as they were, and so it's not uncomfortable to hear his voice come out of a man's face. "Yes?"

He seems to be staring at the fire, though she knows this is an illusion. He can no more see in this form than he can in his previous one. He draws in a deep breath. "I don't blame you."

She inhales sharply. She's afraid to move, to blink, to acknowledge that he's just given voice to her greatest fear. She realizes she's shaking. "It's okay, Spenser. I brought us to the wrong story, then I left you there when you needed me the most. You have a right to be mad. I messed up. No one has ever messed up as badly as me. I-"

"Stop."

Aine swivels, startled by the timbre of Gilgamesh's voice. His eyes are haunted, the flickering fire reflecting off his livid scar. The toadhouse rests between him and Aine. He shoves his hand into it and come out with a book. "I am the only one to blame. For all of this."

He's unable to meet her eyes. Aine recognizes the book he is holding toward her. It is the only book Gilgamesh owns. Her heart is racing. She reaches for it. She reads the front cover.

The Epic of Gilgamesh.

She's breathless. "It's a book about you?"

He looks up, the raw pain on his face difficult to bear. "It's the first book the fairies wrote. It collapsed when I was taken from it. That's the only remaining copy, a gift to me from Kenning." He spits out the word "gift," his mouth twisted excruciatingly.

She pages gently through the yellowed leafs of brittle paper bound in worn soft leather. "You were quite the hero," she observes, after reading a passage. "Why'd you leave?"

"I was commanded to by Finvarra. Gloriana's brother, current king of the Fairies. He wanted me to be his private pilot."

Aine raises her eyebrows. "He destroyed your whole world for that?"

"Yes. He's a man of…whims."

Aine closes the book with a snap and hands it back. She doesn't want to hold this much sadness. All that's left of his world, everything familiar to him, his home, has been destroyed. She'd felt that same level of loss when she'd thought Spenser was dead. "How old are you, Gilgamesh?"

"I was seventeen when Finvarra wrenched me from my story, and seventeen I'll always be. Humans age in their stories, and fairies age wherever they are, albeit more slowly. A human snatched from his story, however, is frozen in time."

"At least you can still read about your world."

Gilgamesh shakes his head, an ashy mix of sadness and fury on his face. "Pages disappear from it every day. Its structure isn't sound without me. I belong nowhere. I've been cast out of Tir Na Nog, cursed to forever travel between stories until Biblos is booktrapped."

"Why?" Aine asks, and she means *everything*.

Gilgamesh's face seems to slide, and he looks down at his hands. They are tan, rough, scarred. His voice echoes off his ribs when he speaks. "On one of our journeys, Finvarra fell in love. Wars had already been waged in the woman's name, so great was her beauty. She'd been stolen from her rightful husband by the man who was to become Biblos. Finvarra then stole her from Biblos and that book."

Aine completes the thought. "Destroying her story like he'd destroyed yours."

"Yes, but not before nearly killing Biblos, who was out of his mind at the thought of losing his love. He charged Finvarra. Finvarra uttered a single spell—tuaslagadh—and Biblos should have dissolved. But just as the spell hurtled toward him, he jumped behind his story's toadhouse. Part of the spell got him, part hit the toadhouse, and it somehow melted them together into a man-creature with some of the warped power of the toadhouse. He can grow and shrink, throw word curses, and, some say, speak babble in your mind that will make you crazy.

"Finvarra didn't realize this immediately, of course. Biblos appeared mutilated and dying, a bloody breathing lump of smoking flesh. Certain Biblos was dead, he ordered me to transport him and his new bride to Tir Na Nog. I did, thus ensuring destruction for everyone in that story." Gilgamesh poked at the fire. In the main camp, someone took out a wooden flute and began playing a soft, sad melody.

"Just as your story had been destroyed."

Gilgamesh clenches his jaw. "Exactly. Which is why I went back for Biblos without Finvarra's knowledge. I couldn't leave that man to suffer any more than he had. Imagine my surprise when I returned to find him healing, and able to sit up and speak. I assumed the toadhouse he'd been melded with had imparted some of its magic, but at the time, I had no idea how much. Taking pity on him, I transported him to the *Apocrypha*, where I was certain Finvarra would never find him. I told him a bit about the fairy world. I also warned him not to change the outcome of the story or he would become booktrapped forever and die at the end." Gilgamesh draws a ragged breath before continuing.

"Biblos was clever, and he was driven by anger so sharp that it warped into madness. Shortly after I left him, he located the agent in the story and tortured him for the secret of escaping it. He also, for spite, killed Thomas, the man who'd befriended him in the *Apocrypha*. Then he found the toadhouse in that story and set out for revenge. Biblos still doesn't know how to travel to Tir Na Nog, where Finvarra lives with his wife, but he's gathered enough information to get close. Finvarra became aware of him, eventually, but it was too late. Biblos Skulas has destroyed thousands of books in his hunt to reclaim his lover and destroy the fairy kingdom as Finvarra destroyed his."

Aine is silent for a time. "This is your great mistake Sura referred to." It's not a question.

Gilgamesh nods, his shoulders heavy under the weight. "I am the reason Biblos has become the monster he is. I unleashed him on the stories. I am the reason Gloriana is dead."

"Finvarra has something to answer for," Aine says fiercely.

"But I didn't learn, did I?" Gilgamesh abruptly locks eyes with her. Her skin tingles from her tips to her toes. He almost drops the gaze but holds fast, his cheeks blazing. "Finvarra told me that only one of you is destined to return to Tir Na Nog, that there would come a moment when I would have to choose between the two of you, and that only one would survive. I believed him. Spenser." He drops Aine's eyes. His voice is urgent. "I took your sister away from you. I knocked her unconscious and took her from your side when you needed her the most."

Spenser had been quiet during Gilgamesh's entire confession. "I know," he says simply.

"What?"

He shifts. "Well, I didn't know that you knocked her unconscious, but I knew that Aine would never leave me. She smothers me sometimes, but she's my sister."

"Spenser?" Aine asks. She hears her voice quivering.

"It's true," he says, talking over her rapidly. "You need to trust me more and let me make more of my own choices. I know you love me, but I'm not a baby. You have to let me grow up."

"But when you came to in *Dr. Jekyll and Mr. Hyde*, you told me..." She can't finish the sentence.

Tru doesn't have the same compunction. "You accused her of not being there for you. Sounded like you were mad."

The Arabian face Spenser is wearing looks confused. "I would never say that."

"It was the pain," Gilgamesh says gruffly. "It can take us outside of ourselves."

Aine suddenly feels so light she could dance. She lunges over to hug Spenser. The flute playing stops for a moment, then a cheer goes up from the crowd of men. Aine realizes they are being stared at and sits back down, embarrassed. The music picks up again, this time playing a rollicking, capering tune.

"I forgive you too, Gilgamesh," Spenser says around the music. "If you thought you could only save one, you were smart to do that rather than let both of us die. If you're a hero in your book like Aine says, I'm sure you know all about making tough decisions."

"I'm not the hero," Gilgamesh says.

Aine realizes he's staring at her again. She looks over. His expression is intense, his eyes burning so brightly that she wonders what he could possibly say. "Someone once said something very wise to me: 'You have to fight for what's important to you, not what's important to someone else.'"

He reaches into his shirt and unclasps the silver chain around his neck. She sees for the first time that a quarter-sized medallion etched with two tiny waves dangles off the end. She flushes as he stands to place it around her neck. When his hand accidentally brushes the sensitive spot near her ear, she shivers with the same electricity she feels when resizing. He finishes clasping it and returns quickly to his seat by the fire. The necklace, warm from his body heat, rests directly above her heart.

He stares into the flames. "I received that amulet from my mother the day I was crowned king. I give it to you with pride, Aine, and my thanks for saving Tru and Spenser, and ultimately, for showing me the way back." His voice is hoarse. The fire reflects off the water in his eyes. "I also give you my solemn vow that from this day forward we fight as a team, no matter what comes our way."

Aine is too stunned to respond. Spenser speaks for both of them. "That's a deal," he says.

"Look!" Tru says, breaking the moment.

They all turn. On the other side of the gathering, Sinbad has entered a heated discussion with one of the travelers. The two men appear to reach an agreement. Sinbad hands the golden staff to the man he rescued, who bows deeply and begins to gather his bedding. Then Sinbad walks down the hill with the man he'd just been arguing with.

"They made the switch!" Aine says. "But where is the man with the staff going?"

"He probably wants to protect his new treasure," Gilgamesh says. "Let's follow him."

They quickly douse the fire and put the remaining food inside the toadhouse, which Gilgamesh carries. They just manage to get everything packed as the man disappears over the hill, following the path up the mountain. Fortunately, he doesn't go far. He sets up camp in a small natural cave off to one side of the path. The den is dangerously near the steep edge of the mountain but has a natural lip that shields him from a fall and provides protection from the elements and passing travelers.

They duck behind an enormous banyan root and peer out. They are lucky they trailed closely. The man is not so far away that a tossed stone wouldn't hit him, but from any other angle, he'd be invisible.

"What now?" Tru asks.

Gilgamesh glances up at the moon. "He falls asleep, and we take the staff."

"There's no time." Aine holds up the archetyper. The moon glints off of it. Even in the descending dark, it is clear there's only one page left. "With Sinbad gone, we can take the staff without affecting the story. It's now or never."

"I'll go," Gilgamesh says.

Aine shakes her head. "I'm the fastest and the best climber, even with my sore arm." Before they can argue, she drops her bag and the archetyper then shoots across the open expanse. The ground is hard-packed outside of the tree cover. Plumes of dust rise from her moonlit footsteps. The air is perfumed with spicy-sweet ylang ylang and frangipani. Exotic night birds strike up their calls, cawing a mysterious language across the tree tops. Aine senses all this around her, but her focus is on the door-sized opening of the cave. She reaches the side of it in three seconds.

Hugging the stone with her back, she peers into the opening. It's shadowed, but the moon gleams off an edge of gold at the far end. It would be dangerous to approach that edge from the front. She'd be in full moonlight, visible to the man inside and vulnerable to his attack. She needs to nab the rod without him every noticing, and that leaves only one route: across the roof of the cave.

Aine scrambles up the side of the rock, favoring her good arm and clinging to vines. The top is five feet across and slopes down toward a lip that marks the edge of the mountain. The drop beyond that is thousands of feet. Aine glances toward the forest. She sees Gilgamesh is staring at her with steely eyes, concern written plainly on his face. Tru has taken her bag and the archetyper. Spenser is twisting his hair.

She crosses the five feet marking the roof of the den. The vines hold securely. She stops when she's climbed as close as she can to the drop without tumbling to a certain death. She refuses to look down, though she can hear the distant shushing of a river from far below. A thick rope of vine leads off into the abyss. She yanks on it and finds it firm. Holding the thick fiber with one hand, she scoots to the mouth of the cave and peers down. The golden staff is only two feet away. The man has left it near the cliff's edge, confident no one can approach from that side.

Aine spots him at the rear of the narrow, shallow cave. It's shadowy, but she can tell his back is to her. It's time to act. She reaches forward, upside down, her upper body stretched across the mouth of the cave. Her left hand holds the vine while her right reaches for the staff. It's a foot from the staff, then eight inches, then six. She can almost feel the cool metal, hear the directions to the next clue, see the beautiful face of her mom. She is smiling grimly, her fingers two inches from the metal. The moon lights it up as if it's golden fire. This surely is the correct rod.

Her trembling fingers barely touch the edge of the gleaming staff. The nearness sends shivers up her arm. She needs just a hair of give from the vine to grasp the gold. A tug buys her another half an inch. Her fingers curl around the metal.

"Thief!" The man appears at the edge the cave, his angry face shoved in hers. He grasps her wrist and pulls, sending Aine tumbling into the chasm.

Chapter 34

Her first sensation is shock, then icy white terror. She grasps at air, rock, earth, spots a flash of gold fly past. Then a crunch, and she stops. The narrowest ledge has caught her twelve feet below the mouth of the cave. Her panic is so deep that nausea overcomes her. She peers down. The bottom of the chasm stretches so deep that the moon can't plumb its depths. But what's that, just below her ledge? The rod! It fell with her and is caught on a scrub bush growing from the side of the cliff face.

She lies flat with her sore arm stretched over the side. It's no use. The golden staff is too far. "Help!"

A voice from above rings with disbelief. "What? You're a woman?"

"Out of my way. Aine, are you all right?" It's Gilgamesh. She can't see his face with the moon behind him, but she recognizes his outline.

"I'm okay. I landed on a ledge. The staff is below!"

"Hold on."

She hears rustling from above. "Anyone have a knife?"

"I have a pen knife." It's Spenser. He sounds scared. "You're going to be okay, Aine. Gilgamesh is cutting some vines so we can pull you up."

"It won't work! They're too thick. You, do you have a knife?"

"No, and I wouldn't give it to you if I had. This girl tried to steal my golden staff!"

"She just needed to borrow it," Spenser says. "We're friends of Sinbad."

"I don't believe it."

Aine hears Spenser gather his breath. "Sinbad!" he yells, and he keeps yelling.

Aine doesn't think it'll do much good. Tru's archetyper must only have a handful of words left. They'll never cut through one of the vines in time to pull her up and get Tru back, even with Sinbad's help.

"Who-hoah, little Jinn! You found me again."

"Sinbad! My sister has fallen over the ledge. Can you save her?"

"I'm certain I can, and I'd be honored to repay your favor." Aine hears the rustling of cloth, and suddenly a band of white appears. "Grab on to my turban, child."

"Tru!" Aine cries, glancing down at the metal staff. It's so close, this key to her mother and her homeland. "How much time?"

"Fourteen letters left to fall."

Aine's heart drops. She has enough cloth to reach the rod, but it will cost Tru his world. She cinches the end of Sinbad's turban around her waist and begins to climb. A great force tugs her the rest of the way up before she's gone half the distance, and she finds herself in the arms of Gilgamesh, Tru, and Spenser.

"Don't ever scare me like that again, Aine," Gilgamesh says.

It's the first time he's called her by her name. She flushes, and Gilgamesh seems to become aware of how tightly he's squeezing her. He drops his arms and points at the edge of the cave. The toadhouse rests there, next to the dumbfounded owner of the staff and a beaming Sinbad. "We have to leave now."

Aine follows the boys in quickly, ignoring the momentary shrinking sensation. Gilgamesh enters right behind her and goes straight for the plotter. Aine peers outside. Sinbad is on his knees, gigantic, staring at them inside their transportation. "I'll have to tell the story of this in my eighth voyage," he says with wonder.

Gilgamesh is at the plotter, whispering frantically. Tru and Spenser rest on the cot. The toadhouse trembles and turns. Sinbad's face appears at the same time on each rotation, then blurs before disappearing entirely along with the beautifully-scented Indian air. The black closes in.

Tru holds up the archetyper and faces Aine. The last letter drops into its crucible. The crucible spits out a word. The word travels to the book. The page begins to turn.

Chapter 35

The toadhouse crashes into light, screeches against something solid, then drops, upsetting everything inside that isn't nailed down. They've landed with the door to the ground. Thick grass tufts through the window.

"Did we make it?" Spenser cries. He is lying on top of Aine, and Tru is on top of him. He seems unbothered by his arm.

"I don't know." Aine gently disentangles herself. Gilgamesh is across the room, bleeding from his head. "What happened?"

Gilgamesh stands, reaching for a comfort cloth that's come to rest near him. He holds it to his bleeding head "My best guess is that we landed in a tree, and then fell to the ground. Is everyone all right?"

"I think so," Tru says. He holds up the archetyper, which he hadn't released in the fall. "But sir, my time's up." The book is complete.

Gilgamesh scowls. "Let's get outside. If this is your story, we've made it in time. Here, help me push."

They all rock and push on the same wall, rotating the toadhouse enough so they can crawl out the window. Spenser smells it first. "Mimosas!"

"The farmhouse!" Aine points as she jumps to see across the height of the grass.

Across the clearing is Grandma Glori's perfect, weathered home. They are at the edge of their forest. Around them, whispering sycamore leaves rustle in the faint, humid Alabama breeze, and a mockingbird welcomes them back with its song.

"Tru, we're here! We made it." Her relief is intense. Despite the horrors they'd witnessed here, this story has been her home for five years.

"Hallelujah!" Tru crawls out of the window and doesn't bother to stand. Instead he kisses the ground then rolls in it like an itchy dog. Blades of grass tower over him like mighty bamboo. "I'm home."

Spenser giggles. "Everything smells and sounds just like it should."

"Looks that way, too," Tru says, using Spenser's good arm to leverage himself up then hopping so he can see over the stalks of grass. "It's exactly like we left it."

"How long have we been gone?" Aine asks.

"No way of telling for sure, not without a copy of the book," Gilgamesh says. "Each story has its own pace. There's no master clock. We wait here until we resize. I nearly got eaten by a fox last time I was here."

All four of them stay near the house. Spenser and Tru chatter excitedly despite Aine's admonitions. She stands guard with Vishnu's arrow in her hand, on alert for snakes and skunks. Gilgamesh does the same on the opposite side of the toadhouse. The minutes pass with blessed uneventfulness, and they soon return to normal size.

"Look." Gilgamesh appears alongside Aine and points toward

the house. Across the clearing, they can just make out a black slash cutting through the left side of the porch, marking the spot where Biblos' murdered Glori. They have arrived after the attack, that much they know. Aine swallows painfully. Glori's body is likely below the slash, lying in two pieces in a pool of coagulating blood. Gilgamesh tucks the toadhouse under his arm and Aine returns to the moment and the task at hand.

"Spenser, Tru, you two stay in the woods. Gilgamesh and I will check on the house."

"You sure?" Gilgamesh asks, studying her. "I can do this alone."

Aine walks toward the house by way of answer. She knows he wants to protect her from seeing Glori's butchered body. She also knows she can reach the porch in less than a second if she wants, but she's not in a hurry. The familiar smells and sounds make the memory all that much more vivid. Intense, powerful Gloriana, their protector, sliced in two, yelling an unfinished warning to her charges, forever frozen in time. Aine doesn't want to see the body, but she needs to.

"Mondegreen's body is gone," she says as they pass the spot where Biblos' blue, airborne blade pierced Glori's companion. "Biblos?"

Gilgamesh shakes his head. "He wouldn't waste his time. He doesn't value life or death, whether it's human or fairy. It's more likely Tone returned to bury our dead."

They near the porch. Aine imagines she can still smell the sulfur stench of Biblos' weapons, the smoky burn of the thick wood railing, the iron odor of freshly drawn blood. She takes the first step and then the second. She doesn't want to look, doesn't want to see the body of the woman she called grandmother sliced in half, but she owes her that respect.

She's on the porch. She turns her head to the spot where she'd last seen Glori.

The body is gone.

Glori's blood stains the wooden planks, thick and muddy. The rocking chair upset during the battle is still on its side. But she is gone.

A voice comes from the far side of the house on the other side of the porch. "Aine?"

She glances up, startled, as Mondegreen limps toward her. Her absolute astonishment mirrors his. He'd been a steady presence in her life as far back as she could remember. She understands now that he hadn't always played that role, that he'd had a complete family before he'd come to live in this story with Glori, but still, his familiar newsy cap, his broad shoulders and open arms—it all looks like home.

"Mondegreen!" She leaps over the railing and lands at his feet.

He pulls her into a bear hug despite the thick, bloodied bandage around his waist and the purple and green bruises rimming his neck. "You're alive!"

"I could say the same for you," she says into his chest. The squeeze hurts her shoulder, but she doesn't say anything.

"Is Spenser with you?"

She pulls out of the embrace and points toward the forest. "Yes, and Tru. Gilgamesh has made sure we didn't die, though we had plenty of opportunities. How did you survive Biblos' attack?"

"I nearly didn't. He strangled all but the last breath out of me. He must have taken me for dead and gone after Glori. When I came to, you all were gone and Glori was—" His face twists into a mask of pain. "I did the best I could burying her. It'll do until you locate the

262

keys, Finvarra reopens Tir Na Nog, and her body can be returned for a proper ceremony."

Aine calls to the boys. They race across the clearing, where Mondegreen sweeps Spenser into an embrace, each careful of the other's injuries. Mondegreen tries to herd them into Glori's house, but Aine demands to see Glori's grave and pay their respects first. They gather flowers as they walk. It's slow going with Mondegreen able to travel no faster than a shuffle. It must have cost him greatly to put Glori's body to rest.

They walk for nearly ten minutes toward the river, and stop next to a fresh dug area. The earth is rich and black, a dramatic contrast to the bright green horsebalm. It smells of rich loam. A shovel is still perched against a tree. Aine kneels next to the grave, but she has no tears. *I'll retrieve all three keys, Glori, and see that you return to Tir Na Nog. I promise it.*

She feels a hand on her shoulder. She looks up, and Mondegreen offers her a small white box. "Here. She made me promise that if anything ever happened to her, that I'd make sure you got it."

"You've been carrying it around since we left?" Tru asks.

Mondegreen smiles sadly. "I felt like I was carrying a little bit of Gloriana around with me."

Aine opens the lid. Inside, nestled in a bed of cotton, are the tiny golden cylinders that Glori always wore. She'd been moving so quickly the last time Aine'd seen her that the jewelry had been singing. "How long have we been gone?"

Mondegreen's eyebrows shoot up. "Not even a full day. The battle with Biblos happened yesterday afternoon. Are you going to wear the earrings?"

"No, but thank you. My ears aren't pierced." She returns the lid to the box and slides it into the same skirt pocket that only yesterday had held three quarters from Grandma Glori. "Do you have her know globe?"

Mondegreen appears taken aback. "How do you know about those?"

Aine winks. "A fairy told me."

"I'm afraid I haven't seen it."

"It was on the porch where she was killed."

Mondegreen shakes his head. "I certainly would have spotted it if it was still there. Maybe Biblos took it."

This thought chills Aine. She stands. "Spenser, are you ready to leave?"

He'd been crying softly. He leans into Aine when she wraps her good arm around him. "Yeah. Are we leaving for Sinbad?"

Gilgamesh sets his jaw. "We're not going anywhere until the toadhouse is fixed. Our wrong turn in the Sinbad voyages has got one good outcome: it's bought us time. Biblos will have to travel through three different stories to follow our trail here. We'll stay in Glori's house tonight so you can rest while Mondegreen and I look at the toadhouse."

At the last moment, Tru decides he can't separate the hermit crabs. When pressed, he can't take them both away from Spenser, either. "You need them more than me," he tells the boy, rubbing his hand through his winter-colored hair. "You lost your house and your grandma. Me, I got a home, even if it's just with my aunt. I 'spect I might even enjoy her rules now that I've had a taste of life without any."

Aine is cupping her elbows. Spenser stands beside her reluctantly holding the terrarium. Mondegreen and Gilgamesh stand behind them as the warm Alabama sun sets at their back. "I'm sorry that you got dragged into this," Aine says.

Tru appears thoughtful, a gesture she's never seen him wear. "I'm not," he says finally.

"You won't tell anyone what you know?"

"Nobody'd believe me anyways. Fairies write stories, and we all live in a book? Come on. I'd be tarred and feathered. Nope, this is our secret."

Aine smiles and gives him a last hug. Her heart expands as he wraps his strong little arms around her and squeezes her tight. "I appreciate you being a friend to Spenser."

He steps back quickly and drops his eyes, suddenly fascinated by a single dark stone. "Hey, I reckon we're all friends for life now. You'll stop in from time to time?"

"Of course," Aine says, though she knows it isn't true. Something inside of her tells her this will be the last time they ever lay eyes on Tru.

He nods and grabs the stone, smooth and no larger than a quarter. "Hey Spenser?"

The boy smiles bravely but his chin is quivering. "Yeah?"

"Knock knock."

Spenser's smile becomes more certain, and he swipes at a tear threatening to fall. "Who's there?"

"Boo."

"Boo who?"

"Ah, don't cry. We're friends forever." Both boys begin giggling, and Aine rolls her eyes but can't fight the smile. She takes the crab tank from Spenser so they can give each other a short hug that quickly devolves into wrestling. After a few minutes they break apart, and Tru hands Spenser the stone. Then he says his final goodbyes and heads toward town.

Mondegreen and Gilgamesh go with Tru to scavenge parts to repair the toadhouse. Aine watches them walk down the road, holding Spenser close at her side. When all three are out of sight, she takes Spenser back to the house. He insists on refreshing the hermit crabs' food and water then letting them spend the night on the porch so they can readjust to the Alabama air. Aine reluctantly agrees, steering him clear of the blood staining the floorboards.

Inside, she gets busy making him the dinner he requests—cheese dreams. When she's done at the stove, the bread has been toasted to a golden brown in a pool of butter and gooey cheese melts down the sides. She slices each sandwich into four triangles, just as he likes it. Aine smiles as she watches him eat, and she finishes his crusts for him, as she always has. It feels good to feed him, and to return to a routine.

His head starts nodding when he is almost done with his third sandwich. She pulls him away from the table and leads him upstairs to his bedroom. It is gloriously familiar, right down to the four-poster bed with the patchwork quilt. Aine considers requiring her brother to bathe rather than letting him crawl into bed filthy, covered in bug bites, sweat, and dirt. While she's deciding, he falls asleep in the chair by the window.

She wakes him long enough to help him get under the covers. He seems small and vulnerable in the big bed. She rubs his hair and sings to him until she feels better and he is deeply asleep. "Good night, family," she says, and kisses his forehead before tiptoeing out.

She considers sleeping herself but is too restless, too unsettled to finally be alone after so much close time with others. She pads downstairs and approaches the toadhouse sitting on the kitchen table as benignly as a potted plant. Aine considers the tiny grey-green shelter with its elfin curl. It's nondescript, a garden ornament, and the secret to everything. How could something she'd never noticed before change her life so completely?

She enters the tiny toad hut slowly, savoring the shivery buzz of shrinking as it consumes each inch of her body. The table, the chairs, the coat rack, the cupboard, and the plotter greet her. Gilgamesh must have set everything to right. Even though everything is where it should be, the inside of the cramped house smells like close-packed people, dried meat, and stored fruit.

The clay floor is rough on her bare feet. She grinds them in to relish the abrasive sensation. She steps toward the plotter. The ornate surface is smooth and cool to her fingertips. She leans in, thinking of all she's gained and lost since she first entered this room, how close she'd come to the rod, how she'd had to let it slip away.

She is so intent that she almost doesn't hear the kitchen door open.

Chapter 36

Aine shoots out of the toadhouse. She's calculating the quickest route to her brother in her miniature size when Mondegreen enters the kitchen.

"Hello, tiny one," he says, dropping a poke of groceries on the table next to her and adjusting his backwards cap. "You might want to get in the habit of hiding that toadhouse if you're going to enter it. Hate for you to be caught that small by a bad guy."

Gilgamesh follows immediately behind Mondegreen, his expression worried. His face relaxes when he sees Aine. "Spenser is safe?"

She nods.

"We've bought enough food to last in the toadhouse for a full week, and all the necessary parts to fix the toadhouse plus spares," Mondegreen says. "Let's get to work."

Rather than return to natural size, Aine cleans the toadhouse as the men fiddle with the clockworks. She scrubs the inside as best she can, throwing out any waste, sweeping the floor with the broom Gilgamesh passes through the doorway, then scrubbing the floor with a piece of cloth and a dot of soap. The most difficult thing to remove is the crusty fruit that was squashed when Aine upset the toadhouse returning from *The Ramayana*.

In a corner of the cupboard behind the plates, she discovers a hoard of rocks and shells, either Spenser's or Tru's. She cleans around it, dusting all the surfaces, washing the dishes, and hanging up the bedding and comfort cloth to air. Once the interior is clean, she secures everything that might shift in a rough landing, using thread to tie down clothes and a rubber band to keep the cupboard doors closed. She has a hard time admitting it even to herself, but she's excited to continue their journey. There's nothing for them here, but there's a whole world of stories out there.

Once the inside of the house has been thoroughly scrubbed, she decides they need something to store food in. Gilgamesh hands her bath towels and a sewing kit at her request. She stitches the hems of the towels so they can be cinched around the edges like bags. She rigs them from the ceiling to allow for more space in the crowded house.

"You about done in there?" Gilgamesh asks, wiping his oily hands on a bit of rag left over from her efforts.

She steps out of the toadhouse. "I am," she says proudly.

"Mondegreen and I are going to run a test to make sure it's working properly. It'll be short. You'll be okay?"

Aine nods and steps out of the way. Once inside the toadhouse, Mondegreen exclaims loudly and Gilgamesh whistles. "I hardly recognize it," he calls out.

Aine smiles as the toadhouse begins to tremble, then rises off the table before spinning like a top. She experiences a moment of anxiety watching it leave. *What if it never returns?* Then she remembers that Spenser is upstairs. As long as he's near, she'll be okay.

She walks to the edge of the table, slides down a chair back and lands on the seat. Stepping to the edge of the flat surface, she eases herself onto its leg and slips to the ground. The stairs are more time-consuming. Fortunately, her ears pop and her body begins to tingle halfway up the steps. She returns to normal size, relishing the explosions inside of her and pausing until a moment of vertigo passes. Once settled, she checks on Spenser. He's snuggled into the green-and-blue quilt Glori had made for him when he arrived. He's snoring softly.

She smiles at him and walks to her small room with its slanted walls, striding across the braided rug to her bookshelf. She owns nearly a hundred books. Glori made sure the children were readers, and now Aine knows why. Running her hands across the cool leather spines, she thinks of the world inside each one. She'd like to read one now, but she's exhausted to the center of her bones.

She pulls the quilt back on her bed, and the crisp white sheets stare at her. She sighs. It doesn't matter how tired she is; she can't get into a real bed this dirty. She tiptoes down to the kitchen, not bothering with the lights, and fills a metal basin with water from the hand pump. Bringing it back to her room, she sets the washbasin in the cabinet designed for it.

The mirror over the cabinet draws her attention. With only the light of the moon trickling through her window, she studies herself for the first time in days. She's filthy. Her face is streaked with dirt, her hair an angry mass of snarls. Under that, though, she looks different. Her chin doesn't seem as pointy, and her eyes aren't too green after all. They have bags under them, certainly, and one is still swollen from a bug bite, but she realizes they're her mother's eyes, beautiful and clear.

270

She strips off her dress, vowing to burn it tomorrow, and follows with her pale pink camisole and knickers. Standing naked in her room, she drops the washcloth into the cool water, wrings it out, and begins with her shoulders. The cool water feels delicious. The washcloth slides over her flat stomach and across the curve of her hips. She has to wring it out frequently, and the water is soon murky.

She dons a cotton robe, goes downstairs to change the water, and returns to her room to wash and braid her hair. Finally she's as clean as she's going to get. She wants to clean the washbasin, but her eyelids betray her. She simply cannot stay on her feet any longer. She pulls on a clean, soft yellow camisole and matching knickers. Now she is clean enough for her bed.

Before sliding under the welcoming covers, she reaches for the box containing Glori's earrings. She takes a quick peek inside before setting it on her nightstand. Mondegreen was right. The beautiful golden rods that had always dangled from Glori's lobes did bring to mind the very best memories of her.

She lays her head on her down pillow. The soft pillowcase smells like a flower, but she can't pinpoint which one. Primrose? No. Lilac? That wasn't it. Lavender?

The memory seizes her like strong arms. She's back in that strange room, hiding behind the man. Helen stands across from him.

Never again, Helen says, sad but determined.

Aine glances down. Her hands are small. She's a little girl hiding in a closet and peeking through the crack in the door.

Her mother moves, and the man turns. It's Gilgamesh.

Another man steps between Gilgamesh and her mother. He's tall and dark, with eyes like Spenser's except that they're sharp. He puts his arms around Helen, but she pushes him away.

You're right, never again, the dark man says to Helen. *We'll only send them away this once to keep them safe. Biblos will come after you, not the children. Sending them away will protect the bloodline. Once Biblos is captured, they can come back to us. It's for the best. It's only for a short while.*

No. Helen is firm. *If they go, I go with them.*

I can protect all three, Gilgamesh says, his voice strong.

The dark man laughs. *You? The reason Biblos is free and I have to go to these lengths? You couldn't protect my dog.* He turns back to Helen and one of his hands curves into a claw. *I'm afraid I can't live without you, my dear.*

He speaks words that are unfamiliar to Aine, musical words that fill the air like feathers. Helen collapses. She's taken away by two women with rigid faces. Glori steps into the picture. She looks exactly like she had when Aine knew her: fierce, proud, with silver hair curling around her ears, and tiny golden rods dangling. *You might be my brother, but you're also a bastard*, she tells the dark man.

Helen won't remember a thing, the dark man says calmly. *I can protect the kingdom, my wife, and my bloodline. When Biblos is captured, the children will return, and I'll remove the mind-clouding from my wife.*

So this has nothing to do with your safety? Glori sneers. *It seems very convenient that you get rid of the marked child just when it's prophesied that the child will be your demise.*

The dark man's shoulders tighten. *Biblos is the threat, not my children. You know as well as I do that Fear Darrig's prophecies are rarely what they seem. No, I am only protecting my bloodline.* He returns his attention to Gilgamesh. *I am sending agents to every story to booktrap Biblos. Your job is to stay out of the way until Biblos is captured, and come to me with the news. If by chance the children come into your hands, remember this: there will come a point when the end seems near. If you hesitate, both children will die. If you act, one will live. Understand?*

Gilgamesh nods.

Glori steps between them. *Who is going to guard the children? Tone.*

Not good enough. I'll go, and I'll bring Mondegreen, too.

The dark man appears shocked. *Give up your life in Tir Na Nog? You don't need to do that. I'll make sure they're well-hidden.*

Glori's hands are on her hips. Aine recognizes the gesture. Glori's mind will not be swayed. The dark man recognizes it, too.

All right. You understand that I'm locking the kingdom until Biblos is captured. The Unlocking is not to be started until Biblos is booktrapped, no exceptions. The lock requires three objects, each touched by the marked child of Helen. After the third is touched, the door to Tir Na Nog will finally appear, and the fairy kingdom will be open once more. I will give you the rhyme for the first object, no more. It's a precaution so Biblos can't torture the information out of anyone.

Glori snorts. *I'm not afraid of Biblos. But why only one child?*

I've sent the four shadows into the future; they see the possibility of only one child of Helen returning to Tir Na Nog. Even so, a practical fairy can also see the future; it's more likely that one child will survive than two. It would kill Helen to lose both. She could survive with just one. That is all.

Gilgamesh steps aside. The dark man leaves. Glori turns to face Gilgamesh, and Aine can see the rage burning in her eyes. She hisses her commands to Gilgamesh. *Both of those children must survive.*

And I'm giving you another job. If, Elfame forbid, Biblos lands in my story, you retrieve the children and protect them with your life. Do you understand?

Before Aine can witness Gilgamesh's response, Glori senses she's being watched. She turns her glittering eyes at the crack in the closet. *Come out.*

Aine steps out from behind the door. She's nervous, but she holds her head high.

Ah, Titania. I should have known it was you. Gotten an earful, haven't you? Well, the spell that worked on your mother will work on you and your brother. Actually, I might do a deeper mind-clouding. You're already a powerful little one.

Glori gathers her in an embrace, and the cinnamon-scented fog drops.

Chapter 37

Aine sits up in bed, her heart leaping out of her chest. It's hammering, hammering, hammering, but then she realizes it's not her heart. The sound is coming from her window. It's the sharp clink of glass against glass. She leaps off her mattress and runs to the casement. On the other side of the panel, a grapefruit-sized marble is trembling, circling, pounding, behaving for all the world like a bird trying to enter the house.

Aine slides open the window. The giant marble flies into her hand.

Grandma Glori's know globe. Back in *The Time Machine*, she had asked Sura what happened to know globes when their owners died. Sura had shrugged. *It seeks out the nearest next of kin, though just like fairies, it can't travel across stories without a toadhouse.* The whole truth of it rushes into Aine's head like water from a broken dam.

"Spenser!" Aine yanks on a pair of cotton pants and a clean blouse then zooms to his room so fast that her feet barely touch the ground. The globe is warm and solid in her hand. "Wake up!"

He sits up in bed, his patchy hair shooting out at all angles. "Is it morning?"

"Hold this!" She places the globe on his palm.

Spenser uses his free hand to rub sleep from his eyes. "It feels neat. What it is it?"

"Listen." She isn't sure what memory it's bringing for him, but the smile that starts small on his face grows to encompass his whole body.

"Mom and Grandma Glori, together, playing hide and seek with me even though I'm just a fat little baby! And we're someplace that smells like lilacs. I feel a chain of soft flowers on my head. What is this, Aine?"

"Glori's know globe, the storehouse of her memories and the memories of her family." She drops her voice to an awed whisper. "Spenser, we're fairies."

He squeezes the globe. "What?"

She tells him the story, shaking her head in wonder the whole time. She pulls in patches and pieces to create a whole: around the fire in *Sinbad*, Gilgamesh had told them of Finvarra, the king of the fairies, stealing his wife from her story and from the man who became Biblos. What he hadn't mentioned was that the story was *The Iliad*, which had been mandatory reading for Aine in the seventh grade but which she hadn't thought of since.

Helen was the woman Finvarra had stolen, the most beautiful woman in any world, and he stole her from Paris, who became Biblos. Finvarra married Helen, they had two children, then he ensorcelled her to forget them so he could protect his kingdom from Biblos. Glori wasn't their grandmother. She had been their aunt. Helen of Troy, stolen from *The Iliad* by the King of the Fairies, was their mother.

"That makes us half-fairies. But still!" Spenser is beaming.

Aine smiles and hugs him.

276

A slow clapping at the door draws their attention. "Very good."

"Mondegreen?" Aine jumps up to stand between Spenser and the door. His hat is absent, and his trousers are torn and dotted with fresh blood. She's unsettled by the tortured, angry expression on his face. "How was the test of the toadhouse?" She glances behind him. "And where's Gilgamesh?"

Mondegreen pushes himself off of the doorjamb. "Dead, or close to it, in another book. I couldn't kill him directly—such is the fairy curse—but dropping him unarmed into the middle of a war in *Ben-Hur* amounts to the same."

Aine's world slides. She thrusts out her hand to steady herself but there's nothing to grab onto. *Gilgamesh. Dead?* She imagines this is what it feels like to be turned inside out. Gilgamesh's amulet lays cold over her heart. Spenser whimpers from his bed.

"Biblos said I should do the equivalent to one of you," Mondegreen continues, "but I said I couldn't, that you were harmless children. Seems you're smarter than both of us guessed. In any case, Biblos is on his way. He can do with you what he chooses."

Spenser has come to stand alongside Aine, his face pinched. "But you're our friend."

A flash of genuine grief crosses Mondegreen's face, replaced immediately by anger. "I was, until Biblos recently captured my wife in *The Wizard of Oz*. Everyone knows how brutal he is. My sweet, gentle Stanza can't survive much torture. If I deliver you both to him, he'll spare her. He contacted me only last week, somehow using the four shadows. It hasn't given me much time to plan, but what I had in mind would have worked if Gilgamesh wasn't such a good mechanic."

Aine returns to herself. "You broke the plotter!"

"I did. Biblos' word curse hit a little high. It was my tampering before you all left that threw the toadhouse off course, or at least would have if not for Gilgamesh."

"You're not even hurt, are you?" Aine asks. The pain of betrayal mixes with the absolute grief at losing Gilgamesh, and into that spills fear for her brother. Nowhere is safe.

"I'm afraid these injuries are real. Biblos wanted it to look authentic. Plus, he's cruel." Mondegreen gingerly pats the bandage circling his waist. "This will all be over soon. Biblos will arrive any moment. Let's go downstairs and wait."

Mondegreen makes as if to grab Aine, but she steps out of his grasp as quickly as a shadow. A strange glint lights his eyes. "So the half fairy did get some powers. Interesting. And a Wind ravin, too. Not much luck with that one, unfortunately. You'll be able to do little more than move fast or stir up a breeze. I should know, as that's my lot." In a wink, he's standing beside her, his arm holding her tightly, a grim smile on his face. "Bring your brother, and I won't hurt either of you."

Aine's mind is spinning. She nods, and he releases her. She leads Spenser down the stairs, keeping him close. "Did you really bury Grandma Glori?" she asks. She's trying to buy them time until she can think of a plan.

A thunderous crash reaches their ears. Something has begun to storm through the woods, eating trees in its path. Its footsteps rattle the shutters on the windows, and the air is poisoned with the stink of burning, rotting fruit. Biblos. All thoughts of a plan fly out of Aine's head in an icy whitewash of fear.

Mondegreen hurries them along, his voice strained. "You mean *Aunt* Glori? I did. It was one of the hardest things I've ever had to do, truly. She wasn't supposed to die. Biblos said he only needed one of you to return to Tir Na Nog. Glori got in his way."

The splintering sound of trees cracking is replaced with terrible, grass-stomping footsteps across the clearing. Biblos is moving fast, far faster than he had the first time he'd come.

They reach the bottom step, and Aine hurries Spenser across the room to the sink. She stands in front of him, wanting to hide him. "How do you know Biblos hasn't already killed your wife?" As she talks, her eyes scour the kitchen. She'd returned her book bag to the hook behind the door. Inside is Vishnu's arrow. Behind Spenser is a rack of knives. This isn't over yet.

Agony bleeds across Mondegreen's face, but he quickly wipes it away. His voice is gruff. "I don't. I can only hope. I'm sorry I've had to make this choice. If it weren't for your good friend Gilgamesh, I wouldn't have had to, so you can thank his human soul when you reach the other side." He is standing in front of the far kitchen window, away from the door and the bellowing monster charging the front of the house.

The kitchen is so normal, with its green curtains hand-sewn by Glori, the table where Aine'd prepared so many meals, the worn wood-planked floor. She can still smell the faint stink of the grilled cheese sandwich she'd burnt before they'd left underneath the fresher scent of the sandwiches she'd just made. They'd come so far only to have it all end right where it had begun. She pulls Spenser in close.

Suddenly, the kitchen explodes in glass, but it doesn't come from the front of the house. Gilgamesh sails through the window behind Mondegreen with a sword at his waist. He grabs the traitor in his arms, and they roll to the floor. They tangle furiously with one other, deep shards of glass penetrating their skin with every movement.

Aine grabs Spenser's arm and leaps across the kitchen, snatching Vishnu's arrow on the way. She rips open the door and yanks Spenser onto the porch. Biblos is two hundred yards away and growing larger with each step. He doesn't grow proportionately, though. First one blazing blue eye then the other expands to the size of a table. Then his head balloons gruesomely to support them, all odd-shaped and pulsing. His mouth grows next, his wide wicked Cheshire's grin gleaming with saliva. His nose pops out last, a big ugly lump of clay in his distorted face. His body follows, one arm shooting into the air like a rocket before dropping like a log, heavy fist slamming the earth. Next comes the worm arm, shocked and seeking, then a leg grows so quickly it pierces the earth.

"Children," he says, drool spilling out of his lopsided mouth, his forward motion never stopping. "How nice of you to wait for me. Which one of you would like to go on a ride with your Uncle Biblos?"

The horror of him is hypnotizing. He stops twenty yards away. His worm hand reaches forward, nuzzling, seeking. Behind Aine, one of the hermit crabs makes a loud scraping noise. The worm hand stops, moves toward the children, darts to the left, and scoops up Pinch and Shelly like a giant slimy finger. Aine thinks Biblos is going to study the beloved crabs but he doesn't even glance at them. Instead, the worm hand curves like a poisoned elephant trunk and feeds the sweet crabs into a dark wet hole at his wrist. The terrible crunching turns Aine's stomach. Its mouth fed, the worm hand again reaches for Aine and Spenser, seeking, quivering blindly in the air toward them.

The thought of that slimy, strong flesh on her skin breaks Aine's paralysis.

"Spenser!" she screams. She doesn't want to leave him, knows he's

280

only a small boy, is more terrified of losing him than anything in this world, but she has to trust him. It's their only chance at survival. "Sinbad Cthulu pool!" She pushes him off the porch, hoping with all her heart that he understands. She runs toward Biblos with Vishnu's arrow in her hand. "Fire!" She thrusts it over her head.

"That does make it much easier to find you, so thank you," Biblos growls. "Don't think I'll forget about your brother, though. Can't have loose ends. But there will be plenty of time to find him. Now come to your uncle, little firefly."

Aine runs toward him as close as she dares, so close that she witnesses the pulsing letters in the murky whites of his eyes and has to punch down the maddening words that he's babbling inside her head. He grins as she nears and leans down, opening his mouth wide. He washes her in a bath of his putrid, rotten sweet burning stink, his mouth gaping as if to scoop her up and swallow her whole.

She is close enough to reach out and tap a bright white tooth when she abruptly turns heel and races into the woods parallel to the route that Spenser took. She knows he can't move as fast as her, prays that he is heading to the whirlpool. Behind her, trees fall under the enormity of Biblos, who is following the bright light of her arrow. She weaves and bobs, but he can travel twenty-five feet in one footstep. His hot breath beats at her neck. Evil streaks of blue and purple shoot past her, narrowly missing her, scissoring branches off trees around her ears. She can't last much longer. Has she given Spenser enough time? Suddenly, her feet are snared out from under her. She falls painfully on her wounded arm.

"You run like a gazelle, daughter of Finvarra, but that means you can also be trapped like one." Biblos' chuckle sounds like metal ripping. He's cast one of his electric ropes around her leg.

Aine shoves the arrow into the center of it. "Destroy!"

The arrow flares, a fierce red in the heart of the sizzling, writhing blue cable. The red momentarily conquers the blue, and the rope of electricity squeals before slinking like an eel back to Biblos. Aine pushes herself to her feet. She can't toy with Biblos any longer. The monster man is too powerful.

She charges toward the river, over rock, under branch. The sweet shushing sound of running water is ahead, and just below that, the crashing of the rapids upstream. Aine smells the clear cool of the water before she spots the river. She crosses the swimming hole so quickly that her feet don't get wet. She scurries up the bank toward the whirlpool.

Biblos splashes through the water.

She turns. He's near. She extinguishes the arrow with a word but doesn't let go of it. The moon is bright enough that they can see one another clearly. He is stalking her, shrinking several feet with each step. She walks backward, up, up, up until she's at the cliff overlooking Cthulu pool. Below, the water rages and gnashes its teeth as loudly as a crashing train, commanding her to jump.

"There's nowhere to run? So sad. And so easy. I don't need to be very large for this. It doesn't work for the delicate job of harvesting girls." He has shrunk uniformly, until he is almost normal-sized except for his head. This he keeps as large as a watermelon, an acid grin cutting across his tattooed cheeks. "Do you want to simply give me your hand? I can make this quick. You were the one I wanted all along."

Aine holds out her hand. She doesn't know if Spenser is near. This might be her last gesture. Biblos reaches forward with his fingered hand. His skin is hot and dry, like a snake's. He grasps her wrist and slides his worm hand up her naked arm. His smile grows impossibly wide, leaking a pool of brown liquid down his chin.

Aine grabs the wrist holding hers and drops onto her back. Biblos leans forward, exactly as she'd hoped. She plants her foot in the center of his chest and tips him over and into the Cthulu pool. He roars as he plummets. It's all going according to plan. Except Biblos doesn't let go of her wrist.

Aine is yanked over the side of the cliff, tumbling, tumbling, the agony in her dislocated arm excruciating. She hits the water like a wall then is sucked into the churning pool. Her body bounces off rock, twirls, suffocating, twists. She isn't sure which way is up. Water burns inside her nose. She's completely submersed, unable to breathe, sucked down, down. Biblos releases her wrist but it doesn't help. She could no more escape this water prison than she could him.

Still she tries, kicking her feet, pushing against the current with her good arm, except it's coming from all sides, and she might be hurrying her fate by kicking toward the bottom. Her chest is ready to explode. Her lungs cry for air. Her head hits a rock. Her mouth opens. The water rushes in. She can't feel her hands. She's so tired. The rabid water shakes her like a doll, sucking her closer to its hungry mouth at the bottom of the Cthulu pool. She thinks of Spenser and hopes Gilgamesh survives to take care of him.

Then she can't fight any longer.

Chapter 38

Aine recognizes the hand at her throat.

He slips it around her neck, notching her chin in the crook of his elbow. They spin in the vortex together. The current claims them both, but only for a moment.

Aine feels the incredible force of his kicks, but his only useful arm is holding her so he cannot use his full power. The water has filled her lungs like cement, but she finds strength now that she's no longer alone. The strength grows until she realizes she can move through the water nearly as quickly as she does on land. Together they break the surface and kick toward shore, dragging themselves out of the roiling, greedy current.

Spenser's sucks in a deep breath. Aine can't draw air. There's no room inside her. Despite her new-found water powers, the liquid has filled her lungs and she's dying. Spenser navigates the rocks to pull her to the nearest bank, where he slaps her back just as she'd slapped Tru's. It takes ten seconds, then twenty. Finally the water comes out in great, glistening heaves. She draws a ragged breath, and it sounds like a dead woman waking.

She coughs, and breathes, and throws up, and breathes some more. Spenser sits next to her and rubs her back with his good arm. His other hangs limply at his side.

"We did it," he says.

Aine laughs, but it's more of a bark. "Yeah. You saved my life, Spenser." Her voice is hoarse.

Someone speaks from above them, on the river bank. "It's a fine night for a swim."

Aine tries to rise. Spenser leaps to his feet to stand in front of her.

The shadow steps down from the river bank. It's Gilgamesh. Aine's heart leaps and she tries to get off the river bank, but she's too weak. Gilgamesh moves slowly, and his white shirt sticks to his body in bloody patches. The toadhouse is tucked under his arm. "Anyone know a trick for removing glass?"

"Rub it with sand." Aine's jaw is sore but she can't fight the smile. She fingers the silver necklace still clasped securely around her neck. She's surprised she hadn't lost it in her flight. "You're a survivor, aren't you?"

He drops to one knee so they are eye to eye. He pushes a damp lock of hair off her face then gently embraces her. He brushes a soft kiss against her forehead before leaning back on his heels. "Likewise. To both of you. I thought I was never going to see you again."

Aine is flushed, happy, sore. The kiss has left her feeling both confused and certain. "Likewise."

Gilgamesh tips his head. A playful smile touches his lips. "You two won't be offended if I take us to look for sand in a different story, would you? Say one without a traitorous fairy or an evil monster named Biblos, maybe someplace I can get this sword sharpened?"

Spenser points at the water. "Biblos is done for."

Gilgamesh stares grimly at the roaring rapids. "I wouldn't count him out until you see the body. And that I'd chop into pieces first. So what say you? A tropical island, or possibly a land where chocolate flows like a river? We're due for a small break before we return to Sinbad and the golden staff."

"I think that's a great idea," Spenser says, "as long as Aine comes with."

Gilgamesh rests the toadhouse on the bank and holds out his hand. In it is the white box containing Grandma Glori's earrings, and on top of that is balanced her know globe. "We couldn't do it without her. If it helps, I think I've gathered everything you want from this story."

Aine and Spenser simultaneously reach for the globe. Their hands touch it at the same instant, and a brilliant light shoots out followed by the brief and delicate sound of rainfall. The air smells comforting like lilies and paper. The know globe has split in two, and they're each holding a smaller version of it.

"Our own globes!" Aine says. She holds hers close to her face. It plays a movie of her and Spenser playing tag around an unfamiliar house on a rolling green hill. She looks over at Spenser and trusts by his expression that he is experiencing something similarly wonderful.

"Glori was right," Aine says. "Everything I really needed was right under my nose. My family." She ruffles Spenser's hair before taking the white box from Gilgamesh. She's abruptly struck by a thought. It gives her chills. "You don't think…"

"What?" Spenser asks.

"Tell me again what Glori's rhyme was."

Gilgamesh complies. "The adventure of a lifetime is tied to a powerful rod. Reach wisely for the metal one, and remember that man is not god."

"Give me your hand," she orders Spenser.

He shrugs and lets her take his fingers. Removing the cover from the white box, she stares down at the tiny golden cylinders that Glori had worn every day of her life. She leads their joined hands toward the box. They both touch the earrings at the same time. The sky explodes with words, bright and tall:

> *In the world of curiosity's monster*
> *find a trapped image that touches the dead.*
> *Fate has marked them.*
> *They no longer need this thread.*

The air is filled with the smell of sulfur. The words crack and fall to the ground with a jingle like wind chimes. They shatter in a mushroom puff of violet when they hit the earth. The only solid object is a bit of gold that drops from the sky with a soft thud.

Spenser's eyes are wide. "Was that our second clue?"

Aine is laughing. "It is! We did it!" She walks over to the golden object. It's an ornate key, so warm that it feels alive.

Gilgamesh shakes his head. "It was here all along. I don't think she even knew."

"I'm sure she didn't," Aine says firmly. She passes the key to Spenser, who feels it with wonder before passing it to Gilgamesh. "She would have told us. It looks like I'll have one more thing to say to my father when I see him." She takes the key from Gilgamesh and holds it firmly in her palm, nodding toward the toadhouse. "Well, what are we waiting for?"

Gilgamesh sees Spenser and Aine safely into the toadhouse before entering. After a short discussion, he whispers the title of the agreed-upon book into the plotter. The toadhouse shivers, trembles, and spins before saying goodbye to Alabama.

The story they leave behind continues to spool. The sun rises, followed by the moon, and the characters live their lives none the wiser. Meanwhile, a faint but steady blue light pulses at the bottom of the Cthulu pool. An indigo burp clears the surface several days after the toadhouse has departed. When it pops, it emits the scent of rotting fruit and baking tar.

Recommended Reading List

Briggs, Katharine. *An Encyclopedia of Fairies.*
Burton, Sir Richard. *The Seven Voyages of Sinbad the Sailor.*
Dickens, Charles. *A Tale of Two Cities. The Epic of Gilgamesh.*
Lee, Harper. *To Kill a Mockingbird.* (This beautifully-crafted novel
    inspired the world where Glori raises Aine and Spenser.)
Lewis, Sinclair. *Babbitt.*
Marlowe, Christopher. *Dr. Faustus.*
Narayan, R.K.'s version of Valmiki's *The Ramayana.*
Shakespeare, William. *A Midsummer Night's Dream.*
Shaw, George Bernard. *Pygmalion.*
Stevenson, Robert Louis. *Strange Case of Dr. Jekyll and Mr. Hyde.*
    (Mr. Hyde and Mr. Utterson's dialogue was taken directly from
    The Oxford World's Classics edition of *Dr. Jekyll and Mr. Hyde*
    and Other Tales, edited by Roger Luckhurst for Oxford Univer-
    sity Press, 2006. ISBN 978-0-19-953622-1. My thanks.)
Wells, H.G. *The Time Machine.*

Acknowledgments

I'd be remiss if I didn't thank the many writers whose work inspired me to create this story: Cornelia Funke, Rick Riordan, Suzanne Collins, Harper Lee, Mary Pope Osborne. It was while reading your books to and with my kids that the Toadhouse took root. Also, thanks to Zoë and Xander, who remind me that being a kid isn't always as easy as it looks. Extra special thanks also to Zoë, Xander, Esmae, Ray, Diane, Steve, Kellie, and Jen for being my first readers.

My mom and dad instilled in me a love of stories, and for that I'll always be grateful. Your willingness to undertake multiple edits of my work, this one included, is a nice plus. Steve, thank you for talking me through plot snarls while walking Juni.

Jessica Morrell edits all of my work, and she is brilliant. I also brought Laine Cunningham on board for copyediting, and I am grateful for her eye to detail. Any remaining errors are mine alone. My agent, Victoria Skurnick, went above and beyond in trying to sell this book. Her love for it and support got me to this level. Thanks, Victoria. Molly Josephine Hester, Gaelic expert at Harvard

University, I am completely to your patience and knowledge. You helped me to get the fairy commands just right; now get back to writing your own book so I can buy it.

To all of my friends, corporeal and Facebook, I can say thank you, but I worry that you'll never know how much your support was necessary to getting this book out there. Aimee, Dru Ann, Terri, Kathleen, Margery, Reed, Hank, Hallie, Rosemary, Karen, Neil, Lisa, Heather, Alan, Alice, Michael, Rex, Steve, Dana, Kellie, and Christine, thank you thank you thank you, and my apologies to anyone left out.

And finally, to those of you who teach people to interpret, enjoy, or create stories, please accept my appreciation. High school literature and writing teachers in particular—like my mom, for 25 years—deserve respect and gratitude. Your job is often thankless, your workload epic, but what you do is vital. We are all connected by stories.

Jess Lourey is the author of *The Toadhouse Trilogy, Book One*, the first in a young adult series that celebrates the danger and excitement of reading. She also writes the critically-acclaimed Murder-by-Month Mysteries for adults with a sense of humor. She's been teaching writing and sociology at the college level since 1998. When not gardening, writing, or hanging out with her wonderful kids and dorky dog, you can find her reading, watching SyFy-channel original movies, and dreaming big. Visit her at www.jesslourey.com/toadhouse/ttt.html.

CPSIA information can be obtained at www.ICGtesting.com
Printed in the USA
LVOW011426300513

336209LV00022B/1094/P